"I'm here to ruin my she announced firmly. "With you."

Stunned by that scandalous notion, Cade couldn't speak.

But Violet didn't seem to mind.

"I'm here to make some thrilling memories," she went on, "and maybe change my future while I'm at it. And we've already wasted a great deal of time, so—" she smiled perkily "—shall we get started?"

* * *

The Honor-Bound Gambler
Harlequin® Historical #1139—June 2013

Author Note

Thank you for reading *The Honor-Bound Gambler!* I'm so happy to share this story with you. I always fall in love with all my characters while writing about them, and Cade and Violet were no exception. They quickly found a special place in my heart—as did Tobe, Reverend Benson, Adeline, Judah…and even that mysterious rascal Simon Blackhouse!

If you enjoyed this story (and I hope you did!), please try another book in my Morrow Creek series. It includes *Mail-Order Groom*, *The Bride Raffle* and several others (including some short stories), all set in and around my favorite Old West town.

You can learn about all my books at my website, www.lisaplumley.com. While you're there you can also download a complete book list, sign up for new-book alerts, read sneak previews of forthcoming books, request special reader freebies and more. I hope you'll stop by today!

Also, as always, I'd love to hear from you!
You can visit me online at:
www.community.eharlequin.com/users/lisaplumley, send an email to lisa@lisaplumley.com, "friend" me on Facebook at www.facebook.com/pages/Lisa-Plumley/164790176872702, follow me on Twitter @LisaPlumley, or write to me
c/o P.O. Box 7105, Chandler, AZ 85246-7105, U.S.A.

The
HONOR-BOUND
Gambler

LISA PLUMLEY

HARLEQUIN® HISTORICAL

Recycling programs
for this product may
not exist in your area.

ISBN-13: 978-0-373-29739-9

THE HONOR-BOUND GAMBLER

Copyright © 2013 by Lisa Plumley

Printed in U.S.A.

**Did you know that these novels are also
available as ebooks? Visit www.Harlequin.com.**

To John, with all my love,
now and forever.

LISA PLUMLEY

When she found herself living in modern-day Arizona Territory, Lisa Plumley decided to take advantage of it—by immersing herself in the state's fascinating history, visiting ghost towns and historical sites and finding inspiration in the desert and mountains surrounding her. It didn't take long before she got busy creating lighthearted romances like this one, featuring strong-willed women, ruggedly intelligent men and the unexpected situations that bring them together.

When she's not writing Lisa loves to spend time with her husband and two children, traveling, hiking, watching classic movies, reading and defending her trivia-game championship. She enjoys hearing from readers, and invites you to contact her via email at lisa@lisaplumley.com, or visit her website at www.lisaplumley.com.

Chapter One

Morrow Creek, northern Arizona Territory
October 1884

> "A gambler is nothing but a man who makes his
> living out of hope."
>
> —*William Bolitho*

From the moment he saw the boy, dirty faced and shabbily dressed, Cade Foster knew he was in trouble. Darting a glance at the middling horse, wagon and foot traffic surrounding him in the territorial backwater he'd arrived at this afternoon, Cade frowned. He stepped sideways, intent on making a detour.

The little sharper moved in the same direction. "Wanna try your luck, mister? I got me a nickel says I'm luckier than you."

Unhappily distracted, Cade glanced down at the coin the boy brandished. It looked cleaner than all the rest of the urchin combined. From his grimy fingernails to his shabby shirt, the boy looked powerfully worse for wear. Unfortunately, he also looked a little like Judah. Maybe that's why Cade stopped.

The boy grinned, revealing a smile that jabbed at Cade's heart like a sterling-silver knuckle-duster. "Ain't nothing finer than a fast game of craps, sir." The boy, probably twelve years of age or a little more, extracted a pair of dice from his trouser pocket. With élan he shook them in his scrawny fist. "How 'bout we toss 'em over yonder, where it's quiet?"

He nodded toward the nearest alleyway. Hesitating, Cade squinted up the main street toward the two-story brick house that was his destination. All Morrow Creek's movers and shakers were expected to be at the benefit being held there tonight, during which the Territorial Benevolent Association Grand Fair would raise funds for a new public lending library.

"You got yer roulette, el Sapo, rondo, rouge et noir, faro, and vingt-et-un—" the boy rattled off the names of those popular games of chance the way most youngsters recited their ABCs "—but for a fast win and real excitement nothin' beats craps, sir."

Transferring his gaze to the child again, Cade noted the boy's hollow cheeks and the dark smudges below his eyes. He saw the way the pint-size "sporting man" hunched his skinny shoulders against the autumn chill. He assessed the boy's nimble movements even as he listened to more of the imp's patter.

"If you roll those bones as ably as you talk," Cade interrupted, "I'd be a fool to strike a wager with you."

"You'd be a fool *not* to, you mean. It's just a nickel."

To a boy like that, a nickel was the difference between eating and going to bed hungry. Cade knew that more than most.

He also knew, with another proficient glance, that the dice the youngster jiggled were likely a pair of dispatchers—so named because they effectively "dispatched" their intended targets: suckers. Like all gambling men, Cade recognized the tools of a cheat. There was no other way to assure himself a square game.

Not that he ever expected to actually get one. Cade reckoned that every game he went up against was crooked one way or another. But if he ever wanted to find Whittier, he had to follow the gambling circuit. Tonight, at least a few of its members would be scouting for prospects—and showing off—at the Grand Fair. Once Cade made his way up the street to that big brick house, he'd have to do his best to impress them.

Winning was the only way to progress up the circuit—to make it to the high-stakes tables where men like Whittier wagered.

Not that throwing dice with this youngster would help Cade do that. He should have tried harder to go around him—regardless of the boy's resemblance to Judah. Now it was too late.

When Cade glanced up again, wondering if he could sidestep the kid without taking too hard a punch to his conscience, the boy was shrewdly studying his watch chain. Doubtless he was envisioning the expensive gold Jürgensen timepiece—a particular favorite of professional gambling men—that dangled at its tail…and wondering if he could win it.

Seeing no other choice, Cade nodded. He ambled

to the alleyway with the boy leading the way. They set their wager.

"I'm in a hurry." Cade nodded. "Go on and roll."

Smartly, the boy refused. "Let me see your nickel first."

Obligingly, Cade produced a coin. On the verge of throwing it in their makeshift kitty, he frowned. "Tell you what," he said in a tone of studied carelessness. "A nickel's not much of a bet. I'll put up my coat in this bargain, too." He was happy to forfeit the damn thing if it would keep this urchin warm for the coming wintertime. That was the least his problematic conscience demanded. "Just to keep things interesting."

"Yeah?" The boy jabbed up his chin. His eyes gleamed with wanting Cade's warm coat, but his decidedly unchildlike sense of skepticism demanded more. "What do you want of mine, then?"

Cade thought about it. "I want those fine dice of yours."

Reluctantly, the scamp examined his pair of clinkers. He'd probably been earning all the sustenance he had with them. He appeared disinclined to part with them. But the kid would be better off without those cheaters in his hands. They'd only get him in trouble. Nobody was likely to keep the boy from earning some much-needed money with fast gambling—and truthfully, Cade wasn't inclined to try—but at least the practice could be made safer. With a keener pair of loaded or expertly shaved dice—like the pair Cade kept ready in his coat pocket, for instance—the boy's subterfuge would be less detectable. All Cade had to do was slip them to the little sharper, easy as pie.

If the morals of helping a child to cheat were supposed to have bothered him, Cade guessed he was past repentance. Because this boy reminded him of his brother—of those hellacious orphan trains the two of them had been shoved onto and the hopes they'd had crushed for all those long-ago months—and he'd be damned if he'd let one small boy shiver for the sake of his own need for a heavenly reward.

Besides, the boy's future marks weren't any concern of Cade's. Any man who would set out to purposely bilk a down-on-his-luck child at gambling deserved to lose a few coins. Cade wasn't that man. But the boy didn't know that and never would.

At the child's continuing reluctance to strike a weightier wager, Cade heaved a sigh. "No deal? Fine. I'm late already."

"Oh? You goin' to Miss Benson's gala benefit?"

"You stalling for time? It's an easy bet. Yes or no?"

The boy toed the dirt. He eyed Cade's coat. "Add in that nice watch of yours too, an' you got yourself a good wager."

Against all reason, Cade admired the boy's pluck. "I won this watch in the biggest game of my life. It's sentimental."

"You sayin' no? 'Cause I ain't familiar with sentiment."

If Cade had been a softer man, that admission would have broken his heart. As it was, he only sobered his expression, then shook his head. "You can't have my watch."

The boy shrugged. Appearing resigned, he shook his fistful of rigged dice. With elaborate showmanship, he yelled, "Hold on to yer britches then, sir! Here comes the first roll, gents!"

Too late, Cade realized they'd drawn a clump of on-lookers. In the shadows cast by the setting sun, four strangers watched as the dice spewed from the boy's hand, rolled on the ground, bounced theatrically from the nearest lumber wall, then stopped.

A five-spot and a one-spot winked up. Another roll, then.

Cannily, the boy let himself lose the first several throws. All the while, he kept up an animated pitch—a talk meant to reel in Cade and keep him wagering even after he began losing. Such tactics were all part of the game—a prelude to the inevitable swindle after which the boy would walk away victorious.

If a grown man had tried such tactics on Cade, he wouldn't have been so patient. There was a reason he carried a derringer, two wicked blades and a surfeit of suspicion wherever he went.

As the alleyway grew darker and the dice rolled on, side bets sprung up among the spectators. Money rap-idly changed hands; good-natured insults were traded along with the wagers. Cade wasn't surprised. In the West, gambling was as common as breathing. After all, what was mining if not wagering that you'd find more gold than dirt in the nearby hills? Compared with wield-ing a pickax, pitching dice was hardly backbreaking.

As the dice rolled again, a sharp breeze whirled into the alleyway. The boy shivered. So did Cade. He'd upped the ante on their wager several times already. Now it was time to end this.

"My turn." Cade accepted the dice. Deftly, he switched them for the pair from his coat pocket. He rolled. Then he swore.

Exactly as he'd planned, he'd lost everything.

"I won! I won!" the kid crowed. "I get your coat, mister!"

The boy's eyes shone up at him. In that moment, Cade didn't mind that he'd made himself late for the Grand Fair. Then the urchin deliberately schooled his expression into his previous toughness, Cade remembered that he was a hard-nosed gambler who was in town only long enough to find the man he'd hunted through several states and territories…and the world righted itself.

"Tough break," a bystander commiserated. "You was just coming back, mister. You ain't got no kind of luck, do you?"

At that, Cade grinned, pinned by an unexpected sense of irony. This time, with the boy, he'd lost on purpose. But he *hadn't* enjoyed his usual run of good luck lately— that was true.

In fact, if his current unlucky streak continued, Cade didn't know what he'd do. He was *so* close to finagling a way into the high-stakes gambling circuit he'd been chasing. He desperately needed to keep up with that league of professionals.

It was the only way to find Whittier. He ran with that circuit; if not for his vaunted appearances at the table, he might as well have been a ghost. The minute rumors had flown that he'd been spotted here, in Morrow Creek, Cade had pulled foot for the town, too, hoping to catch up with him.

Besides, Cade had already tried everything else he could think of to track the man. His more legitimate search methods had turned up nothing.

"Well, it's like I always say," Cade told the bystanders, "if you must play, decide upon three things at the start—the rules of the game, the stakes…and the quitting time." As he spoke, he slipped off his overcoat. He dropped it, covertly divested of all the items he wanted to keep, on the boy's shoulders. "Now it's quitting time."

"What? You ain't even gonna try to win your money back?"

"Not tonight." Cade turned away. Behind him, he heard two awestruck whistles and several gruff, gossipy murmurs. Whoever said women were the only ones with flapping jaws was dead wrong.

"Hell! I'd say we got ourselves a new sporting man in town, boys!" one of the local men said with a chortle. "And he's droppin' money like he's got holes in his pockets, too."

The urchin ignored the chattering men. He chased down Cade, the oversize coat trailing on the ground behind him, then tugged at his suit sleeve. "Hey, mister! I know I won and all, but…I don't reckon you meant to leave *this* behind. I found it in your coat pocket."

He held up a wad of greenbacks, fastened with an ivory clip, which Cade had won off a cotton merchant down South.

Cade *had* meant to leave that money with the raga-muffin. He didn't have much use for his winnings—aside from their ability to stake his reputation, admit him into the elite high rollers' circle and eventually get him invited into their next private faro tournament. If he was lucky, that's where he'd find Whittier. Cade had already skimmed off a sufficient quantity of cash for his own incidentals. He had a fair bankroll set aside at his hotel. And there was always his benefactor, Simon Blackhouse, to rely on if he needed more funding, too.

But what concerned Cade now wasn't his own well-being. Because behind the boy, out of sight of his stupe-fied gaze, all those onlookers stared at Cade's carelessly lost money with hungry eyes. Surely they wouldn't ac-tually *steal* from a *child*?

Cade didn't know. All he knew was that some things—not many, in his experience, but some—weren't wager-ing material.

"You show me how to get to the Territorial Benevo-lent Association Grand Fair," Cade said, "and you can keep it all."

Wide-eyed, the boy nodded. Quick as a wink, he shoved the wad of cash down his pants for safekeep-ing. "For this much scratch I'll take you there myself! But I ain't stayin'. I done heard of kids bein' lured in by Miss Benson and then they ain't never seen again! I don't want no reformer gettin' ahold of me."

Cade only shrugged. "I don't care much for those do-gooder types myself." He started walking, with the boy eagerly dogging his every booted step. Something about the urchin's sudden devotion bothered him, but

Cade shrugged that off, too. "Give me a bottle of mescal, a pretty girl, a fair hand and a chance to square off against Lady Luck, and I don't need much else."

The boy skipped ahead, belatedly taking the lead as he'd agreed to do. He pointed to their destination. "The fair's up yonder at that ole' brick house." He eyed Cade. "You fixin' to steal all the raffle money for the new library or somethin'?"

"Nope. I've never stolen anything in my life. I've never had to, and I'm not starting now." Speaking in all honesty, Cade leveled his gaze on the house. Morrow Creek residents came and went in all their meager territorial finery. Music and lights spilled from inside, foretelling exactly the frolic he expected. "I'm here for something even better than raffle money."

The boy scoffed. "*Nothing's* better than money."

"At least one thing is," Cade disagreed.

At that, the boy made a disgusted face. "What? *Love*?"

Cade laughed. "Nope. Not love."

He wasn't even sure what love was. He cared for Judah; that was true. Everyone else he kept at arm's length for good reason.

"If it ain't money, and it ain't love, then what is it you're after?" the child demanded to know.

"Answers," Cade told him. "I want answers."

Then, for the fourth time in as many months, he headed toward the celebration he hoped might change his life...all over again.

Standing at the edge of the boisterous Territorial Benevolent Association Grand Fair with her toes tapping and her arms full of discarded shawls, wraps and overcoats, Violet Benson felt like nothing so much as a human coat hanger—a coat hanger who wanted desperately to join in the fun.

All around her, the finest and largest house in all of Morrow Creek was packed to the gills with revelers. Her friends and neighbors were dancing, drinking and trying their luck at the evening's games of chance, including the fancifully painted wheel of fortune donated by Jack Murphy. Now that the device wasn't situated in his saloon, even the ladies felt free to place bets. Violet hadn't yet done so herself, but she thought she might later if she ever divested herself of her burden.

"Oh! Violet! How nice to see you!" One of her longtime friends bustled over, all smiles. "Are you collecting wraps? Here—take mine." She flung off her lace shawl, then added it to the pile in Violet's arms. "You're so kind. Thanks so much!"

"You're welcome." Rearranging the wraps, Violet glanced at her friend's dance card. A number of gentlemen's names adorned it already. "My, look at your card! Aren't you popular tonight."

"Yes!" Her friend beamed. "My card is almost full already, and I've only just arrived. But *you* must be in demand, too!"

In unison, their gazes dropped to the dance card at the very tips of Violet's fingers. She hadn't even claimed it by printing her own name in the designated space at the top yet. She'd been too busy fancifully perusing her card's many blank *partner* spaces—imagining lots of suitors writing in their names with the small ribbon-attached pencil—when the first partygoer, another friend, had assigned her his overcoat for safekeeping.

Unfortunately her dance card remained conspicuously empty.

"Well—" her friend offered a cheering grin "—don't worry. It's early yet. Partners will be clamoring for you later on!"

Gamely, Violet grinned back. They both knew that wasn't likely. As far as people in Morrow Creek were concerned, Violet—the minister's plain-featured daughter—was better suited to doing good works than enjoying good times. Eventually, Violet reasoned, she would adjust herself completely to that fate.

In the meantime, she couldn't quit tapping her toes. The latest song was a fully frolicsome one, and she loved dancing.

"Look! I see Adeline Wilson and Clayton Davis!" her friend exclaimed. "I must congratulate them on their engagement."

Just like that, Violet was left alone again, stuck pinning up a wall with her shoulder blades and pining for a chance to dance. She watched as her very best friend, Adeline Wilson, gracefully accepted a fresh dose of congratulations, appearing typically beautiful and amiable all the while. Everything that Violet was *not*, Adeline *was*: pretty, dainty and sought-after.

But Violet possessed her own good qualities, she reminded herself staunchly. She was kindhearted, brave and intelligent. She was effective in her charity work. She was clever. She truly enjoyed doing good works. She had many close friends, as well.

So what if she had an empty dance card? That didn't matter.

Except it *did* matter, Violet admitted to herself as she heaved a resigned sigh and went to put away all those bundled overcoats. In her heart of hearts, it mattered a great deal. Worthy pursuits were rewarding, that was true; but so was dancing!

There was nothing to be done about her empty dance card now, though. Nor was there any point in torturing herself with it any longer. Almost to the cloakroom, Violet tossed her dance card toward a nearby trash bin.

Likely there were several helpful tasks she ought to be doing anyway, and there'd be cleaning up to do later, too.

She should concentrate on practical matters, just as she always did…and leave the daydreaming to women like Adeline—women who stood a chance of having their fantasies come true.

At the conclusion of his initial assessment of the Territorial Benevolent Association Grand Fair, Cade noticed the woman who tossed away a dance card. With nimble movements, Cade snatched the card from midair. He was surprised to see it was empty. But empty or full, that didn't matter for his purposes.

A man never knew when an accoutrement of belonging someplace, like a dance card, would come in handy. With a cursory glance at the primly dressed woman, Cade pocketed it. It might prove useful as an introduction to a conversation later.

He didn't know anyone in Morrow Creek; except for

his sponsor, the notoriously private Simon Blackhouse, Cade was alone. That's why he'd made it a point to perform his usual analysis with extra caution, identifying every entrance and exit and cataloging every potentially dangerous character in attendance. A man couldn't be too prepared. As Cade patted down his pristine suit coat pocket, assuring himself the empty dance card was secure, he reminded himself a man couldn't be too vigilant either. In his line of work, surprises could be deadly.

Despite his expectations, though, it seemed the Grand Fair was nothing more than an ordinary rural raffle. On the stage across the ballroom, a wire cage held the raffle entries, ready for the drawing. A locked cash box stood beside it; foolishly, there was no guard in the vicinity to protect its contents. Near the refreshments table, partygoers bid on cakes and pies and other wholesome goodies. Banners and bunting hung gaily from the rafters. Gullible townspeople danced blithely beneath them.

To Cade's jaundiced eye, the whole place seemed improbably virtuous. But no place was *that* good. No *person* was that good. Hell, even that mousy woman with her armful of coats and her downcast gaze probably had scandalous secrets to tell.

Cade simply needed to look closer. If he did, he knew he'd find the bad behavior he expected—and along with it, the inevitable wagering that he hoped would lead him to the elusive Percy Whittier—professional gambler, runaway family man and odds-on favorite to win the upcoming private faro tournament.

Unless, of course, Cade got to Whittier first.

And that's exactly what he'd promised to do.

Another circuit of the Grand Fair later, after a few informative chats, some flirting and a bolt of whiskey, Cade found it: his first proper game of chance in Morrow Creek.

It was time to get to work.

Sliding in place between a dandified farmer—whose Saturday night shirt couldn't disguise the grime of Friday's labor—and a soberly dressed minister, Cade flexed his fingers. He offered his most charming smile. Then he hoped like hell his unlucky streak was at an end, because he needed a win.

Chapter Two

As typically happened at parties, Violet found herself at the spinsters' table in short order. She'd already made the rounds of the gala's volunteer helpers, offering her assistance wherever it was needed. She'd sat in with a fiddle for one of the musicians' simpler songs at the horn player's urgings. She'd also earned hearty laughs among the members of the ladies' auxiliary club with her anecdotes about baking apple-spice jumbles as her contribution to the Grand Fair bake sale. Now she was earnestly engaged in boosting the spirits of her fellow wallflowers. She simply couldn't stand seeing anyone unhappy.

"Even if we *don't* do any dancing tonight," Violet was telling the women nearest her, "that doesn't mean we have to abandon the notion of fun altogether! The evening is still young. Besides, I'm having a wonderful time talking with you!"

The town's most outspoken widow, Mrs. Sunley, snorted over her glass of mescal. "That's very kind of you, Miss Benson. But *I'd* prefer to trot around in the arms of a handsome young buck."

Everyone tittered. Mrs. Sunley typically spoke her mind, sometimes to the point of impropriety. Privately, Violet admired her for it—and for her enviable sense of independence, too. Most likely, her own future would be similar to Mrs. Sunley's, Violet knew—save the aforesaid marriage to begin it, of course.

"That would be delightful, Mrs. Sunley," Violet agreed, "*if* there were any handsome new 'young bucks' here in town."

"Oh! But there *is* a handsome new man in town!" one of the wallflowers said. "We were talking about him earlier!"

At that, everyone launched into a spirited dissertation of the mystery man's rugged good looks, sophisticated suit and rakish air of *je ne sais quoi*. One woman described his smile ("It made me dizzy! I swear it did!"); another rhapsodized over his masculine demeanor ("My brother, Big Horace, looked like a wee girl standing next to him!"); a third waxed lyrical about his elegant manners ("Yes! He *bowed* to me, just like a gentleman in a *Harper's Weekly* story! I almost swooned on the spot!").

"I think he must be here for the private faro tournament," one woman confided in hushed tones. "I heard from my Oscar that all the finest sporting men are coming to town to participate."

Everyone nodded in approbation. Out West, professional gamblers were accorded a great deal of respect, especially when they were winning. Even Jack Murphy, one of Morrow Creek's most reputable citizens, employed professional sporting men to run the tables at his saloon.

"I'll bet he's a big winner!" someone said, still prattling on about the mysterious stranger. "He certainly looked it, with that self-assured air he had. And those *eyes*!"

The women all sighed with romantic delight. Even curmudgeonly Mrs. Sunley fluttered her fan in a coquettish fashion. The gossip went on, but Violet couldn't help laughing.

"Gambler or not, no man is *that* fascinating," she insisted. "In my experience, men are usually clumsy, smelly, unable to properly choose their own neckties and in dire need of moral rehabilitation—which my father is always happy to provide."

"You've been meeting all the wrong men," a friend said.

"Or all the right ones," Mrs. Sunley put in with a knowing grin. "The most interesting men need a little reforming."

Tactfully, no one mentioned that it didn't matter which men Violet met. With a few notable and short-term exceptions, most men hadn't seen her as a potential sweetheart; instead, they'd usually approached her for an introduction to the beautiful Adeline Wilson. Now that Adeline was officially engaged to Clayton Davis, even that role had become obsolete.

As everyone belatedly pondered that dismal realization, silence fell. All the wallflowers exchanged embarrassed glances. Violet studied her still-tapping toes, wishing she didn't make people feel so awkward. Another friend cleared her throat.

"Speaking of moral rehabilitation," she said into

the uncomfortable silence, evidently hoping to end it quickly, "where could I find your father? I have something to discuss with him. I saw him earlier, but he seems to have disappeared."

"He has?" Newly concerned, Violet bit her lip. All thoughts of the dazzling, wholly unlikely new mystery man—and her own unpopularity with such men—were forgotten. At an event like this one, chockablock with wheels of fortune, raffle tickets and—undoubtedly— backroom wagering, there was only one place Reverend Benson would likely be found. "Don't worry. I'll find him," she told her friend. "I'll ask him to speak with you straightaway."

Then, scarcely waiting for her friend to acknowledge her offer, Violet excused herself from the wallflowers' circle. She suddenly had a mission more important than consoling her fellow nondancing, non-sought-after companions: finding her father before he did something foolish.

Cade was down almost three hundred dollars when the first of his gambling companions quit. In disgust, the man hurled down his cards. His chair scraped back. "You keep 'em. I'm out."

The other men at the table protested. Cade did not. After a little conversation, a little gambling and much careful observation, he knew the man's retreat had been inevitable. Like the grubby farmer and the soft-handed minister who remained at the table, the man had been in over his head. All the same, Cade had the good sense and the good manners to keep his gaze fixed on the baize-covered table, tabulating the money in the kitty.

His unlucky streak had not yet ended. Nothing less than an impressive win would get him invited to the private, high-stakes faro tables where he expected to find Percy Whittier and to make him pay for his sins. With so much at stake, Cade couldn't relax. He couldn't quit. He couldn't fold. He could only focus on the game with the same taut intensity he always employed.

The departing man opened the back room's door. The lively sounds of the Grand Fair's music and dancing swept inside. So did the earthy, aromatic scent of Kentucky's finest tobacco.

Nostrils flaring, Cade looked up.

He knew that blend. Its fragrance was melded with his earliest memories. It was forever tied to loneliness and loss…and to questions he'd never been able to find the answers to.

It was the signature blend smoked by Percy Whittier.

Frozen in place, Cade stared blindly at his cards. Could he be this lucky? He'd believed the rumor had been true. He'd believed Whittier was in Morrow Creek; otherwise, Cade wouldn't have come there, with or without Simon Blackhouse's aid. But to find Whittier by chance this way, *tonight…*

It defied the odds laid in by even the most hopeful gambler. And Cade had never been hopeful.

Hope was for people who fooled themselves into forgetting the truth: that life was short, fickle and cruel. More than anyone, Cade knew better than to put his faith in long odds. Doubtless, he told himself as he went on studying his hand, many men smoked that particular Kentucky blend, not just Whittier.

An instant later, a burst of raucous fiddle music restored his usual sense of purpose. What was he doing just sitting there?

Anyone looking at him would have thought Cade didn't *really* want to find Whittier. The notion was daft. He might not be hopeful, Cade reminded himself, but he *was* determined. He'd made promises to Judah. He intended to keep them or die trying.

"I'm out, too." Heart pounding, Cade made himself stand. He schooled his face in an impassive expression, needing to hide the damnably naive hopefulness he felt. The answers he needed felt tantalizingly close. "Night, all. Good luck, Reverend."

Startled, the minister glanced up. He couldn't have known that Cade had already taken pity on his foolish wagering and slipped him an "improving" card when everyone else had been watching their easily defeated companion leave the game. But Cade knew it. He hoped the minister took the boon and quit, too. Otherwise, the way he'd been wagering, he'd lose for sure.

Cade hadn't wanted to let that happen. Not because the minister was a holy man; Cade didn't have much use for preaching. But according to their chin-wagging, the widowed minister had a daughter—as it happened, the same mousy woman who'd tossed away her dance card—and Cade hadn't wanted the man's family to pay for his witlessness.

Giving the minister that improving card had meant setting back his own game, Cade knew. But he'd had faith he could regain his edge. The hapless holy man didn't have the same advantage.

The door creaked. Through the slowly narrowing gap in the doorway, Cade glimpsed swirls of dancers, a wisp of smoke…and the profile of a cigar-smoking man. Was it really Whittier?

Cade couldn't be certain. In Omaha, he'd spooked Whittier with a too-aggressive pursuit. He'd lost him for weeks. Now Cade had to be smarter. Otherwise, he might ruin his advantage.

As far as he knew, Whittier didn't know Cade was still in pursuit of him. Cade meant to keep it that way… until he caught up altogether.

"Don't forget our weekly game at the Lorndorff!" one of the men called from behind him. "We can always use one more man."

"'Specially a losing man!" Another yokel gambler guffawed.

Too intent to argue with their wrongheaded assessment of his skills, Cade raised his hand in acknowledgment of their invitation. It wasn't quite the wagering offer he needed, but he reckoned it was a start. From here, word of his ability would travel upward to the elite circuit and eventually—he hoped—garner him an invitation to those sought-after tables.

Decisively, Cade slipped into the giddy fray of the Grand Fair. He was almost close enough, he saw, to identify Whittier for certain. With only a faded tintype and his own hazy memory to go on, it was hard to tell. But the smell of the man's distinctive tobacco blend tantalized Cade with its nearness.

He needed a plan. The moment he saw the minister's daughter—no longer burdened with overcoats—determinedly on her way to the back room, Cade hit upon one. This time, he would keep his distance from Whittier until the moment was right. This time, he would be smart. This time, he would win.

In the meantime, he had to get a little closer. So...

"There you are!" Smiling, Cade pulled the woman into his arms, keeping Whittier in sight. "You're missing our dance!"

"Oh no I'm not!" the woman said. "I'd never miss a dance!"

Then, to Cade's immense relief and improbable good fortune, the woman allowed him to dance them both into the frolicsome melee...straight toward the spot where Cade had last glimpsed his quarry.

This must be what it felt like to fly, Violet thought as the handsome stranger whirled her around the dance floor. Guided by his strong arms and innate dexterity, she nearly laughed.

This was what she'd been wanting all night.

This...and maybe more.

Enchanted, Violet gazed up into the stranger's arresting face. Clearly, this was the man who'd had all the town's wallflowers aflutter. Indeed, as she examined his wavy dark hair, piercing blue eyes and impeccably arrayed features, she *did* feel a bit dizzy. A bit bedazzled. A bit swoony.

He was...*perfect.*

He delivered her an abashed smile. "Thank you for

letting me sweep you away just now. I'm in your debt, Miss...?"

"Benson. Violet Benson." Beset by her rapidly galloping heartbeat, Violet sucked down a breath. She executed another turn in the dance. This had to be some sort of mistake, but she'd be jiggered if she'd miss this opportunity to kick up her heels. Politely, she asked, "And you are?"

"Cade Foster. I'm very pleased to meet you, Miss Benson."

Hearing her name on his lips made Violet feel downright light-headed. How did he manage to make her ordinary name sound so extraordinarily intimate? So intriguing? So...wonderful?

On the verge of asking him exactly that question, Violet stopped herself. Instead she blurted, "You're new in town."

It was not a smooth entrée to further conversation. But a person would not have guessed as much to look at Cade Foster's appealing smile—a smile that engaged twin dimples in his cheeks.

"Not anymore." He tightened his hand on hers, sweeping them both in an elegant arc across the room. "In your company, Miss Benson, I suddenly feel quite welcomed to Morrow Creek."

Goodness, he was charming. And he was charming *her*! Awed by the realization, Violet prayed her feet wouldn't lose all sense of rhythm. She glanced downward. Blessedly, her feet seemed to be keeping up very well...even while the rest of her dithered.

"Well, I have that effect on people," she confessed.

"My friends say I'm a veritable one-woman hospitality committee. Probably owing to all my charity work. You see, I do a great deal of volunteering among the destitute, the sick, the needy—"

"They're fortunate to have you. As am I, tonight."

"Oh. Now you're teasing me."

"Not at all." Mr. Foster danced them both near the raffle cage and its attendant cash box. "I'm enjoying you. I think you're enjoying me, too—at least if your smile is any proof."

Caught, Violet tried to tamp down her wide, telltale smile. But it was no use. It was simply too delightful to be *flirted with* this way! Especially by such a dashing man. Also, she couldn't help noticing that several conversations had quit at the edge of the dance floor. A few dancers had even slowed to gawk. The whole place, it seemed, was fixated on Violet and her gallant dance partner. The sensation was altogether novel.

She, Violet Benson, was the center of attention!

This must be what her friend Adeline experienced every day.

Encouraged by that realization, Violet gazed up at him. "My smile doesn't prove a thing about my supposed feelings for you, Mr. Foster," she said in her most coquettish tone. Until now she had only employed that tone in her imagination. It felt much more fun in truth. "I always smile when performing a good deed. It makes me happy to lend a hand to those in need."

Mr. Foster appeared dumbfounded. "Charity? You're likening *me* to a charity case?" He raised his eyebrows.

"I assure you, Miss Benson, I do not need help. Not from you or anyone else."

"Are you sure?" Violet angled her head, studying him. "When you first invited me to dance, I felt sure I detected a certain air of…desperation about you. I know it sounds strange, but—"

He stumbled. For an instant, they both lost the cadence of the dance. Then his hand closed more securely around hers, they both recaptured the necessary steps, and Violet reconsidered.

Undoubtedly, Cade Foster had never been desperate for anything in his life. He seemed the sort of man for whom everything fell into place, lickety-split. Still, during those first few moments, she had definitely felt… *something* from him.

Something, if not desperate, then very, very needful.

"You move very well, Miss Benson." Cade Foster presented her with his flawless profile. If he noticed the avid stares and gossipy whispers directed their way, he gave no sign of it. "The men in town must be bereft that you threw away your dance card."

She gawked at him, all thoughts of his potential desperation forgotten. "You saw that? You saw…me?"

"Of course I did." Mr. Foster glanced sideways. He frowned. "Why did you do it? Why did you throw away your dance card?"

Still enraptured with the notion that she might *move well,* as he'd said, Violet felt a shiver race through her. *He* was the one who moved well—the one who danced with effortless poise. Cade Foster's skill was to make his partner seem equally adept.

Doubtless he possessed several similar talents…all of which would be scintillating and assured and unlikely to be shared with Violet beyond this night and this dance. Maybe that's why she let herself fling her usual caution to the wind.

"Why did I throw away my dance card? The answer to that question, Mr. Foster, will cost you another dance."

He smiled, seeming impressed. "You're bold. I wouldn't have expected that from a self-confessed do-gooder."

"I prefer 'aid worker.' And a straight answer."

Mr. Foster laughed. "And bolder still." He twirled her as the last flourish of music played. He glanced sideways, then muttered a swearword under his breath. "But I have to refuse."

"Why?" Violet kept her tone light. "Are you afraid I might save you with a dose of well-placed charity work?"

"No." Inexplicably, he paled. "I'm beyond redemption."

His voice sounded fraught. Troubled, Violet dared to touch his shoulder. "I'm sorry. I was being flippant. I didn't mean—"

"Take this." As the next dance began, Mr. Foster gave her something: a dance card. *Her* dance card. "You'll be needing it."

Violet boggled at it. How had he come to possess her dance card? "I don't need it. There was a reason it was empty."

He didn't seem to hear her. "Thank you for the dance."

"We could have another. I still haven't answered your—"

"Your father is headed to the mescal booth to celebrate his recent win at cards." Mr. Foster nodded. "I'm guessing you'll want to intercept him before he gets two fistfuls and a snort."

Her father? Winning and *drinking?* But how could Mr. Foster possibly have identified both the Reverend Benson *and* his worst foibles, all in a single glance? Confused, Violet turned.

It was true, she saw. However unaccountably, Cade Foster had summed up the situation. Papa did appear to have won.

He also appeared to be intent on memorializing his victory at the gambling table by pickling himself in locally brewed liquor. Her father, although devout and bookish by nature, had never refused a whiskey. He considered it a fair restorative.

"Next time I see you, you'll be overrun with suitors." With another beguiling smile and a touch of her hand, Cade Foster bowed to Violet. He didn't seem to realize how preposterous his statement really was. "I'm happy to have danced with you first."

Violet didn't have time to elucidate matters to him. Nor did she want to. Cade Foster had enjoyed dancing with her! Why should she spoil that by telling him that she typically spent more time decorating for parties than dancing at them?

"Thank you very much. I'm happy to have danced

with you, too!" Eagerly, she nodded. "But now I really must dash!"

Then, with Cade Foster's enthralling features still dancing in her mind, Violet picked up her skirts and went to do her duty. Her turn at being belle of the ball was over. For her it was back to everyday existence— without the pleasure of a man's hand in hers to help guide her through…or to share her smiles.

"Papa!" she cried an instant later. "What have you done?"

"Violet, my dear!" Her father embraced her happily. "You're just who I wanted to see. Look! I won fistfuls of money!"

"Oh, dear." Nibbling her lip, Violet swept her father's winnings with a chary look. Probably he would add them to the collection plate on Sunday, but until then there was always the chance he would wager most or all of it. She didn't approve of gambling, but it seemed to give Papa a happiness he'd lost since the death of her poor mother years ago. "Congratulations!"

"That's my girl!" He kissed her cheek, then delivered her a quelling frown. "But shouldn't you be conducting the drawing?"

The drawing. She'd forgotten about the raffle entirely. As organizer of the gala, Violet was responsible for determining the winner and for delivering the money raised to the committee.

"Yes! I was just about to do that." Reminded of her pressing duties, Violet sighed. Dancing had been *so* much nicer!

Turning back for one last compelling look, Violet

glimpsed Cade Foster striding through the dancers. He was leaving her behind just as abruptly as he'd swept her into the dance.

It was only too bad, Violet thought as she watched him go, that she'd had a taste of flying with him at all. Now she knew, for the first time ever, exactly what she'd been missing in her life.

Strangely enough, it had taken an enigmatic and downright captivating man to show her the truth: she *needed* to fly. Perhaps recklessly. Perhaps foolishly. But regularly and soon, preferably with a companion by her side. But…how?

Chapter Three

Seated across the table from Cade in his suite at the Lorndorff Hotel, Simon Blackhouse smiled. That's how Cade knew something significant was afoot. Blackhouse never smiled, not while there were cards in his hand or dice within his reach. Blackhouse took gambling as seriously as he did nothing else.

"What's the matter with you? Are you drunk?" Cade peered out the hotel suite's lavishly curtained window. A slice of autumnal blue sky greeted him. "It's only ten in the morning."

"I'm not drunk. I'm *thinking*."

"Aha. That explains it." With sham concern, Cade leaned nearer. "You're new at making an effort with things, so I should probably warn you—*thinking*, once begun, is hard to stop."

"Very funny." Unperturbed, Blackhouse smiled anew at his cards, making Cade feel doubly wary. "I can't help it if things come easily to me," his sponsor argued. "It's in my nature."

"It's in your inheritance." Cade gestured. "New game?"

With a murmur of agreement, Blackhouse rounded up the cards. He dealt. For a while, the only sounds were the ticking of the mantelpiece clock and the shuffling of cards.

At the conclusion of their game, Blackhouse smiled again.

"That's the fourth game straight you've won today." He studied Cade from over the tops of his losing cards. "You know what this means, don't you? Your unlucky streak has ended."

Cade wasn't so sure. "If I were playing a *skilled* gambler—"

"You'd still win," Blackhouse told him, ignoring his genial gibe. "You're the luckiest son of a bitch I've ever known." With his shirt half buttoned and his suit coat askew, Blackhouse seemed the very picture of privileged, happy-go-lucky young bachelorhood. "Aside from myself, of course. I'm damnably lucky, too." Appearing characteristically pleased by that, he lit a cheroot. He gazed at Cade through its upward-curling smoke. "What happened? Did you bed a Gypsy who broke the curse?"

"I wish it had been that simple. I would have done that months ago." It had been almost that long since he'd had a break in his search for Percy Whittier. Last night hadn't changed much in that regard. Cade had lost sight of Whittier while dancing with Violet Benson. Although he'd tried not to be, he'd been distracted by her—especially by her too-astute claim that he'd appeared desperate. *Desperate!* "I'm afraid the only woman I've been with lately was a naive reformer. She threatened to 'save' me." Cade shuddered at the remembrance. "I can't stand do-gooders. They remind me of orphan trains and foundling homes."

"So?" Blackhouse arched his brow. With nimble fingers, he scooped up the playing cards. "I've established a few foundling homes myself. They're not all bad." As though considering those altruistic efforts—along with the prestigious family name and attendant family fortune that had facilitated them—Blackhouse paused. He shook his head, then shuffled expertly. "A Rom woman would have been wilder," he alleged, grinning again.

Disturbed by the return of that grin, Cade frowned, uncomfortably reminded that he didn't truly know Blackhouse well enough to discern his intentions but had to trust him anyway.

Although charming, wealthy and advantageously footloose—with a private luxury train car and a loyal valet to prove it—Blackhouse was nonetheless a mysterious figure to Cade. They had met at a poker table in San Francisco and had become friends (of a kind) while outlasting every other player at the table. When Blackhouse had unexpectedly offered to finance Cade's search for Percy Whittier, Cade had cautiously agreed. He hadn't had the stakes to continue alone. Likely, Blackhouse had known that and had decided to exploit it…for whatever reasons.

He still didn't know what Blackhouse's interest in Whittier was. Knowing Blackhouse, it was something frivolous. All Cade knew was that Blackhouse had the money, Cade had the tenacity, and between them they could bring Whittier to heel.

"I don't have time for *any* women," Cade said. "Rom or not." He told Blackhouse about spotting Whittier at the Grand Fair and about losing him during the dance. "He must still be in town."

"Yes. Faro is his game. He'd be unlikely to miss the tournament." Agreeably, Blackhouse cut the cards. He arranged them on the table between them, then nodded cannily at Cade. "Go ahead. Choose four. If you pick out all the aces, I'll lay out an extra thousand for tonight's gaming. And maybe lend you my overcoat, too." An amused look. "You seem to have lost yours."

Cade didn't take the bait. He didn't want to discuss giving his warm overcoat to the grimy-faced child sharper in the Morrow Creek alleyway. "I don't need any more of your money." *Not yet.* "Besides, the odds of choosing all four aces in a row are—"

"Inordinate. I know. That's the point." With a leisurely gesture, Blackhouse summoned Adams, his valet. "Do it."

"Fine." Exasperated, Cade flipped up four cards.

In short order, a queen and three aces stared up at him.

"See? Just as I thought." Blackhouse pointed. "Not all four aces, that's true, but still a good enough draw to prove I'm right. You should be delighted." Yawning, Blackhouse selected a postmarked envelope from the silver tray that Adams offered him. He tossed it in front of Cade. "By the way, this letter from your brother arrived this morning. I hope Judah is well?"

Cade nodded, still boggling at his chosen cards. Turning up three aces was unbelievable. "His leg should be almost healed by now." Distractedly, Cade frowned. "You must be double dealing."

Blackhouse scoffed. "I'm not double dealing. I'm not trimming cards. I'm not even wearing a holdout, despite my enthusiasm for collecting such things." He spread his arms, showing he was free of mechanical cheating devices. "It's *you,* Foster. Just you. Your usual good luck has clearly returned."

Dubiously, Cade regarded the cards. Like most sporting men, he believed in superstition. It was foolhardy and unreasonable not to. A man needed all the breaks he could get. But *this…*

"I think it must be your reformer who did it," Blackhouse opined. "She's your lucky charm. That's the only explanation."

Lucky charm. Cade could use one of those, especially now.

Still filled with disbelief, he scowled at the cards. He didn't want to agree with Blackhouse. He didn't want to believe in luck alone. But with no other leads readily available….

"Well, there's only one way to find out, isn't there?" Cade asked. "That's to find my 'lucky charm' and see what happens."

Then he threw on a necktie, grabbed his suit coat and hat, and went in search of his very own private do-gooder and (potential) good-luck charm.

God help him, he seemed to need her.

* * *

When Violet glimpsed the town newcomer, Cade Foster, from across the room at the charity kitchen she'd organized with the help of Grace Murphy and her ladies' auxiliary club, she knew she had to be imagining things…which wasn't altogether surprising, given how preoccupied she'd been since yesterday.

All afternoon long, even while ladling up soup and passing out bread donated by Molly Copeland's popular bakery, Violet had relived last night's dance at the Grand Fair. She'd recalled Cade Foster's smile. She'd remembered his features. She'd contemplated his intriguingly muscular personhood and sighed over his eyes. She'd even envisioned herself seeing him again.

So a part of her wasn't at all surprised to catch sight of him there. The rest of her knew that she should pinch herself—especially when Cade Foster spied her, raised his hand in a masculine greeting, then determinedly headed in her direction.

"Yes!" someone whispered nearby. "It's definitely *him*!"

"Did you see them *dancing* together?" someone else added.

"I saw her *leave him* standing heartbroken on the dance floor!" a third gossip added in breathless tones. "Imagine that! Plain Violet Benson, the minister's daughter, having the cheek to turn her back on a man who's willing to dance with her!"

Well. Being the subject of such vaguely uncharitable gossip took some of the fun out of things, Violet thought. That was a new and unwelcome experience for her—one she'd helped Adeline through a time or two, though. Besides, she retorted to herself silently, she hadn't left Cade on the dance floor. She'd gone to fetch her father—it was an entirely different thing. Tightening her hold on her soup ladle, she went on watching Cade approach.

Plainly, he was close enough to hear everything her fellow helpers were saying, Violet realized. Because almost imperceptibly, he angled his head toward that chatty clump of gossips, flashed them a brief but brilliant grin, then kept right on going.

Collectively, the three women swooned. For herself, Violet only stood there with her ladle at the ready. *This,* she realized with another flutter of excitement, might be her chance to fly!

Cade Foster might be her chance to dance through *every* part of her life—her chance to have some *fun*. It was exactly what she'd yearned for at the Grand Fair last night. Violet certainly didn't have much to lose by trying something new. So that's exactly what she meant to do—beginning right now, with Cade.

Maybe the local men hadn't been able to glimpse Violet's charms past Adeline Wilson's dazzle, it occurred to her, but Cade had. That made him special. That made him worthy of joining her in her newfound quest to spread her wings.

At least that way, when she was Mrs. Sunley's age, Violet reasoned, she'd have some thrilling memories to look back on.

Oblivious to her hasty decision making, Cade reached her.

"You're a difficult woman to find." This time, his

smile touched *her* alone, leaving aside her sharp-tongued cohorts. "I've been to the jailhouse, Dr. Finney's medical office, your father's church and the schoolhouse— I was told you sometimes volunteer with schoolmarm McCabe. And now here you are in the very last place I thought to look."

"Well, you always find everything in the very last place you look, don't you?" Violet couldn't help staring. She felt defenseless against his charisma, spellbound by his voice, fascinated by his just-for-her smile. With Cade Foster inside it, her charity kitchen suddenly felt much too small and meager. "If you kept on searching after that it would be silly."

Cade Foster blinked. Then he laughed. "That's true."

"You may be glib, Mr. Foster, but I'm sensible." Violet ladled up some soup for the next recipient. She gave the needy woman a smile, then received a warm thank-you in return. The line of recipients moved up a pace. "As you can see, I'm quite busy here, as well. So if you want to talk charming nonsense to me, I'm afraid you'll just have to do it later."

A shared gasp came from nearby. Evidently, her colleagues were still eavesdropping, and they fully expected her to fall at Cade's feet, lovesick with longing, at the first opportunity.

He gave her another grin. "You think I'm charming, then?"

"And glib. I also said 'glib.' Didn't you hear that part?"

"I heard it. But I don't think you believe it."

Violet smiled. "I wouldn't say it if I didn't."

"Truly?" Mr. Foster seemed intrigued by that notion, commonplace as it was. He moved closer, nearly shoulder to shoulder with her. "Do you always say exactly what you think?"

"Why not?" Violet stirred her soup. "Don't you?"

"I'm a professional sporting man, Miss Benson. I make my living on hope and happenstance. Honesty doesn't enter into it."

"It seemed to do so last night. Between us."

At her words, he seemed taken aback. "Well, I *was* honest with you about *not* being a desperate man," Mr. Foster said, "so if that's what you mean regarding honesty between us—"

"No," Violet interrupted gently. "I mean that, after we danced, you told me I would be swamped with suitors. That's what you said. *Honestly.* I didn't believe you, but you were right!" Gleefully, she confided further, "After you left the Grand Fair, I went through *two* more dance cards!"

Alone in her bedroom afterward—with care and no small measure of disbelief—she'd pressed those signature-filled dance cards between her Bible pages for safekeeping. She'd thought they might be her only mementos of that extraordinary night. But now that Cade Foster had arrived, all broad shouldered and fascinating, at her charity kitchen, the world felt ripe with possibilities. Given his occupation, he seemed twice as likely to be capable of satisfying her urge for extra zest in her dutiful, workaday life.

"*Two* dance cards? You danced that much?" Relief

softened his features, lending sparkle to his vivid eyes. "That must have been fun."

"It was unprecedented," Violet told him candidly. She handed a hunk of bread to the next recipient. "I've never danced so much in all my life! I'm sure it was because of you. By dancing with me last night, you seem to have kindled some sort of curiosity about me, Mr. Foster."

"The men in Morrow Creek aren't alone in being curious about you." Intimately, he lowered his voice. "I am, too. I haven't been able to stop thinking about you."

"I'll only be sorry when it's over." Violet sighed, still reminiscing about last night. "Before long, folks in town will forget this, and I'll be back to cheering up the wall-flowers at parties while everyone else…" She paused, belatedly realizing the astonishing admission he'd made. "*You?* Thinking about *me*?"

She nearly had to use her soup ladle to close her gaping jaw. The very notion was dumbfounding. And thrilling too!

"Yes. You're going to be very important to me, Miss Benson. I can feel it." Pausing to study the visitors to the charity kitchen, Cade Foster stepped into place beside Violet. Adeptly, he handed a bowl of soup and some bread to the next person in line. The poor woman who received it nearly fainted with glee at being served by him. He didn't seem to notice her obvious ardor. "I'd like to become equally important to you, if you'll let me."

Violet flashed him a dubious look. She might be hopeful, but she was not an imbecile. Nor was she especially naive.

"You could have the company of any woman in

town." As proof, Violet gestured to the other volunteers. To a woman, they were gazing swoonily, chin in hand, at Cade Foster's handsome countenance. All three of them sighed. One waved. "Do you expect me to believe that of all the ladies in town, you are interested in me? I know what I look like, Mr. Foster. As a minister's daughter, I can't bring you a fine dowry, either. So—"

"I'm not asking for your hand in marriage." He seemed disturbed by her rebuttal and maybe a mite perplexed, too. "Is there someplace we can talk about this privately?"

Violet shook her head. As much as she wanted to be more venturesome, she did have obligations to consider. Besides, *thinking* about adventuring was not the same as *doing* it.

"Not unless I quit work," she said, "and that's—"

Impossible, Violet meant to say.

But before she could, her fellow volunteers interrupted.

"Very easily done!" one of them said.

Chattering and smiling, they stripped Violet of her soup ladle. They untied her apron and smoothed her upswept hair. They filled in her place in line, then all but shoved her forcibly out the door with the gambler. At that, Violet couldn't help forgiving them their unkind gossip earlier. She wasn't a woman who held a grudge. No doubt they'd simply been surprised that she'd been so popular with Mr. Foster last night…and today.

That made four of them. Because she was surprised, too.

"Go on!" one of her friends urged cheerfully. "You

work all the time! If anyone deserves a break, Violet, it's you."

"Yes. Have fun." Another friend winked. "We'll take care of everything here. Don't you worry about a thing. He's a gambler, isn't he? So why don't *you* take a chance for a change? On *him*!"

So, with no further avenue of protest available to her and with Cade Foster standing patiently nearby, Violet did just that: she took a chance…on a gambler.

Sitting beside Cade on a narrow bench outside the charity kitchen next to a sweeping ponderosa pine tree and a branching rivulet of the nearby creek, Violet Benson shook her head.

Plainly surprised, she asked, "You want me to do *what*?"

Cade didn't answer at first. He simply felt too distracted by what she'd said earlier: *I know what I look like, Mr. Foster.*

That admission was telling. It was, as Cade was rapidly learning, characteristically direct, too. If he'd been a crueler man, he would have used Miss Benson's feelings about her appearance to gain an advantage. As it was, Cade could only examine her through clear eyes, wondering what it must be like to live as Violet Benson did: plain featured and overlooked.

Unexpectedly, a kinship arose inside him. He knew what it felt like to be overlooked—to be left behind. He didn't want that for her or anyone.

Of a certain, Violet's pale red hair was not quite as stylishly arranged as the other ladies' was. Her complexion was a mite too ruddy to be called fashionably pale. Her teeth sported a gap in front, and her nose was too assertive to be considered strictly "pretty." But her hazel eyes were vivacious, her mouth was full and gentle looking, and her hands...

Well, her hands stirred in Cade an unlikely wish to be blessed by her touch—to be granted that salvation she'd alluded to last night when they'd danced. Appalled by the realization, he frowned. He repeated the proposition he'd just made to her.

"I want you to be my good-luck charm. To be available to me at a moment's notice before faro games and hands of poker." He spied her mistrustful expression and added, "I'll pay you for the privilege, of course. I wouldn't consider asking you to do this otherwise. It's only fair that you're compensated."

She made a face. "You really believe in good-luck charms?"

"I can't afford not to. Mine is a precarious business."

"And you believe *I* am yours?" She sounded amused. And intrigued. And unexpectedly compassionate, too. Her very presence exuded kindheartedness and care and a certain special exuberance that intrigued him. "Your good-luck charm, I mean?"

"After I met you," Cade said simply, "my luck changed."

For a moment, Violet Benson gazed across the street that bordered the charity kitchen. Wagons and buggies passed by; the clomping of hooves raised drifts of dust. Those drifts reminded Cade of cigar smoke—and of losing sight of Percy Whittier.

He might be a fool, it occurred to Cade, to ally himself with the same woman who'd disastrously distracted him from his search for Whittier last night. He hoped he didn't regret this.

"If you have enough money to pay me, why do you need luck?" Violet Benson asked astutely. "Why do you need to win at all?"

That was easy. "Because I don't gamble to win money."

"Then you're not doing it properly." She gave a pert smile.

Unable to resist as he should have done, Cade returned that smile. "I entered the gambling circuit to track down a man I'm searching for," he explained. "It's been several years now. I've come close. I've had clues and false leads and near misses. But I've never faced him across a gambling table. I've never caught up with him long enough to get what I want from him. To do that, I need to win. I need to get invited to all the best tables. I need to fit in among the men he runs with."

"If you plan to kill him, I won't help you." Suddenly chilly where she'd once been warm, Violet Benson examined him. "I'll help Sheriff Caffey track you down, in fact. I have a fair sense of what you look like, as does every other woman in town."

This time, Cade smiled more artfully. "I'm flattered by your attention," he said in a teasing tone. Deliberately, he flashed both dimples. "I have every intention of rewarding it, too, in ways I think we'd both enjoy… very, *very* much."

"Right now," Violet clarified drily, "I'm memorizing

your features so I can help the deputy draw a wanted poster."

Hmm. Charming female subjects was something Cade had learned to excel at. Perversely, he felt impressed that Violet Benson appeared too levelheaded to fall for his misdirection.

"I want answers from him, that's all." Cade leveled a square look at Violet. "I want to know why he ran out on his family back East. They loved him and needed him, and he—"

Unexpectedly, Cade heard his voice break. A powerful sense of bereavement and anger and solitude welled inside him.

He scarcely knew what to make of it. Irately, he reasoned that Violet Benson and her damnable compassion had caused it. For the second time that day, he wondered if he was making a terrible mistake by coming to her— by trusting her even this far.

"He must have had a good reason for leaving," she said in a thoughtful tone, proving his caution was warranted. Naively, she added, "No man would ever abandon his family unless—"

"*Percy Whittier did.*" Hard-faced, Cade stared at her. He needed to hold on to his fury and hurt. It fueled him when he didn't want to continue searching. He didn't need Violet Benson's natural empathy to awaken something soft inside him—something that was better left to wither and die, as it had been on its way to doing before he'd met her. "Percy Whittier left his family. There's no reason in the world that excuses that."

"I see." Violet inhaled. "You seem very intent on

finding this man. Are you a detective, then, hired by his family?"

"No." Cade noticed his hands were shaking. He clenched them, hoping to make the shaking stop.

"A U.S. Marshal? A lawman of some sort?"

"No." Hellfire. Why couldn't he quit shaking? "Neither."

"Hmm. You're going to have to be a bit more forthcoming if you expect me to help you." Through inquisitive eyes, Violet studied him. Lightly, she touched his fisted hand. Like magic, he stopped trembling. Awed, Cade stared as she stroked him, soothingly, the same way a parent might calm a frightened child or a caregiver might help a wounded man. "I might be plain and sensible and occasionally overlooked," she said, "but I'm also—"

"Forbidden to talk about yourself that way," Cade interrupted in his sternest tone. It aggrieved him that she kept on referring to herself as ugly and passed over. Surely the folks in this little creekside town weren't so blind that they couldn't see she had worth beyond bland prettiness. "I won't have it. If we're going to strike a bargain between us, you'll have to quit reminding me of how 'unattractive' you are."

"I know, I know." Self-consciously, Violet Benson ducked her head. She rubbed her thumb over the back of his hand, a bit nervously now. "What God gave me is just fine. The Lord doesn't make mistakes in creating us. My father's told me those things many, many times." She lifted her gaze to his face, her eyes flashing with a glimmer of defiance. "But that doesn't mean, Mr. Foster, that you have license to call me unattractive!"

Stricken, Cade gazed at her. "I hurt you. I'm sorry."

"I've made peace with my looks," Violet went on rather huffily, "but I still expect common decency from people. Even you! That was thoughtless and unkind. You must know that."

He hadn't known that. He'd only been repeating what she'd said herself. Maybe he'd been on this hunt for Whittier for too long. Maybe he was becoming unfit for society. Maybe, with every hand of cards and risky wager, he was losing…everything.

"I'm *very* sorry." He was, too. Very rapidly, she was becoming more than a means to restoring his good luck. She was becoming…*essential*. Carefully, Cade raised his free hand to her slender jaw. He turned her face to his. "I like looking at you. I've never known anyone whose emotions were so evident."

"That doesn't sound like much of a compliment."

"It *is* a compliment. From a man who spends all day being as poker-faced as possible." He smiled. "I find you…fascinating."

"Truly?" Violet's lips quirked. Her wide hazel eyes held a challenge. "Can you guess what emotion I'm feeling right now?"

"Suspicion." Cade stroked her cheek, just once, then made himself let her go. He missed her softness almost immediately. "But you don't have to be suspicious of me, Miss Benson."

"Call me Violet. Then perhaps I won't be."

That brought a smile to his face. "I'd be honored to do so. And you should call me Cade. *Please* call me Cade."

"All right. Cade." She gave a self-deprecating laugh. "Heaven knows, you might be the only man who ever invites such familiarity from me. I guess I might as well enjoy it!"

Again, Cade looked at her sternly. "I can make sure you enjoy it. I can make sure every man in Morrow Creek wants you."

She arched her brow at his certainty, seeming more than a little bit doubtful. "You're not a detective, a marshal or a lawman." Her smile turned playful. "You're a miracle worker!"

He'd had enough. "The real tragedy in life isn't failing to believe that hope exists, Violet. It's convincing yourself that you don't want any hope, even when it's right in front of you."

"Are you talking about me? Or about you?"

Cade snorted. "I'm talking about the likelihood of your choosing from among a dozen smitten suitors if you help me."

"You mean if I behave as your lucky charm?"

A nod. "Once everyone sees us together, people will look at you with new eyes. They'll wonder why *I* want you—why I'm captivated with you. They'll imagine… all manner of things."

She inhaled again, steadying herself. "Good things?"

The lilt of hopefulness in her voice was heartrending.

"Good things," Cade affirmed, feeling touched by her beyond all reason. He didn't know why he wanted to help her—why he wanted to erase her wrongheaded notion that she was undesirable and unnoticed. He only knew that he did. "Everyone wants what they can't have. Especially men. I know more about human nature than I want to, after all these years of wagering, and I know that's true. Let me show you, Violet. Let's strike a deal."

Hesitating, she bit her lip. "Who will know about this?"

"As far as your friends and neighbors are concerned, I'll be courting you," Cade swore, taking her hand. "That's all."

A glance. "But really *I'll* be bringing *you* good luck."

She was smart, he realized. And much less naive than he'd thought. That made Cade feel better about this whole endeavor.

"Yes," he said. "You'll be bringing me good luck." He offered her a winning smile—one he knew was persuasive. "But hopefully that good luck will be shared by us both."

"You know," she mused, giving him another of her patented, too-observant looks, "I think you're an optimist at heart."

"I think you've only just met me," Cade disagreed, "and it shows."

Her smile touched him, suddenly mysterious. "Well, you'd better find some optimism, then. Because I can only do this if my father agrees. That means you'll have to impress him at dinner tonight and obtain his blessing. Will I see you at six?"

Sunnily and capably, Violet gave him the particulars.

Dumbstruck at the realization that he'd have to impress a straitlaced minister to put his good-luck-charm plan in motion, Cade hesitated. Then he nodded. The minute he did so, Violet Benson jumped up from her bench, briskly said goodbye, then left him alone while she returned to her charitable good works.

That was twice she'd left him stranded, Cade realized as he watched her leave. The first time, on the Grand Fair dance floor, he'd purposely allowed her to do so. The second time…

Well, the second time, just now, he hadn't. Damnation. Was it possible that an innocent small-town girl had outmaneuvered him?

Worse, was it possible that a *reformer* had outfoxed him?

No. He was worldly, intelligent and determined. No one could outwit him. Except maybe Percy Whittier. And even then only a few times.

But the man wasn't a god, and he wasn't infallible. He was only irredeemable. With a little more effort, Cade knew he would find him. Then he would get the answers he needed.

The answers he'd promised Judah.

In the meantime, Cade had a few more hours to spend before dinnertime at the Benson household. That was just enough time, he reckoned, to write to his brother, beat Blackhouse at cards a few more times…and strategize how best to turn Violet Benson into an irresistible temptress, all before Cade left town in the next week or two.

Chapter Four

When Violet heard a decisive knock at the door at precisely fifteen minutes before six o'clock that evening, she felt her heartbeat perk up a notch. Jittery and breathless, she untied her ruffled apron. She hung it on its hook in the kitchen. She smoothed down her skirts, then hastened to the front door.

There, she stopped. Staring at that ordinary white-painted, wooden-framed door, so familiar and yet so unremarkable, Violet couldn't resist feeling that something *momentous* was about to occur. For the first time ever, she'd invited a man to dinner. He'd accepted. And now...who knew what might happen.

Fastening a smile on her face, Violet tugged open the door.

The gambler Cade Foster stood on her front porch, with the setting sun and all of Morrow Creek behind him, attired in yet another of his well-designed suits. His dark hair, brushed from his face in waves, framed his features superbly. His white shirt looked crisp. His necktie looked silky. His coat set off his broad-shoul-dered physique to perfection. He looked...*wonderful*.

The only thing missing in his appearance was—

A smile. Just as she thought it, Cade gifted her with one. At the sight of it, Violet's poor heart pitter-pattered twice as energetically. He really was *so* handsome. And *so* charming!

Unfortunately, while Violet was savoring the sight of *him*, Cade was enjoying an equal opportunity to scrutinize *her.* He sent his gaze roving over her flowing calico skirts, her dress's high-buttoned bodice, her lace-trimmed shawl…and nodded.

"You look lovely." He took her hand in greeting. His fingers felt warm over hers—warm and deft and masculine. "That dress brings out the green in your eyes. They're sparkling."

"That's because I'm happy to see you. Please, come in!"

Violet stepped back with a flourish, feeling uncommonly pleased that he'd approved of her ensemble. The oak plank floorboards creaked under her feet; the scent of roast chicken and root vegetables wafted from the kitchen's cast-iron stove. Expectantly, she clasped her hands, waiting for him to enter.

Cade didn't move. Instead he gave her a doubtful frown. "I hope it's all right if there's one more for dinner."

From behind him, Cade reached for something. He dragged it forward. At first it looked like a bundle of cast-off clothing. Then it resolved itself into a scrawny child—a boy with wary eyes, sharp features and an overall air of shameful neglect.

"Tobe Larkin, I'd like you to meet Miss Violet Benson," Cade said. To Violet he added, "Tobe is one of the first people I met in Morrow Creek. I…ran into him on my way here and decided to bring him along."

"Why, that's fine," Violet began. "One more is always—"

"He shanghaied me!" The boy, Tobe, jerked his arm out of Cade's grasp. He glowered at Violet. "I tole him, that lady done *dropped* her reticule! I was only gonna return it to her, is all. Nothin' more'n that. Until *this* here knuck picked me up clean off'n the depot platform and said it was the sheriff or *you*—".

Cade kicked his foot. As though recognizing that signal, Tobe quit talking. Instead he raised his chin. Then he sniffed.

"Is that chicken I smell?" Enthusiastically, the boy strode inside the house. "Chicken and biscuits, maybe? Mmm, mmm, mmm."

With a confidence that belied his few years, Tobe stepped farther into the entryway. He propped both hands on his hips. "This might be all right, I reckon. Only don't you get no ideas about sellin' me into white slavery or nothin', Miss Benson," he warned. "I done heard'a you plenty. I aim to be on my guard the whole time I'm here, and that's for certain. I ain't no fool."

"Well, I—" Mystified by his wrongheaded notions about her, Violet hesitated. "We've only just met. I wouldn't think to—"

She glanced to Cade for guidance. He was watching Tobe with a strange, mingled sense of stoniness and nostalgia on his face.

"—*sell* anyone," she continued, wondering all the

while at Cade's unusual expression. "I'm certainly not a white slaver!"

Where in the world had the boy gotten such a nonsensical idea? Violet could scarcely fathom it. Indeed, she helped many different people in town, including children, but the people whom she helped were generally grateful for her assistance.

"He's afraid you'll send him to a foundling home," Cade explained, doubtless recognizing her confusion. "He told me so on the way here. Screamed it, more precisely. Not that I can blame him. Those orphanages are nasty places sometimes."

As he made that curious statement, Cade stepped inside, too. He shut the door behind him. His presence filled the entryway. Instantly her household felt twice as exciting with him in it.

"Tobe insists he's happier on the streets," Cade went on, giving the child another odd look, "among his felonious little friends. He says he has everything he could ever need."

"Oh. I see." That couldn't possibly be true. Could it? Where were the boy's parents? Violet might yet suggest that Tobe go to a temporary home of some kind, she knew. Everyone deserved a home and a family who loved them. Violet was fortunate enough to have both and deeply cherished them. "Well, then there's no need to rush to an orphanage, is there?" At Tobe's still-wary expression, Violet tried another tack. "I mean, I'm *very* pleased to meet you, Tobe! Why don't you tell me about yourself."

Tobe regarded her with evident suspicion. His little

face was filthy. His hair might once have been blond; now it was tangled and too dirty to discern its true color. A knit cap, doubtless pilfered, partly shaded his eyes. His britches sported holes in the knees. His shirt needed mending, too. Only his woolen overcoat, which was so large it hid his hands and dragged on the floor behind him, appeared to be in reputable shape.

Concerned, Violet gave him a smile. "Are you new to town?"

"I come in off'n the train. With my mam. Only she's—" Tobe broke off. "Gone," the boy finished flatly. As Violet and Cade exchanged a troubled glance over Tobe's head, he looked with interest at the Benson household. "So...how 'bout that chicken?"

Deciding that further questions could wait, Violet nodded. "It will be ready very soon. I made oyster stew to start, a lovely braise of kale and turnips, and chicken with dumplings."

Tobe shot a triumphant look at Cade. "Tole you so!" He held out his small grubby hand, fingers waggling. "Pay up, chump."

With a resigned grin, Cade plunked a nickel into the boy's palm. To Violet, he explained, "We had a small wager going."

"On the constituents of my dinner?" Violet shook her head in disbelief. "I wonder what you'll make of my dessert then?"

On her cue, both males—one tall and one small—raised their heads to sniff the air like the most persistent of bloodhounds.

"Something with cinnamon." Tobe perked up. "Pumpkin pie?"

"No." With a mien of concentration, Cade inhaled once more. "It's apples. Apple pie… No. Apple pandowdy. With cream."

Slack-jawed, Violet stared. "It *is* apple pandowdy!"

With a genial chortle, the males traded that very same nickel once again. Glimpsing the surprising camaraderie between them, Violet felt unexpectedly moved. Cade Foster seemed like a hard man. He seemed tough and unwavering and more than a little bullheaded. But when it came to a child in need, apparently, he was entirely mush-hearted.

"You two are almost as incorrigible as Papa," she confided with a shake of her head. "He's at a congregant's, offering them counsel, by the way. That means he'll likely be late to dinner."

Cade gave her a piercing look. "Does that happen a lot?"

She shrugged. "Sometimes. Papa's flock needs him."

"So do you." As though guessing at the loneliness that Violet sometimes felt, alone inside the quiet, tidy and modest house she'd grown up in, Cade squeezed her hand. "I aim to give you everything you might need and want, Violet. *Everything.*"

For a long moment, his gaze met hers, private and enthralling. His promise of giving her *everything* swam in Violet's head, making her feel downright giddy. When Cade had first made his unusual proposition to her this afternoon, she'd been taken aback, it was true. But now that she'd had time to consider matters, Violet was entirely in favor of helping to bring Cade good luck. His proposition provided a handy cover for her own plans to become more adventuresome, without forcing her to risk rejection. It would probably be fun, as well.

Provided Papa approved the idea, of course.

"Don't worry, Cade. You needn't keep wooing me. I've already made up my mind. Besides, there'll be plenty of time to clarify those particulars between us later on. In private." She shifted her attention to Tobe, who'd wandered into the adjacent parlor. Surrounded by its humble but comfortable furnishings, the boy appeared even more down on his luck than he had before. "After I ask little Tobe to unhand the statuette he's about to pinch *and* unburden his pockets of my prize collection of sterling-silver spoons."

Cade only gawked at her. "He's been stealing? *Here?*"

"Well, either that," Violet clarified with a nod, "or his pants are growing elephantine pockets all on their own."

Cade scowled. "I'm sorry. I'll handle this."

With a laugh, Violet put her hand on his shirtfront. Beneath her fingers, Cade's chest felt warm and solid and— *No*. She had to concentrate. "You've done enough by bringing him here," she assured Cade. "It was the right thing to do. But if you confront Tobe now, you'll likely scare him away for good."

"Stealing is not polite." Cade clenched his jaw. "I've been spending most of my time at gambling tables, that's true, but I still possess sufficient manners to recognize that much."

"I have no doubt you're *wonderfully* well mannered." In fact, she was counting on that. His inherent gentlemanliness would allow Violet to behave more daringly without risk of getting in over her head. Comfortingly, she patted his chest. It still felt superb. "But you relax now. I'll take care of this."

Cade gave a reluctant grunt. She accepted that as consent.

"In the meantime," she volunteered sunnily, "you can consider when you would like your next dose of good luck!"

Then she left with a smile to deal with Tobe.

Even after he'd savored a delectable meal of home-cooked dishes, prepared with a love and care he'd *swear* he could detect outright, Cade could not stop thinking about what Violet had said before she'd gone to cope with Tobe's thieving tendencies.

You can consider when you would like your next dose of good luck!

Gazing at Violet now from across the gingham tablecloth–covered table, set with its simple pottery and hand-me-down cutlery, Cade wanted his next dose of good luck soon. *Very* soon.

He didn't know how Violet had done it, but somehow she'd captivated him. Her cooking was magnificent, her caretaking was even better and her skills at affable conversation left him as full of contentment as her meal had left him full of chicken and dumplings. He'd come here expecting to employ his usual methods of strategy and artifice and charm. It had turned out, to his surprise, that he'd needed none of those things to earn Violet Benson's goodwill—especially since her father had yet to appear for dinner—or to discern the most important fact about her.

She was *wonderful*. To be precise, Cade decided as he watched her while spooning up the last sugary, cinnamony bites of his portion of apple pandowdy, she was soft and sweet and quick with a joke. She was capable and smart and loyal. She was not beautiful; that was still true. She was not flirtatious or trivial or full of flattering niceties, the way some women were.

Violet spoke her mind, sometimes even to her own detriment. She blushed at the drop of a hat—a hat not unlike the expensive, flat-brimmed model Cade had respectfully removed while entering her household—and she lacked all sophistication. She would not have fared well in San Francisco or New York or any of the myriad big cities Cade frequented and sometimes called home temporarily.

Simon Blackhouse, he knew, would have found Violet both gauche and probably unlovely, with her easy laughter and broad gestures. But Cade, to his incredulity and satisfaction, found Violet to be…endearing. Being around her was stimulating in a way that keeping company with other people never had been.

Violet never failed to surprise him, the way she'd done with Tobe tonight. She hadn't shirked from welcoming the boy *or* from reprimanding him when necessary. Even though Violet was admittedly ordinary in looks, her high-spiritedness and wit more than made up for her lack of rosebud lips or alabaster skin or any of the other features that prettier women were lauded for.

The plain fact was, Cade realized, Violet's face drew

him to truly look at her…and to keep right on looking, helplessly entertained and absorbed by wondering what she'd say or do next.

With genuine warmth, Violet leaned closer to Tobe, urging him to take another spoonful of apple pandowdy. Doubtless she hadn't noticed him stuffing his wee pockets full of the yeasted rolls and nuts she'd served earlier, but Cade had. The boy had fast hands and sprightly thieving fingers—fingers that currently clutched Violet's flatware and likely intended to steal it, too.

At Violet's offer, Tobe gave an eager nod. His cheeks bulged like a chipmunk's. Even as Violet served him his extra dessert, Tobe went on spooning up his pandowdy. He ate as though someone might steal it before he was through. In his rough-and-tumble world, Cade knew, someone might. He didn't know why he'd brought Tobe with him tonight; he only knew it had felt right.

It wasn't like him to interfere in someone else's affairs—even the affairs of one small, larcenous boy. Cade reckoned he'd already started going soft, owing to Violet's pure-hearted ways.

He should have known, by now, to steer clear of a reformer.

"Apple pandowdy is not the loveliest of desserts, I'll grant you that," Violet said, "but it's quick and delicious."

Tobe grunted his assent, still eagerly fisting his spoon.

"It's *beyond* delicious," Cade assured her. His own flatware clinked into his serving dish as he set it aside.

"And there are many things more valuable than merely being lovely."

"Like…being lucky?" Her smile looked mischievous.

"And being here, right now, to enjoy all this."

"Ah. I see." Violet's eyes sparkled at him. She set aside her own plate. "You're a man who lives for the moment, then."

"I'm a man who lives for enjoyment. I just said so."

"But what about planning for tomorrow?"

Cade glanced at Tobe. "Plans go awry. Only a fool counts on tomorrow. All you really have is the hand you're dealt today."

"Or the dice," Tobe put in matter-of-factly. "You might have dice to use." He finally set aside his spoon, then gave an exaggerated groan of contentment. "Thanks for them new cheaters, by the way," he told Cade. "I seen right away that you swapped 'em out for my old rough pair the other night. Soon's I've practiced enough, I oughtta clean up plenty."

"I'll give you a few tips after dinner," Cade volunteered.

Openmouthed, Violet stared at them both. "Are you offering to help Tobe learn to *cheat* more effectively?"

The boy nodded guilelessly. Cade did, too, unable to see what the problem was. "It will keep him safer in the long run."

"What would keep him safer is a secure home to live in," Violet disagreed, rallying handily. "And his mother to care for him!" Concerned, she turned to Tobe. "Where's your father?"

The child shrugged. "Dunno. He run off a while back."

"Before you got on the train to come here?" Violet pressed. "Or after you and your mother arrived in Morrow Creek?"

Tobe squirmed, plainly uncomfortable at being questioned.

"You can tell me, Tobe," Violet urged. "It's important that you do, so I know how best to help you. Unless I know where your mother and father are, I won't know how to proceed. Please, isn't there anything you can tell me about their whereabouts?"

With panicky eyes and a quarrelsome expression, the boy glanced at Cade. His whole demeanor seemed a plea for help—a plea for rescue from Violet's questioning. Tobe seemed either unwilling or unable to answer her…at least right now.

"Can't we leave now? I done ate everythin' I got given."

"And then some." Mustering a courteous smile, Cade pushed back his chair. It was just as well Tobe had spoken up. Cade suddenly felt less than cozy here himself… especially with Tobe's entreating gaze—so much like Judah's—fastened on him that way.

His brother wasn't as tough as Cade was. He never had been. Their orphan life had been harder for Judah than it had been for Cade. That's why Cade, as the eldest brother, had taken it upon himself to settle the discontent he knew Judah must feel.

He'd taken it upon himself to help Judah feel *whole* again.

For himself, Cade figured, it was already too late.

"I guess we'd better get going." Signaling as much, Cade rose. "Thank you for dinner, Violet. Everything was delicious."

"You're welcome." Violet gawked at him, seeming entirely taken aback. "But you're not really *leaving* already, are you?"

"It's time." Cade summoned Tobe with a nod, rescuing them both from further questions. "I'm sorry I didn't have a chance to see Reverend Benson again. I would have liked to say hello—and to get this deal squared between us, of course."

"'Again'?" Violet repeated, seeming stuck on the word. "But when did you and my father ever—" She broke off, her gaze sharpening. "Did you help Papa cheat, too, like you did Tobe? Is that how you knew Papa won at cards the other night?"

Beside her, Tobe rose from his seat. Taking advantage of Violet's distractedness, he swiped a butter knife. He slid the utensil's long silver handle up his shirtsleeve for safekeeping.

Cade raised an eyebrow. The little troublemaker was on his way to becoming a full-bore criminal, the way he was behaving.

"I may have slipped your father an improving card or two," Cade acknowledged. Reverend Benson had been on the verge of losing his clerical collar *and* his shirt in the game they'd played together. "But whether he used it or not, I can't say."

"Oh, *I* can say." Violet folded her arms. "You'll be happy to know that those winnings of his went to the church collection basket, though. My father is completely incorruptible."

Cade frowned. "I'm not trying to corrupt anyone."

Her raised eyebrows suggested otherwise. "Even me?"

That was easy. "*Especially* you."

"Oh." Paradoxically, she seemed almost disappointed.

That made no sense. At a loss to understand her—and wondering why he wanted to—Cade deepened his frown. Who cared what pious Violet Benson thought or felt? By the time the first snowfall blanketed Morrow Creek, he would be gone from here.

He would be gone from her life, likely for the better.

Tobe wriggled impatiently. "Are we pullin' foot or not?"

"Yes." Cade headed for the entryway. "It's time to go."

Tobe and Violet trailed after him. So did an odd sense of disappointment. He'd been having a nice time…until Violet had kicked off her damn reformer routine and ruined everything.

He should have known that taking up with a do-gooder was an endeavor doomed to failure. The two of them were like oil and water. Trying to put them together was like trying to glue down dice and expecting them to still produce a win. It didn't work.

"You can't leave yet," Violet protested. "What about our…" She cast an aggrieved glance at Tobe, plainly hesitant to speak openly in front of him, then finished, "agreement?"

She meant his reckless offer that she behave as his

lucky charm, Cade knew, in exchange for his pretense of a courtship.

"I reckon that's worked about as much as it's likely to."

"For today, you mean?" Violet specified, hurrying in Cade's wake to the front entryway. She handed him his hat along with a perplexed, entirely too-wounded look. "But tomorrow—"

"I don't plan on tomorrow." Cade reminded her. "Besides, your father hasn't given his blessing yet. He might never."

"But you can't just leave!" Violet insisted. Her expression turned insightful. "If you're merely being protective of Tobe—"

Cade scoffed, irked that she'd read his intentions so effortlessly. "Why would I be? I barely know the boy."

"There's no need for that," Violet hastened on. "In fact, I was thinking—Papa and I have plenty of room. Tobe could stay here with us if he wants to. Just until he finds his family."

Now it was Tobe's turn to scoff. "I ain't no charity case."

Reminded of something similar that he'd told Violet himself just yesterday, Cade shifted uneasily. Like Tobe, he didn't want charity from Violet. He wanted… nothing at all.

Except maybe a pinch of good fortune. And another smile.

Hellfire! What was wrong with him? He was behaving like a besotted fool—and all over a woman whose feminine curves scarcely showed beneath her prim, starched-and-pressed gown.

"I have no claim on the boy. He can do what he likes."

As though freed—unreasoningly—by his statement, Violet crouched in front of little Tobe. Gently, she smiled at him.

"I'd be very pleased if you'd agree to stay here awhile, Tobe. You can have plenty of food and a nice soft bed, and I think we even have some spare clothes in the church's donation box to lend you. You can wear them while I mend yours for you."

"Not my overcoat!" The boy hugged it. "It's new!"

Giving Cade's former outerwear an overly observant glance, Violet agreed. "That's fine. Of course, you'll want a bath—"

Now Tobe looked petrified. "A bath?"

"Careful there," Cade warned, unable to hold back a grin. "If you scrub off the grime, there'll be nothing left of him."

Violet tossed him an amused glance. Unreasonably, Cade felt blessed by her approval…and warmed clean through. too. He *liked* being included in their comfy, bantering conversation this way. It felt curiously as though the three of them were…a family.

That thought hardened Cade's resolve instantly. He had all the family he needed in Judah. Everyone else could go hang. Including spinsterish Violet Benson and her interfering ways.

"Pish posh. There'll be plenty of him left over!" Oblivious to Cade's glowering look, Violet gave Tobe's gaunt shoulders a heartfelt squeeze. She addressed the boy directly next. "I, for one, can't wait to see what color your hair is!"

"It's blond!" Tobe blurted. "Blond like my mama's."

"Truly?" Violet pretended to be flabbergasted. "Blond?"

At that, the boy actually *giggled*. "Yep! You'll see!"

Cade couldn't help staring. He went right on staring as Violet, with no evident persuasion at all, convinced Tobe to stay.

Disbelievingly, Cade stood by as Violet divested Tobe of his overcoat, his various pilfered household goods and even his hoarded-for-later foodstuffs. The latter she wrapped securely in a big plaid napkin and set on top of a cupboard in the kitchen.

"I'll leave this right here for you, in case you get hungry later tonight," she assured the boy. "No one will touch it."

Cade shook his head. "When your father comes home—" Reverend Benson had not yet returned from his counseling mission "—he might mistake that food for his. He might take it himself."

At his blunt statement, Violet blinked. She appeared surprised to find Cade still there. He'd followed her and Tobe into the kitchen from the entryway…just to watch over the boy.

"No one will take it. I wouldn't promise otherwise."

"Tobe, you should put that food with your things," Cade advised gruffly. "Keep it close to you. You might need it later."

Plainly perplexed, Violet turned to Cade. "He'll have it later," she insisted. "It's right there. He doesn't need to hide it." She touched Cade's arm. "Why would you say such a thing?"

Hard-won experience, Cade knew. A long time ago, he'd learned to keep the necessities close and to trust no one.

But he refused to say so. He didn't want to engender any more reformer's pity from Violet…or to reveal any more of his own vulnerabilities. He'd thought he'd erased those long ago.

He had. Damnation, *he had*. But Violet didn't seem to think so. She gazed thoughtfully at him, seeming on the verge of offering Cade a consoling emergency food packet of his own.

He, foolishly, almost longed for a chance to take it, if only it would please her. Hell. Would his gullibility to her never find an end? Cade had never experienced its like.

Fortunately, Tobe broke the silence between them.

"All right. That's good enough for me, I reckon." Happily, the boy took off his hat. He set to work on his shoes. "Where's that bath? 'Cause I been itchin' somethin' fierce lately."

To her credit, Violet didn't even recoil. "I'll get it."

Still feeling baffled and discomfited in ways he didn't understand, Cade stepped into her path. Determinedly, he took hold of Violet's arm. He pulled her into an alcove where they could speak privately, then lowered his head. "Don't do this."

"Do what?" In the midst of capably rolling up her sleeves, Violet paused, plainly baffled. "Haul some bathwater? Heat it? I assure you, Cade, that I'm more than up to the challenge."

Her cheerful smile touched him again. Cade resisted it. Frustrated by his inability to make her see the damage she might do to Tobe, he raked his hand through his hair. He fixed her with a warning look, determined nonetheless to have his say.

"Don't give that boy too much hope. It's not fair."

"Oh." In a heartbeat, her face softened. "I see."

He wasn't sure she did. "You don't know what you're doing. If you get Tobe used to a soft bed and regular meals and—" *warm hugs*, he'd been about to say, but he stopped himself just in time "—plenty of silver spoons to line his delinquent pockets with, it will be doubly hard for him when he has to leave."

Violet appeared to consider that. In the hallway they'd found themselves in—lantern-lit, safe and intractably homey—she edged nearer to him. Confidently and somehow sadly, she gave him a long look. "You know, a wise man once told me that the problem isn't giving up on hope. It's convincing yourself you don't want any hope, even when it's standing right in front of you."

Recognizing his own foolhardy words, Cade looked away.

He hoped she didn't mean him. *He* truly *didn't* need hope.

"I agree," Violet continued staunchly. "So I can't see anything wrong with trying to make sure Tobe never gives up on himself. I *can* help him find his parents, Cade. I can! I know almost everyone in town. I volunteer everywhere. I have access to records most people don't.

Everyone from Sheriff Caffey to the folks down at the train depot will help me get information. I'm dogged, too. I promise you, I can help Tobe. And I will."

"You shouldn't." Hoping to make exactly that point, however he could, Cade backed them up to the hallway wall. He caged in Violet with his arms, then ladled as much seriousness into his voice as he could. "You heard Tobe before. He doesn't want to talk about his parents, or where they went, or why he's alone."

"He's only just met me," Violet insisted, not daunted in the least by Cade's intimidating posture. "He'll talk later."

Cade couldn't help admiring her spunk. "Now who's the miracle worker?" he asked. With an amused sound, Cade slipped on his hat. He touched Violet's chin, then smiled. "All right, then. Have it your way." He shook his head, knowing she was much too confident about her plans to find Tobe's parents. "I'd wish you good luck, but I don't seem to have any to spare right now."

She grinned. "Does that mean I'll see you again tomorrow?"

"I can't rightly say."

"You *won't* say, you mean."

Cade shrugged. Determinedly, Violet straightened her spine. Her maneuver put her chest right up against his. It turned out that her shape wasn't quite as washboard flat as he'd imagined it was. Violet Benson was not curvaceous, but she was...affecting.

As though sensing her unexpected advantage, Violet tipped her face to his. She offered a kittenish smile. The mingled fragrances of castile soap, laundry starch and warm, feminine skin reached him next, making Cade go stock-still with longing.

Men at a gambling table didn't smell like that. Neither did roving train cars or impersonal hotel rooms or bathhouses. Cade couldn't remember when he'd enjoyed inhaling quite so much.

"I'd be very happy," Violet said, touching his arm with an utter lack of guile, "if you'd come back to see me tomorrow."

Yes. *Yes.* On the brink of agreeing instantly just to see her smile again, Cade flashed his dimples at her instead. "Mmm. And *I'd* be happy if you'd rub up against me some more, sugar." Deliberately, he gestured at her position. "But this time, move a little slower, please. I want a little more time to enjoy it."

Just as he'd expected, Violet widened her eyes. She blinked, seeming to awaken to their compromising position. Then she smiled up at him. "You're the one who backed us up here. Anyone watching would think *you* wanted to be this close to *me.*"

Damnation. She had him there. Cade put down his arms.

"You do, don't you?" Defying his expectations this time, Violet stayed put, arms crossed. "You can't scare me, Cade. As I said, I've done a lot of charity work. I'm not meek or naive."

"But you are inexperienced. And I'm plenty skilled."

She appeared to ponder that. Her expression turned subdued.

"Well," she said. "If you don't turn tail after this

one evening together, I guess we'll find out about that, won't we?"

Her expression now appeared downright challenging.

Cade gaped. "I can't believe you're baiting me. *Me*."

"Then we're even. Because I can't believe you're trying to seduce me into *not* helping one small, innocent boy who's all alone in the world! Even though *you* helped him first. You must have brought Tobe here for a reason." Tilting her head, Violet examined Cade with uncomfortable perceptiveness. "I think I know what it was, too. Cade…how many orphanages did you stay in?"

Shocked, Cade stiffened. Memories rushed at him, black and lonesome and bitter to recall. He'd thought he'd buried them.

It took him a minute to recover. Dimly aware of Violet watching him, Cade sucked in a deep breath. Somehow he made himself toss off a smile. It was not his most dazzling effort.

"I've just decided," he told Violet, "that I won't be back tomorrow. It turns out, if *this* is good luck…I don't much like how it feels."

Then he tipped his hat to her and took himself away.

Violet Benson might have succeeded in "saving" one male of her acquaintance tonight, Cade told himself darkly as he stepped into the chilly evening air outside on the front porch, but she wasn't getting her angelic hands on both of them. Not if he could help it.

And he damn well could.

Chapter Five

$\diamond\!\!\!\sim\!\!\!\diamond\!\!\!\sim\!\!\!\diamond$

The nice thing about Sunday services, Violet thought as she sat, hands clasped atop her hymnal, clad as usual in her best jade-colored, worsted-wool bustled gown, in her customary place in the front pew of her father's church, was that they afforded folks a much-needed chance to socialize after a busy week.

Of course, church services *also* helped save people's immortal souls. That was of utmost importance, too. But from a secular, practical perspective, everyone liked to mingle. It was as simple as that. Church provided the best possible place to deepen old friendships and forge new ones, which was precisely what Violet had been doing ever since the gambler Cade Foster had left her standing in her own hallway, all flushed and breathless and feeling as hot as a Thursday afternoon in July.

I'd be happy if you'd rub up against me some more, sugar, she remembered him saying in that low, rumbly, undeniably shiver-inducing voice of his. *But this time, move a little slower, please. I want a little more time to enjoy it.*

Heavens! Just thinking about their encounter now—
in Sunday service, of all places, while her father droned
on with his sermon!—made Violet feel all...*tingly* inside. She hadn't realized exactly how close she'd gotten
to Cade in that hallway. She'd been too busy wondering about him, trying to understand him, searching for
a reason that explained his odd resistance to her plans
to help Tobe. Who was doing just fine now, by the way.

After a hasty glance at the boy—who for today was
being watched over by sweet Miss Mellie Reardon, one
of her friends, and seemed to be enjoying all the attention—Violet reclasped her hands, then thought about
Cade some more. She believed she was right about his
having spent time in an orphanage. He'd been too dis-
trustful of foundling homes to dismiss the idea outright.

But why? Why would Cade be so cynical about a
place that only existed to help forlorn and abandoned
children? She couldn't think of a single reason. For a
man who'd lectured Violet about the need for hopefulness, she decided, Cade seemed in miserably short sup-
ply of it himself. In the end, he hadn't even been able to
believe in his own gambler's superstition.

If this is good luck...I don't much like how it feels.

Well, that was doubtless because Cade hadn't experienced its full effect yet! He certainly hadn't given *her* a
fair chance as a lucky charm, Violet thought in her own
defense. At the rate things were going, he might never
do so. She hadn't so much as clapped eyes on Cade since
he'd left her house the other night.

She knew he was still in town. Morrow Creek's tire-
less gossipy grapevine—and all her friends, besides—

had kept her informed of that much. But Cade hadn't returned to ask for Reverend Benson's blessing of their supposed "courtship" and attendant lucky-charm scheme, and Violet hadn't sought out Cade herself, either.

Why should she? she asked herself as she shifted in her seat. Word had gotten out about the dinner she and Cade had shared. The knowledge that the mysterious new sporting man in town had paid a deliberate social call on plain, unremarkable Violet Benson had already perked up her prospects considerably.

Exactly as their dance at the Grand Fair had done, their convivial dinner had provoked new curiosity about Violet among the menfolk in town. They'd paid her more attention of late than ever before. She was trying not to become *too* foolishly accustomed to their interest. But it was thrilling, all the same.

Not as thrilling as Cade was, she'd admit. But still…

Unable to properly describe *why* Cade's attention was so much more stimulating than the attention of other men, Violet was saved from continuing the effort by the one thing that never failed her: good works. It was time to pass the collection basket, and Violet was responsible for doing so.

Turning her thoughts to that duty, Violet made her way to the back of the church. Her fellow congregants smiled at her; her father's familiar voice comforted her. She wasn't *sure* that his gambling winnings had wound up in the church's charitable offerings, as she'd insisted to Cade, but she felt hopeful they had.

She stood at the backmost pew, then offered the

collection basket to the first congregant. He put in his contribution. The basket passed from hand to hand. Absently, Violet watched it.

A fat wad of rolled-up currency landed in the basket.

Startled, Violet stared at it. That was a great deal of money! Even if all the bills beneath the top one were the lowest possible denomination, there had to be…a *lot* of cash there.

Aching to know who was so generous, Violet nonetheless kept her gaze lowered. She strived to remain neutral to the offerings her friends and neighbors made to the church. Everyone gave what they could; sometimes people took help when they needed to.

But *this* was beyond unusual. Only a lucky gold miner, a railroad magnate or maybe a touring European could afford to give so much to a Sunday collection plate. It was unprecedented.

Interestedly, Violet let her gaze roam down the pew. Near the far edge where the basket was, she glimpsed quality shoes, a pair of strong legs clad in gray trousers, two masculine hands—

The people on either side of the mysterious donor gasped. Loudly. As one, the whole congregation turned to see what the fuss was about. Caught staring, Violet felt herself flush.

The basket moved on. Throughout the small church, the congregants' rumblings rose a little higher. More people spied the wad of cash in the basket. Each row of worshippers swiveled their heads in turn, trying to glimpse the charitable benefactor in their midst. Her father cleared his throat, then preached on.

Steadfastly, Violet collected the basket at the end of its rounds. The unknown donor's contribution appeared to have kicked up some sense of competitive giving among the congregants. There were more coins and bills than ever before—and one small but valuable gold-dust packet, as well. It smelled like whiskey.

Happy for it all the same, Violet carried the collection to her father's modest office. Located in a small room behind the chancel, it contained a rolltop desk for Papa's books, papers and the church register, a well-worn chair, a window, a seldom-used door that led to the church-yard and a reliable safe. In the West, even a man of God couldn't be too careful with money.

Crouching before the safe, Violet made fast work of depositing the collection funds. Ordinarily she would have sorted them. Today she felt much too curious about the identity of the mysterious donor to be too persnick-ety about organizing the money. Instead, she shoved the whole lot inside, then clanged shut the safe's door. She gave the dial a hasty spin.

"You missed your calling. You should have been a gambler."

At the sound of that familiar voice, Violet started. She rose, her green worsted skirts swirling around her ankles, to see Cade Foster standing there in her father's office. He looked exactly as handsome—and as darkly enigmatic—as she remembered.

"When I dropped my latest bundle of winnings in your basket, everyone around me gasped," Cade said. "But you didn't even bat an eyelash. I'm impressed—you have quite a poker face."

"That's not what you said the other day," she disagreed. "You said my emotions are unusually evident on my face."

"That's true." He came a little closer. "I did say that."

At his nearness, her heartbeat surged. Breathlessly, Violet stood her ground, feeling suddenly impatient and exhilarated and anxious, all at once. She'd thought she might never see Cade again, she realized. She'd thought her turn as belle of the ball might end as quickly as it had begun. Evidently, she'd been wrong. She'd never felt *so* happy to be wrong about something.

She ought to be more cautious this time, though. It had shaken her when Cade had skedaddled from her house so abruptly.

To that end, Violet lifted her chin, striving to sound as though she bantered on a regular basis with worldly, roguish gamblers like him. "You also said that was a compliment."

"It was." Cade peered at her more carefully. His expression looked unreadable. "But I reserve the right to change my mind."

She couldn't help feeling stung. "About the compliment?"

"About your ability to bluff. Maybe your poker face only applies to other people, not me. Maybe with me, you can't help showing how you feel." Cade nodded. "You're doing it right now."

She was? "No, I'm not."

"You are." Another careful, interested look. "You look as though you feel…excited. Do you, Violet? Do you feel excited?"

More than she ever had. She could scarcely keep her knees from wobbling, she felt so unendurably curious about why he was there. Had Cade only come to assuage his guilty gambler's conscience by dropping off a contribution to the church? Or was there another reason the gambler had come there? To see her?

"I guess it's probably not smart to tip your hand to a renowned gambler." Rallying, Violet smiled. "I'll make more of an effort to be cryptic and unreadable." She did. "See?"

"Nice try." Cade appeared improbably amused by her efforts—and possibly a bit charmed, too…even though that made no sense. "But even when you're trying, you're still you, Violet."

"Meaning what, exactly? Why are you here, anyway?"

"Meaning," Cade clarified as he came a bit nearer, all the way into a patch of October-morning sunlight, "that you're about as mysterious as an open book on a sunny day. At least to me."

She couldn't help feeling vaguely disappointed. Everyone knew that gentlemen liked pretty ladies who kept them guessing.

"And I'm here," Cade added as Violet pondered the devilish impracticality of that, "because I missed looking at your face."

She glanced up. "Oh." That *might* be a good thing. It might be as good as the way he looked just then, with his dark wavy hair all burnished by sunshine and his eyes bluer than blue.

"*You* can't stop being open to me, it seems." Now

Cade was close enough to touch her. So he did. He took hold of her elbow, then drew her nearer. "And despite my efforts to stay away—"

"So you *were* avoiding me on purpose!"

"—*I* can't stop wanting to be near you."

Heaven help her, he looked as though he meant it. His gaze roamed over her features, full of enjoyment and remembrance and…surrender? Violet didn't know what to make of that.

"I won that money for your collection plate shortly after we had dinner together," Cade told her. "I even got invited to the next level of play in the qualifying rounds for the private faro tournament. I glimpsed Whittier, too." He dropped his gaze to her bodice. Most likely, he could see her heaving in eager, restive breaths. "But I haven't won a damn thing since then."

"Oh. I'm very sorry to hear that."

"No, you're not." Cade's eyes sparkled at her, full of mischief and something darker…something needful. "Neither am I. Because it's brought me back here to you." He lifted his hand to her cheek. Rousingly, he stroked her. Tellingly, his voice lowered. Huskily, he said, "You see…I need more good luck."

He was going to kiss her. Violet could tell. She'd not been courted much, that was true; but she recognized something primal in Cade's eyes. Possibly because she felt a bit passionate just then herself. Her knees quaked. Her hands trembled. She *needed* to be kissed, it occurred to her. How else to truly know Cade?

How else to know if she could trust him? Rely on him?

"I need more good luck," Cade repeated, "and it

seems I can only get that from touching you. Maybe... from kissing you."

From the rest of the church, the sounds of her father's sermon echoed from the pulpit. Its usual emotive vibrancy was muted by the walls that stood, quite properly, between Reverend Benson and Violet. The effect was surreal—and inhibiting, too.

"You can't...get your good luck here. *Now*," she breathed, thoroughly scandalized by his suggestion. "We're in church! Everyone I know is in there, a few feet away!"

Rakishly, Cade quirked his eyebrow. "So?"

"So..." Vigorously, Violet gestured. "They'll know what we're doing in here! I'll be ruined." She gave him a quelling look. "You might be leaving Morrow Creek soon, but I'm not."

He laughed, then squeezed her hand as though to reassure her. "I left quite prominently after making my contribution to the church coffers. As far as anyone knows, you're alone here."

Well...that might be true. Cade *had* used the exterior office door very effectively to enter without her noticing. More important...*he was still going to kiss her.* No matter who was nearby to know it or to happen upon them or even to disapprove.

Agog at the realization, Violet backed up. Her bustle bumped into her father's desk, stopping her retreat abruptly.

She guessed this was what she got for toying with a notorious gambler—for pretending to be more sophisticated than she really was. In a last-ditch effort to retain her virtue, Violet tried some distracting chitchat. She pointed to Cade's fine leather brogues. "I thought I recognized those shoes."

Another smile. "Don't be afraid, Violet. I'll be gentle."

"You'll be…" Envisioning the possibilities inherent in that soft promise, Violet sighed. Tellingly. Swallowing hard, she nodded. "You'll be very, *very* gentle? And quick?" She cast a hasty glance at the doorway. "Very, very, *very* quick?"

"You're new at scandalous behavior. I can tell."

"Try not to seem so amused by that. It's rude."

"I'm sorry. I do admire your enthusiasm for the task at hand though. Not every sinner wants to conduct their sins quite so…efficiently as you." Contritely and somehow wickedly, Cade took her other hand. "I never mean to be unkind to you, Violet. Please allow me to make up for my rudeness…with pleasure."

Oh my. "*Gently,*" Violet specified shakily. "And *quickly!*"

"Hmm." A low, speculative rumble escaped him. "I can't rightly promise either…seeing as how I've been hungering for this every day since I saw you last." Cade squeezed her hands again, almost longingly. "I want you, Violet. Let me have you."

Let me have you. No one had ever spoken to her that way before. So passionately, so stirringly…so *commandingly.*

At Cade's roughly voiced request, Violet could hardly refuse. Willfully, she nodded. Her entire midsection tightened with eagerness, filled with uncertainty about what came next.

"Yes," she began primly. "Yes, if you like, you may—"

Kiss me, she was about to say, but Cade's mouth came down on hers just as that last puff of breath was about to escape.

Every bit of what she'd been thinking flew from her head. All that remained were Cade's lips, surprisingly warm and firm and soft on hers, and Cade's hands, releasing her hands to pull her whole body tight against his, and Cade's hips, pressing against her skirts, crowding them against the desk behind her.

His kiss was not gentle. It was not quick. It was hard and slow and probing and remarkable, and Violet wasn't quite sure how—given how dizzy she felt with shock and amazement—she remained upright beneath it. Cade's hands cradled her back; his lips slid over hers, making her mouth come alive with new sensations. A wild burst of…it could only be *longing*, she knew, rushed to her toes. Avidly, Violet grabbed his lapels and held on, but even that was not enough to steady her. She needed… *more.*

"Oh, Violet." Moaning with enjoyment, Cade pressed his forehead to hers. Intimacy rushed between them, heady and new. He stroked her cheek, pushing back a few errant tendrils of hair. He curled his knuckles against her jaw. "You're so…"

Helplessly, she froze, waiting for him to say something thoughtless or unkind. Once, a blacksmith's apprentice who'd courted her briefly had kissed her, also.

I never thought I'd find myself kissing you! he'd tactlessly burst out afterward.

It had taken her days to stop feeling ashamed of that.

"—so perfect," Cade said at last. Seeming truly to mean it, he blessed her with a smile. "So perfect in every way."

"You're joking," she burst out. "You *must* be—"

"Give me more," he urged. "I'll try to be gentler."

Warily, Violet raised her eyebrow.

Sensing her skepticism—and feeling inexpressibly saddened by it—Cade stroked her cheek again. "I promise I won't hurt you," he said.

Markedly unsure of that, all at once, Violet exhaled. She shook her head. "You can't promise me that."

"I just did." A *very* gentle kiss. "Believe me, Violet."

But it was too late. She'd already been reminded of the way her infrequent suitors usually reacted to her. She couldn't help wondering: Exactly what, if anything, made Cade different?

Astutely, the gambler gazed at her. "How many?"

Violet blinked, surprised. "How many what?"

"How many men have hurt you? How many have disappointed you? How many have made you believe in them, then let you down?"

Shakily, Violet scoffed. "None," she lied, subtracting every single man who'd courted her briefly, then revealed that he didn't want to marry her, had found someone else, or had only wanted to meet Adeline. Irked that he could read her feelings and her past so well, she raised her chin. "None at all."

His gaze met hers. "Someday you'll tell me the truth."

"How do you know I haven't already?"

"Because your whole body tells me you haven't." Tenderly, Cade ran his fingers down her arm. He stroked his thumb over her wrist. "I can feel you leaning toward me, wanting more—"

She felt herself flush. Compared with him, she was so inexperienced. So gullible. So defenseless to protect her heart.

"But a part of you always stays behind." Cade's coaxing hand swept along her arm. He watched its progress, seeming transfixed by the sight of his masculine hand against her lace-trimmed gown. "Give me more. I won't disappoint you, I swear."

Violet tried to laugh. She tried to appear worldly and sure. Maybe if Cade believed she was sophisticated and carefree, he wouldn't recognize the disappointment and worry she tried so hard to keep hidden. But it was too late. He already had.

"Give over, Violet," he urged. "Do it. It's the only way to feel alive."

That was a reckless philosophy. Violet opened her mouth to tell him so, but Cade met her with another kiss. She lifted her chin to muster up a more assertive, more convincing stance, but Cade took advantage of her position to kiss her neck. Shocked to feel his mouth there above the lacy collar of her dress, Violet stiffened. Ardently, Cade kissed her there again. This time, a tiny, barely perceptible squeal of enjoyment escaped her.

"See there?" Cade grinned. "*Now* you feel alive."

She *did*. Her plan to fly to new heights was working, Violet thought in a daze. Never had she felt anything so wondrous as Cade's warm mouth, his faint, raspy beard stubble, his hands and his breath and his body—so much bigger and stronger than hers—holding her close against him. His kisses moved onward, sliding from her neck to her jaw, and all the while he kept on speaking.

"All I want is for you to feel wonderful," Cade said in a low voice. "I want your heart to race…just like it's doing right now." Proving he'd noticed it, he laid her hand, covered with his, atop her heart. The gesture felt almost impossibly intimate. "I want your breath to pant and your knees to weaken."

Obligingly, her body complied. Violet didn't understand. If she didn't yet trust him, how could she be so responsive to him?

"I want you to touch me, too, Violet." Cade delivered another kiss, potent and sweet, just at the junction of her neck and jaw. "I want to feel your hands on me… just like this. Mmm."

At his soft moan, Violet opened her eyes. When had she closed them? Swoonily, she saw that Cade had moved their joined hands from *her* heart to *his*. Specifically, to his chest. Upon finding herself touching him so boldly, she widened her gaze.

But there was more. "*Your* heart is pounding, too!" she said.

His nod exhilarated her. "I like kissing you," Cade said in a matter-of-fact tone. "I *love* kissing you. I knew I would."

Violet disagreed. "You couldn't have known that."

His dimples flashed. "Only you would argue the point."

She smiled. "Only you would dare such an enormous bluff."

Cade merely shook his head. "What will it take for you to believe me? I'm right about us. I'm right about us *together*."

His blue-eyed gaze suggested there was something about them being *together* that Cade knew...and she did not. Trying not to blush any more forcefully than she already had, Violet fluttered her fingers over his shirtfront. What did he look like underneath it? she wondered suddenly. Was he burly? Hairy? Both?

She bet he looked like an Adonis, splendidly come to life.

Shocked by her own prurient curiosity, Violet lowered her hands. Evidently, Cade brought out all kinds of new qualities in her. If this continued, he wouldn't need any persuasive ability to make her do...whatever he wanted. And wasn't that the trouble?

"You can trust me, Violet," Cade said. "You know you can."

He was probably right. Of everyone she knew, Cade was the only one who'd never tried to sugarcoat his opinions of the way she looked or the way she behaved. Cade had never pretended to love her. He'd never even gone out of his way to be particularly solicitous of her. He was characteristically blunt and fully undaunted by the attitudes of other people. He was...*himself.*

On the other hand, Violet remembered, Cade took chances for a living. He wagered on everything from playing cards to dice to her own homemade apple pan-dowdy. *I make my living on hope and happenstance,* he'd told her once. *Honesty doesn't enter into it.*

Did that mean she could trust him? Or not?

Unhappily, she recalled what her best friend, Adeline, had said upon learning of Cade's interest in Violet. *You'd better be cautious,* Adeline had told her. *You don't want to get hurt.*

What Adeline *hadn't* said was what they both knew: that Cade's newfound devotion might be both short-lived and heartbreaking for Violet to lose…now that she'd sampled it.

"Well, I guess you probably have about a week's worth of luck by now," Violet settled on saying, sidestepping the issue of trust altogether. Brightly, she smiled. "That'll do, right?"

"No." Cade frowned. "Because this isn't about good luck."

"It isn't?"

"Not anymore. You make me want *more* than luck. Much more."

"You're a gambler, Cade." Violet turned away, hoping to divert herself by straightening the papers on her father's cluttered desk. "What more is there for you, besides luck?"

Silence. But only for a moment.

"I was hoping you could tell me that," Cade said.

Violet didn't have the first notion how to do so. Hedging, she said, "Until my father agrees that I may see you on a social basis, I'm afraid I can't comment on our… relationship."

"Then there is one. Good." There was a smile in his voice. "That's a start, at least. That means both of us are anteing up."

"I'm not a poker game," Violet protested, "to be bet upon!"

"I guess we'll see about that." As she turned to him again, Cade tipped his hat to her. "I'll be back. You can bet on that yourself—even without an infamous gambler's credentials to your name."

Then, with an audacious wink, Cade exited to the churchyard, leaving Violet to wonder exactly what he meant—and if she should bet on anything at all where the gambler was concerned.

Outside under a ponderosa pine tree, Simon Blackhouse stood smoking a cheroot. A farmer wandered past, giving the itinerant bachelor an inquisitive look—undoubtedly owing to Blackhouse's fancy suit, air of privilege…and close-at-hand valet, Adams.

Approaching his benefactor, Cade didn't feel as awkward as that farmer undoubtedly did. But he did feel unaccountably grim.

"Will she do it?" Blackhouse asked.

Cade gave a curt nod. Behind him in the church, the people of Morrow Creek went about their Sunday worship—unknowingly, with a freshly kissed Violet Benson beaming in their midst.

She hadn't been kissed much, Cade decided. Or she hadn't been kissed very well. But what Violet lacked in tutoring, she made up for in sheer, stirring responsiveness. With Violet all warm and pliant and soft in his arms, Cade had felt luckier than a riverboat gambler with a handful of aces and no table limit.

"Good. You'll need her." Expansively, Blackhouse offered Cade a cheroot—or rather, at his signal, Adams proffered the box of elegant, square-tipped cigars. Cade accepted one. "I was beginning to think you couldn't catch up with Whittier on your own. I was considering calling in a fallback to make certain."

"I'll catch up with Whittier." Discontentedly, Cade eyed the small, white-painted church. In a minute, congregants would begin streaming out, full of chatter and kindheartedness. Men would stretch and collect their wagons; women would tidy their children's hair; youngsters would let loose the energy they'd kept pent up while stuck in their pews. They'd holler their glee at being free from confinement for the rest of the afternoon.

Dimly, Cade recalled doing all those things with Judah…and his parents. But the memories felt faded and bittersweet, almost too hazy to believe they'd happened to anyone…least of all him.

"Someone else might be even more motivated to find Whittier," Blackhouse was saying. He withdrew his favorite match safe, a shiny gold model engraved with a full house of cards. In a whiff of sulfur and a crackle of fire, he struck a match to light Cade's cheroot. "Your brother, for instance?"

Over the glowing tip of his newly lit cheroot, Cade eyed Blackhouse. "Judah and I agreed. When I won that Jürgensen, I earned the right to track down Whittier. *I* did. No one else."

"Ah, yes. The famed 'luckiest game of your life.'"

"That's right."

Dubiously, Blackhouse perused the gold chain that secured Cade's watch, tucked safely in the pocket of his ornate wool vest. "If only you'd known that it was Whittier across the table from you that night," he said. "That it was *his* watch you were winning. Things might have unfolded very differently."

Cade wished they had. But he refused to say so.

"I've often wondered..." Blackhouse went on in a cryptic fashion. "Do you think Whittier lost on purpose? Maybe he *wanted* you to have that Jürgensen. Just because you didn't know who he was doesn't mean he didn't know who you were...even then."

At that, Cade felt even less talkative. Drawing on his cheroot, he gazed contemplatively at the church. From inside it, the homespun sound of the congregants' singing reached its crescendo. That meant the service was almost over, he reckoned.

"I always liked that hymn," he remarked without thinking.

Blackhouse's raised eyebrow brought him back to himself quickly. Cade didn't want hymns. He wanted answers. Period.

"All this goodness and God talk is giving me a headache." With a jerk of his head, Cade indicated the dusty street nearby. "How about a bolt of mescal and a fast round of Mexican monte?"

"Yes!" Blackhouse appeared immeasurably cheered. "As a matter of fact, I wouldn't feel I'd visited the Arizona Territory properly if I didn't sample more of...

both those things," he said. "Come along, Adams! We have winning to do."

Just as the worshippers began filing out into the churchyard, Cade escaped in the opposite direction with Blackhouse and Adams hard on his heels. That made twice now that he'd eluded redemption, it occurred to him, and by a narrow margin each time, too. But Cade couldn't help wondering as he headed away from the church and all its virtuous believers: Would he ever stop running...if Violet ever asked him to?

Chapter Six

It was near midnight by the time Cade looked up from the gambling table. Mexican monte with Blackhouse had turned into roulette with Adams, which had led to craps with Sheriff Caffey, which had segued into "bucking the tiger" with a new batch of local gamesters and everyone's favorite sin: faro.

Now, with an almost empty whiskey bottle at his elbow, a pile of cash winnings beside it and a too-friendly saloon girl eyeing both him *and* his latest hand of cards, Cade knew he should have felt on top of his game. Instead he felt morose and brooding and downright solitary. He wasn't alone; not precisely. But he felt as detached from his opulent, risk-engendering, sinfulness-stoking surroundings as he possibly could have.

When had green baize and playing cards become so dull? How had scantily clad women and wagering opponents stopped being stimulating? Where was he supposed to go for satisfaction now?

He hadn't entered into the gambling world for thrills, Cade reminded himself. But somewhere along the way, while searching for Whittier and tracking his movements within the circuit, he'd become used to the distracting pleasures that world offered him.

Glancing around the table now as he idly placed his next bet, Cade couldn't help wondering: When he got the answers he needed from Whittier…what then? What would be left for him then?

As if in answer to that question, a gray-haired man stepped through the crowd of saloon goers. He wore a sober pressed suit, a minister's clerical collar and a starched-looking hat. From beneath its dark brim, his full, silvery whiskers were plainly evident; so was his determined expression. Whatever Reverend Benson had come to the saloon for, it was important to him.

"Foster!" Reverend Benson barked. "I want a word with you."

Aha. The minister had come regarding Violet, then. Cade had been expecting this—for quite a while, in fact.

"Just *one* word?" Cade gave the older man's lowered eyebrows and indomitable features a chary look. He set down his cards, readying himself. "I reckon you want more than that, don't you?"

"Don't be impertinent."

"I'm guessing you've got a whole passel of words saved up, all ready to unleash on me." Cade clinked together his winnings. With deft movements, he pocketed his money. Beside him, the showily painted saloon girl blinked, obviously surprised at his speedy movements. "Let me guess—they start with 'stay away' and end with 'my daughter.' Am I close, Reverend?"

The older man compressed his mouth, seeming displeased.

Knowingly, Cade grinned. "You're not the first father I've run into during my travels. I doubt you'll be the last."

But he was the only one Cade had ever felt disappointed to be having this conversation with. The realization puzzled him.

"That only makes my business with you all the more urgent."

"To you? Maybe." Cade shrugged. "But to me, this is just the latest town. The latest game. The latest overprotective father, determined to guard his daughter's virtue." Aware of their observers' curious looks, Cade met Reverend Benson's gaze squarely. If the reverend thought they'd forged some sort of friendship just because Cade had slipped the man an improving card... well, he'd better think again. Cade didn't form alliances. "The only thing that makes you different, Reverend, is you're less likely to swear at me. Or to try to swing a punch."

"Keep talking." Frowning, Reverend Benson made a fist. "You might inspire me to show you that you're wrong about that."

Impressed, Cade raised his eyebrows. Maybe he had misjudged this particular soft-spoken father. "Violet wouldn't like that."

"You don't know what my daughter likes."

"Mmm. I think I do." He had when he'd been kissing her. But admitting as much would be beyond indiscreet—and Cade was nothing if not restrained. His lonely life had taught him to be. Carelessly, he dragged on his suit coat. He adjusted his lapels, then made himself smile. "You're here later than I expected," he observed, glancing up at the minister again. "Most fathers would have voiced their objections to me long before now."

Reverend Benson straightened. "*I* am not most fathers."

"Violet is not most women." Lazily, Cade rose. "So I'm curious to know. Why have you waited this long to protect her?"

Benson's eyes bulged. Growing red faced, he pointed a shaky finger at Cade. "Your intentions *are* dishonorable, then?"

Another smile. "If they were, would I admit it?"

"Talk straight with me!" The reverend raised his voice. "I'm here, man to man, to manage this situation between you and Violet. To offer you a wager! But if you insist on speaking in riddles with me, then it will be impossible for us to—"

"A wager?" His curiosity piqued, Cade went still. No domineering papa or interfering uncle or matchmaking mother had ever suggested a wager. Not to him. Especially not with regard to a woman like Violet. He'd been hoping he could use charm and conviviality to earn Reverend Benson's blessing to call on Violet—eventually—but that tactic no longer seemed available…not given the man's current combativeness. "What sort of wager?"

Reverend Benson glanced around. Across Jack Murphy's boisterous saloon, the piano still pinged out a bawdy tune. Gamblers still placed their bets. But near the table where Cade had done his wagering so far, all was silent in anticipation.

"A private one," Benson said firmly. "Let's talk alone."

That seemed fair. With another shrug, Cade left behind his latest game. "Keep the table warm, gents," he said over his shoulder. "I'll be back directly to clean your pockets."

Amid the genial, profanity-filled objections of his fellow sporting men, Cade followed Reverend Benson to the saloon's back room. Whatever Violet had done to bewitch him into wanting her by his side, Cade realized, it must be nigh irresistible.

Otherwise, how else to explain the fact that he was about to risk angering a man of God—and maybe the Almighty Himself—in a wager that was sure to be foolish at best?

But he didn't have much to lose, Cade reminded himself as he shut the door behind himself and Reverend Benson. His search for Whittier was leaching away whatever hopefulness he'd once had. If a fresh bet could enliven his night, what was the harm?

Standing in the minuscule, inadequately heated Morrow Creek train station office on a brisk autumn morning, Violet accepted a stack of registers and paperwork from Joseph Abernathy, the clerk. It was an awkward exchange. Joseph had lost partial use of his hand and arm a few years ago during a sawing accident at the Copeland Lumber Mill, so his grasp on the records was a bit precarious. But his smile, which he offered her in conjunction with the leather-bound books, appeared every bit as bright and boyish as it always had.

"Here you go, Miss Benson," he said cheerfully. "All our receipts from last spring all the way up to last week."

"That will be fine. I shouldn't need any more than that." Knowing the records in her grasp ought to provide her with at least a first step in tracking Tobe's arrival with his mother in Morrow Creek, Violet smiled. "Thank you very much, Joseph. I can't tell you how much I appreciate your help. Again. This must be the fourth favor you've done for me in as many months."

"Pshaw. It's no problem at all!" Joseph insisted. "After everything you've done for me, it's the least I could do. If it weren't for you, I don't know what would have happened to me."

He meant after he'd lost his job at the lumber mill, Violet knew. He'd been deeply distraught. But all that was behind him.

"The depot is fortunate to have you." Joseph's position there—wrangled by the combination of Violet and mill owner Marcus Copeland, working together—had been a snap to procure. "You're smart and hardworking, and that uniform suits you, too."

This time Joseph blushed, all the way to his ears. "That's what Miss Hartford told me. That she likes me in my uniform."

"Really?" Intrigued and pleased, Violet hugged the records to her chest. "How are things progressing between you two?"

Somewhat shyly, Joseph confided his plans to propose to his longtime beloved, Miss Letitia Hartford. Violet liked Joseph; she was happy for him. For the first time when hearing such romantic news, she didn't feel even a twinge of jealousy or self-pity. *She* had some-one to care for, too, Violet remembered—someone who cared for her, also. Someone who wanted to kiss her!

Cade might be an unusual partner, but he was a dazzling one. His interest in her now made up for years of disregard.

"Well, good luck with your proposal." Warmly, Violet gave Joseph a parting squeeze to his upper arm. "I have business to conduct at the Lorndorff Hotel—" meaning she had more records to retrieve there "—a few letters to mail and then a sewing bee to get to. My women's group is making quilts for needy families this year, and there's a great deal of work left to be done."

"That's mighty kindhearted of you, Miss Benson."

Violet merely shrugged. "It's as much for me as it is for anyone else. I'm so blessed—how could I *not* share that?"

"Knowing you? You couldn't." Joseph tipped his cap. With a leading look, he added, "I only hope you and your Mr. Foster will be as happy together as me and Miss Hartford are."

"If you're angling for grist for the gossip mill, I'm afraid you're going to be disappointed." Violet grinned. "Despite rumors to the contrary, Mr. Foster and I share a simple friendship." *With kisses. Lots and lots of kisses.* "That's all."

At least until Papa agrees I may see Cade. And then....

"Absolutely," Joseph agreed, eyes wide with sham naïveté. "No one is expecting a wintertime engagement for you at all!"

An engagement. Wouldn't that be extraordinary?

With the notion taking root in her heart for the first time, Violet considered precisely what such a remarkable event would mean: that she was loved…*beloved.* That she could finally give herself to someone on a more personal basis than the broad generosity required for quilted coverlets or charity kitchens.

That would be the fulfillment of her dreams for certain. But did *she*—plain-featured, overlooked Violet Benson—truly dare to hope for such a momentous occurrence? Cade insisted he wanted her. Joseph and several of her friends seemed to agree that they could become a credible couple. So what was stopping her?

"Well, perhaps everyone *should* expect that!" Violet dared to say. At the immenseness of her boast, her heartbeat hammered madly. If she wasn't careful, soon she'd be bluffing as often and as recklessly as Cade. But at the same time, she couldn't help remembering exactly what Cade had told her the other day.

Give over, Violet. Do it. It's the only way to feel alive.

She *wanted* to give over to her wildest impulses. She did. Cade had helped her to recognize that from their very first dance. Already, Violet realized, she was well on her way.

Perhaps now she could go even further.

Joseph blinked, appearing slightly less teasing—and slightly less sure. "We should expect an engagement? For *you*?"

Heedless of the hesitation now edging into her friend's voice, Violet brightened. She *should* do it! she

decided. She should do *something*, at least. She should…
seize this rare opportunity at courtship and gamble on
love herself! Everyone seemed to believe she'd done so
already. So why not do it?

After all, Cade believed she could bring him good
luck. There was no reason to suspect she couldn't improve her own fortunes at the same time. With Cade still
ensconced, so far as she knew, in his luxurious room at
the Lorndorff Hotel—her next intended destination—
there was no time like the present.

There was no time like now to truly *fly*. With Cade.

Fired up now and full of newfound verve—not to
mention a budding hope that what existed between her
and Cade might grow into something more—Violet gave
Joseph's arm another squeeze.

Then she turned hurriedly to leave.

"By the first snowfall, we could *both* be engaged
to be married," Violet told Joseph as she left. "Let's
hope so!"

"For your sake," Joseph vowed sincerely, "I *do* hope
so!"

Was that more *doubt* suffusing his voice, making
him sound uncertain and wary? Violet didn't think so.
Assuring herself she was doing the right thing, she offered Joseph a heartfelt goodbye. Then, with her docu-
ments hugged to her chest and her heart filled with a
heady mix of bravado and sheer until-now-untapped determination, Violet left the train depot and headed for
the tall, two-story opulence of the Lorndorff Hotel…
and somewhere inside it, Cade Foster's scandalously
enjoyable embrace.

* * *

To be a good gambler, a man had to be both observant and detached, interested and wary. He had to be willing to risk everything on the turn of a card or the roll of a dice. He had to possess sufficient grit to stay the course even when fortune didn't spin his way. Most of all, he had to keep his word. Otherwise, he'd rightly be labeled a liar and a cheat, and the gambling world would snap shut to him for the rest of his days.

That's why, last night when Cade had lost his wager with Reverend Benson, he'd had to accept the consequences. He'd had to move forward like a man. For the sake of his reputation, he'd had to smile at Violet's father, nod in acceptance of his fate and move on straightaway.

Last night, Cade had done all those things. Today, in the unforgiving light of a bleak new morning, he almost wished he hadn't. The stakes that Reverend Benson had set—and Cade had foolishly and arrogantly accepted— were just too high.

If you win, the minister had said, *you may court my daughter. You may call on Violet and entertain her in public. Eventually, if she agrees, you may even marry her.*

And because, to a whiskey-soaked and overconfident Cade, that prize had sounded nigh irresistible, he'd agreed readily.

But if you lose, the minister had gone on to caution him, wearing a peculiar smile, *you must agree to find yourself honest work, as an honest laborer, and give up all your gambling ways.*

Even the "gambling ways" that have benefited your church coffers and your own pocketbook? Cade had asked with a grin. It was just like a pious man, he'd reckoned then, to try to reform him…even while he profited from his supposed debauchery.

But the wager had been all but set at that point. There'd been no way Cade could foresee losing a bet to a fumble-fingered, outlandishly overoptimistic minister—especially one who let tender emotions overrule common sense. No self-respecting professional sporting man could have. So Cade had merely shook hands with Violet's father, requested a fresh deck of cards from Harry, Jack Murphy's able barkeep, and begun a new game.

Two hours later, Cade had stared in patent disbelief as gray-haired, newly jocular Reverend Benson had scraped all his winnings into his overturned hat, issued an incomprehensible bit of scripture as a final condolence, then bade him farewell.

Don't forget! his parting words had rung out. *Honest work! In an honest trade, with a fair exchange of labor for wages.*

Cade scarcely knew what that meant. And he scarcely knew how to explain this disastrous misstep to Blackhouse, what's more. His benefactor wouldn't be pleased with this wrinkle in their plans. Whatever Blackhouse's reasons for wanting to find Whittier were, they'd kept him in the hunt for a long while. The bachelor ne'er-do-well of the rails was unlikely to quit now.

Considering the thorny issue of explaining himself to Blackhouse, Cade dragged his arm over his eyes. He wanted to shield himself both from the daylight shoving its way through his hotel room draperies *and* from his own recriminations.

How could he have been so brash? So reckless? Not only had he put his search for Whittier in jeopardy, but he'd also cut himself off from seeing Violet. She would never understand this.

Wondering if the reverend would tell his daughter the truth about their situation, Cade groaned. Of course he wouldn't. He'd wanted to force Cade to stay away from Violet, and he had—in a fashion that Cade could neither argue with nor back down from.

I believe you're a man of honor, Reverend Benson had told Cade as he'd made ready to leave the gambling table and Murphy's saloon last night. *For Violet's sake, I'm glad of it.*

That was him, Cade thought now with a new sense of irony. An honor-bound gambler: the first and last of his kind. Because when it came to Violet and what she deserved from him, honesty was paramount...but honor came hard on its heels. For Violet, Cade would have clung to the merest of honorable intentions. How else to explain why he'd entered into such a foolish wager at all?

Sprawled amid his tangled bed linens, beset with regret and the rough aftereffects of too much Old Orchard whiskey, Cade groaned again. The only thing to do was get on with it. If he went on lying here, turning over the events of last night in his mind, he'd surely lose the will to get up altogether. Judah had found him that way once, Cade recalled unwillingly, half-drunk and entirely naked, stuck in a nameless hotel room from which he'd felt no inclination to leave for almost a week.

He'd lost track of Whittier on that occasion, too. That had been years ago now—years and many disappointments…the latest of which had left Cade completely averse to carry on fighting.

Get up, his brother had urged him. *You're scaring me.*

Judah's blue eyes—so like their father's—had looked especially large and fearful that day, set against the youthful features of his familiar face. He'd been not quite twenty then. Cade had just turned twenty-four. It felt a million years ago now.

Please, Judah had said then. *I need you to keep trying.*

But now Cade's brother was hundreds of miles away. There was no one to rouse him from his bed this time. There was no one to lie to him and tell him there was still hopefulness left.

A sharp rap at the door startled Cade.

Judah? he couldn't help thinking. Had Blackhouse really brought him there, as he'd suggested he'd do so many times now?

Impossible. "Go away."

Another knock. It sounded more determined this time.

"Leave me alone." Maybe it was the maid. Yesterday she'd flirtatiously suggested using her feather duster to tickle his fancy. Cade hadn't been interested. "I don't need anything."

That was a lie. He did need things. He needed answers and resolve and maybe a kind word or two. He needed Violet Benson.

"I don't need anything you can give me," he clarified with a certain belligerence. He swore. "Go bother someone else."

The knocking quit. An instant later, the doorknob turned.

Cade gawked at it. It rattled vigorously. Next came the distinctive click of a key being inserted into the lock.

Hellfire. Probably Blackhouse had bribed a hotel employee into unlocking Cade's room—possibly for the express purpose of gloating over Cade's loss to Reverend Benson last night. Cade didn't think anyone knew about the outcome of their wager. But during their acquaintance, Blackhouse had proven surprisingly adept at collecting information—at least when he could be bothered to bestir himself from his usual pleasurable pursuits.

With an even more raw and heartfelt swearword, Cade heaved himself from his bed. Bleary-eyed and shirtless, he padded across his hotel room's plush Oriental rug. With one eye on the door, Cade dragged on his trousers. He'd just buttoned them when the lock finally gave way. The door burst open with a bang.

Violet Benson stood there, her arms full of books and ledgers and papers, all held higgledy-piggledy in her grasp. Her face was flushed, her breath was hurried and her smile was enchanting. Cade knew he must have imagined her. He must have conjured her from some devilish mixture of despair and regret, specifically to taunt himself over losing the chance to be with her. He could be unforgiving that way, he knew. He could be cruel, especially when it came to himself and what he needed.

"I don't want to bother anyone else," Violet piped up with giddy, adorably girlish certainty. "I only want to bother *you*!"

She *looked* real enough. She sounded real enough. She even reacted realistically enough when she belatedly noticed that Cade was tellingly tousle haired and mostly undressed.

Unlike him, Violet did not appear at ease with his near nudity. Blushing even more furiously, she gave a one-handed wave in his direction. "But I can wait until you're dressed. To bother you, I mean. I don't mind waiting for, um, you to—" She broke off, obviously floundering. "That is, I did come here on purpose, you see, but I was not quite prepared for such a speedy entrée into the world of, well, courtship and…things."

"Courtship? And things?"

"Indeed." A nod. "Although I believe it's customary to be dressed, at least for the initial stages. So you should—"

"You haven't spoken with your father yet, then?"

Violet gave him a puzzled look. That only convinced Cade he was probably losing his mind—or maybe was still a little drunk.

Perhaps, he thought with the sudden insight of the formerly sober, he shouldn't have chased his Old Orchard with mescal.

"My father was ministering to a congregant this morning," Violet informed him. "So no, I haven't spoken with him today. But if you're concerned about earning Papa's permission—"

"I'm not." Not with *this* Violet, Cade wasn't. With *this* Violet, he still had a chance to indulge all his fantasies.

Intrigued by the possibility—even if he *had* fabricated an inconveniently prim version of her—Cade took a step nearer.

Violet's upswept hair was mussed, he noticed. Her skirts were askew, as though she'd run all the way upstairs to his room. Which she couldn't have done, of course. Because a proper young woman like Violet Benson— a minister's straitlaced daughter, no less!—certainly wouldn't risk her reputation by taking herself alone to visit a scurrilous gambler like him.

That all but proved he'd conjured her somehow. Whether through some consequence of the liquor he'd drunk or simply his own overwhelming desire to see her, he'd imagined her there in his room. Still watching her, Cade realized that if *this* Violet wasn't real—if this wasn't really happening at all between them—then he didn't need to be gentlemanly or restrained. He didn't even need to watch what he said for fear of scaring her away.

"You're lucky I'm wearing even this much," he said as a test of his theory, gesturing at his low-slung trousers. "Until I heard the knock at the door, I was lying in bed entirely naked."

Her gaze skittered to the unmade bed. Her eyes widened. She was picturing the sight, Cade reckoned…exactly as he'd meant for her to do. If this was the real Violet, she'd scurry away now.

Instead, she lifted her chin. "I bet that was…comfortable."

Cade raised his brow. His imaginary Violet was sassy. He liked that about her. "It was. You should try it sometime."

She nodded, biting her lip in apparent deliberation. At that, Cade's imagination truly galloped away with him. Wholly unbidden, it offered up a tantalizing vision of Violet lying there in his bed, with her skin bare and her luscious curves ready for him to touch. Swallowing hard, Cade shook his head to clear it...even as Violet nodded in thought once more.

"Yes. That's a marvelous idea. Perhaps I will try lying in bed naked." She eyed the bed and its rumpled covers as though considering the notion more carefully. "Perhaps very soon."

As if that outrageous statement were simply a long-expected promise, she met his gaze squarely. Cade scarcely dared to wonder what his make-believe Violet would say or do next.

"I'm here to ruin my reputation, Cade," she announced firmly. "With you."

Stunned by that scandalous notion, Cade couldn't speak.

But Violet didn't seem to mind. "I'm here to make some thrilling memories," she went on, "and maybe change my future while I'm at it. And we've already wasted a great deal of time, so—" perkily, she smiled "—shall we get started?"

Chapter Seven

"Get started?" Cade repeated. Did she really mean what he thought she meant? That they should be together...intimately?

"Yes." With an air of plucky certainty, Violet set down her books and papers and leather-bound ledgers. "We should have all the time we need, so don't worry about that. I told the hotel clerk that I was here on a charitable mission for the church."

"The church?" Cade repeated dumbly, still stuck on the possibility that Violet might willingly lie naked in his bed.

"Yes. I embark on altruistic works all the time, you know," Violet assured him. "Everyone in Morrow Creek is aware of that. So they won't find it the least bit questionable that I'm here visiting you like this. After all, you're new in town, and you're most certainly in need of ministering to. It's undeniable. I mean, just *look* at you!" She beamed at him as if delighted by his debauchery. "I felt immensely clever when I realized that on my way here. Isn't it utterly convenient?"

"Yes." It *was* convenient, Cade realized. Ingenious, too.

Contrary to all expectation, Violet's logic suggested that a virtuous woman could misbehave far more readily than a scandalous one could…and not be suspected of being anything less than upright in the process. No wonder Violet seemed so all-fired pleased with herself. She had a veritable license to sin.

And she wanted to use it with Cade.

"No! No, it isn't convenient," he blurted, realizing too late that he had to backtrack. For honor's sake. "Everyone will find it *very* questionable that you're here. Alone. With me."

I'm here to ruin my reputation, Cade. With you!

"You can't ruin your reputation," he insisted. "You made me promise that *I* wouldn't ruin your reputation. This is madness."

"It's not. It's actually quite sensible. Besides, my feelings have changed on the matter of my reputation. Given our newfound…closeness, I think this will be fine." Her satisfied smile seemed to settle the matter. "The desk clerk remembered you coming in intoxicated last night. He remembered you swearing about losing your latest wager. Because of that, he was fully prepared to believe I'm here to reform you." Violet paused to deliver him a suggestive look. "However long it takes to do so."

For a moment, Cade couldn't breathe. His entire existence was taken up with imagining the authentic Violet Benson seducing him this way…with wondering if she would have wanted him like this. He thought she would have. After all, he *hadn't* concocted the attraction between them. It had seemed unlikely to him at first. But very quickly it had felt real and true—and tempting.

"I think you're mistaken about what 'reform' means, Miss Benson." Cade couldn't help cracking a grin. Damnation, he wished she was real. He wished Violet's idea of "reforming" him really did include alluring looks and promises to lie abed naked with him. "But I confess to liking your take on the notion."

"Yes. I thought you might." Surprisingly, Violet grinned too, leaving him feeling overcome by the impish beauty of her smile. "The truth is, I wasn't intending to go this far when I set out for the Lorndorff a little while ago. But partway here I realized this might be my only chance to experience lovemaking, Cade. *You* might be my only chance. I don't want to miss it."

"Miss...lovemaking?" Cade repeated, scarcely able to form the words. Her frank way of talking left him electrified. He'd never expected to hear such things coming from Violet's mouth.

Then, too, he *wanted* to be her only chance, just as she'd said. God help him, he *wanted* to be the one to introduce her to lovemaking and all the pleasures it had to offer. He wanted *her*.

But this...wasn't real. It couldn't be.

Trying to recover his wits, Cade shook his head. Somehow his harmless fantasy had grown fangs. Now it was torturing him.

Violet was off-limits. Violet was proper and good. Violet didn't want a man like him—a man without a future to offer her.

"Yes. Lovemaking," Violet said firmly. "I might never be married—not the way things are going, anyway—and I can't see why I should be penalized for that.

So I have to make this good. I have to do whatever I can to *feel alive* before it's too late!"

Recognizing his own words on her lips, Cade groaned. He aimed his gaze heavenward, desperate now to end this reverie—if that's what it was. He was beginning to have serious doubts.

"I'll never touch a drop of whiskey again," he swore fervently, hoping to snap out of his fantasy. "I swear it."

"See?" Violet's ever-comforting smile touched him. "That's very well done of you to play along! Anyone passing by would believe I've been partially effective in reforming you already."

As if tardily realizing then that any idle passersby could indeed glimpse them, Violet punctuated her statement by pushing Cade's hotel room door completely closed. Its thudding slam alerted him to the fact that perhaps—almost certainly—he wasn't imagining things. He wasn't imagining *her*.

What, exactly, was happening here?

"But even if I've licked your awful problem with drinking, there's still the matter of your *terrible* gambling impulses to deal with, Mr. Foster." Violet's expression turned alarmingly teasing. She seemed almost cocksure…for her. "You need my help. You really do," she insisted earnestly, crossing the room to come nearer to him. When she arrived to stand almost atop his big bare feet, she smiled up at Cade coquettishly. "When Henry—he's the desk clerk…I've known him since we were both in the schoolhouse together—gave me my own key to your hotel room, he wished me good luck in coping with your…uncontrollable urges."

Uncontrollable. Yes, that was exactly the way Cade would have described his desire for her just then. Trying hard not to think about that, Cade glanced at the hotel room key she'd used. Even now it mocked him from atop the ledgers and things Violet had set aside. Feeling suddenly beset by those selfsame urges she'd alluded to—or at least by a few illicit impulses exactly as passionately felt—he clenched his jaw. *Violet was real.*

She was real, she was here, and Cade could not give in to any of the things she was suggesting. No matter what.

"This is a test," he announced, realizing it must be true—diabolically so. "It's a test to see if I'll keep my word, the way I promised to. Well, you can tell your father that I did." Cade raised his hand to swear it. "This is one honor-bound gambler who won't endanger your heart *or* your reputation."

"Oh, I don't intend to tell my father about this." Violet raised herself on tiptoe. She clasped her hand with his upraised hand for leverage, then pressed a kiss to his mouth. "Or that." Another kiss, followed by a tentative smile. "Or that. Or anything that might happen between us from now till midnight."

"Midnight?" Maybe he'd misunderstood. After all, he'd never been "reformed" before. Maybe he'd been dreading the notion unnecessarily all this time. "What will take until midnight?"

"More kissing," Violet specified. "More touching. More looking." Audaciously, she sent her gaze over his bare torso. "I like the way you look, you know. I like it very much." Another, bolder perusal. She nodded. "You look very strong. And capable."

It was still possible he could deter her before it was too late. Hoping to do exactly that, Cade said, "I *am* capable."

Her mouth parted. Her cheeks turned a pretty shade of pink.

"I'm capable," Cade went on, gazing into her eyes, "of giving you the kind of pleasure you couldn't possibly have imagined. I'm capable of making you yell with enjoyment—of making you writhe and pant beneath me, begging for release."

Violet swallowed hard. But her gaze never left his.

"I want that," she said. "I want you. I trust you."

She shouldn't do that. *Hellfire.* Closing his eyes, Cade tried to summon whatever fortitude and integrity he had left.

"Don't, Violet. Just…don't." This time, paradoxically, Cade was the one begging—and they hadn't even reached his bed. "You don't know what you're doing… what could happen. This is—"

"Perfect," she breathed. "It's going to be perfect, just as soon as you give in. Just as soon as you realize that I *want* this. I want *you*!" Eagerly, Violet shucked her long woolen coat. Beneath it, her calico dress swayed with her movements, showing him a glimpse of stocking-clad ankle. "Please, Cade. I'm not going to beg. But we've had an understanding between us for a while now. You must have known this was inevitable. Because I know you see me as I am, and I see you, too, the same way."

"No, you don't," Cade disagreed, needing to disillusion her. "There are things about me that you can't conceive. Dark things. Things I can't explain and don't have answers to."

"Then you can tell me all about them. I want to know."

He hauled in a ragged breath. If he had no choice…

"Because I've realized something about us, Cade." Violet offered him a bashful smile. "Something about us together." With her eyes shining in anticipation of her coming statement, she inhaled. "Somehow, I think, we're each other's last chance."

Cade didn't understand. "Last chance for what?"

"For feeling loved!" Violet took his hand. "I know I want that. You must want it, too. Wouldn't it be downright foolhardy to throw away that chance just for the sake of propriety?"

He grinned. "You make a compelling argument."

"And you make a surprisingly reluctant participant," she teased. "For a renowned scoundrel and known chance taker."

"I'm not reluctant. These stakes are higher than most."

If he wanted to behave honorably, Cade knew, he'd tell Violet that propriety trumped all. If he wanted to avoid hurting her, he'd tell her that he *had* felt loved, many times over, and had no need of her paltry caring now. But that would be a lie—an especially egregious one—and Cade could not deliver it. Because all at once, he saw Violet in a new and vulnerable light, and he knew that *not* being with her might hurt her more than being with her ever could. And Cade decidedly didn't want that.

"But I reckon it *would* be a sin to throw away a chance at love," he finally agreed with a reckless grin. "A terrible sin."

Her eyes brightened. "I'm happy you see things my way."

"Me, too," Cade agreed after broadening his smile, and with that, he quit resisting altogether. After all, he'd duly warned Violet. He'd described exactly what would happen between them. He'd even alluded to his frightful past. And still she remained there. No one could fault him for giving her what she wanted.

And if this wasn't following precisely the intent of his wager with Reverend Benson…well, that could be forgiven, too. Especially if no one ever found out about it, as he planned.

Because Cade hadn't called on Violet. She'd come to him. She'd come to him and she'd offered herself to him, and he was just a man, with a man's needs and a man's eagerness to pleasure a woman, and no one short of a lunatic would expect him to refuse her. Particularly not while she stood there, seeming so ripe and inventive and intriguingly innocent. He'd never had an innocent woman, it occurred to Cade. From his first paramour— a kindhearted whore who'd lived down the street from Cade's third set of foster parents—to his last, everyone he'd been with had been experienced and jaded. Like him, his partners had been wholly uninterested in any connection beyond lusty pleasure.

But Violet was different. Violet was sweet. She was caring.

All she'd talked about was *feeling* loved, just this once. They'd both be fools to surrender that chance. So with his mind made up, Cade broadened his smile. He gave Violet a lingering, up-and-down perusal…one designed to heighten her innocent awareness of exactly how close they were about to become.

"It *would* be a sin to throw away a chance at love," he repeated. Then, "Do you know what else is a sin?"

Violet swallowed hard. In a shaky voice, she ventured, "Coveting your neighbor's skill with a knitting needle?"

He smiled. Damnation, but he could have fallen for Violet…if he'd been a settling-down kind of man. Which he was not. Giving her a tenderhearted smile nonetheless, Cade said, "Not understanding what your body is capable of feeling. Not experiencing all the sensations that are waiting for you."

"Oh." She bit her lip. "I see. Such as?"

She was so brave, it occurred to him. Even in this. He couldn't help admiring that about her. Moving closer, Cade skimmed his hands along her hips to her waist. With slow, deliberate movements, he traced the curves he found there.

"Such as…this." He lifted his gaze to hers. "Do you feel that? Do you feel the way your body differs from mine?"

She shivered…even while her body radiated warmth to his fingertips. With sham contemplativeness, Violet crinkled her brow. "I'm not sure. Perhaps if you demonstrated some more?"

"Minx." Cade grinned again. "You're deliberately encouraging me to continue."

"Yet you're decidedly *not* continuing. So…"

"So you hadn't reckoned on my self-control, I guess." *He* hadn't either, he realized. He hadn't reckoned on his resolve crumbling so much in the face of Violet's naive allure. "Try to pay attention this time," he said, "and I'll demonstrate again."

Smiling, Violet stood erect. "All right. I'm ready."

So was he. He was ready to lay her down on the waiting bed, strip off those interferingly fussy clothes of hers and make her his. But that wouldn't be nearly as much fun as this…as much fun as carefully sliding his hands from Violet's hips—again—to her waist. To augment his lesson, he kissed her, exceedingly gently.

"Where you're curvy, I'm straight," Cade explained. "Where you're soft and yielding, I'm sturdy…even rigid." *Damnation, he was rigid.* It felt as though his hastily yanked-on trousers had shrunk in the past few minutes. "We fit together, you and me."

"I hope we fit together," Violet quipped. "Otherwise I've been woefully misinformed about what to expect."

He raised his brows. "What do you expect?"

She breathed out, glancing determinedly away from him. "Some good things. Some touching. A bit of… pain." Her gaze skittered back to his. "My married friends do confide in me."

"Your married friends are the ones who are misinformed."

"What do you mean?"

"I mean lovemaking shouldn't hurt." Cade might not have indulged in the sentimental, hearts-and-flowers version of sexual relations, but he knew that much for certain. He knew it should feel good. "If there's any pain, it should be brief and—"

"Oh, it won't hurt *you*! Don't worry about that!" Violet hastened to assure him. She gave a fretful titter, seeming concerned that she might have alarmed him unduly. "*You* will enjoy it, without a doubt! All men do. If my friend Adeline is right, *I* will enjoy some of what goes on between us too, so—"

"*All*," Cade specified fiercely. "You will enjoy all of the things that go on between us. Or I'll know the reason."

Her eyes widened. "You sound so determined."

That was because he cared about her, Cade knew. Because he wanted her to experience the kind of joy she deserved and had been denied until now…and maybe would be denied in the future, too. It wasn't fair that Violet Benson had been overlooked just because she didn't possess apple cheeks or an upturned nose. In that moment, Cade found her beautiful. He wanted her to feel that way, as well. He wanted her to feel…*everything*.

"*You* sound dubious," he replied with another grin. "But that won't last. I promise you that much."

"Oh? And how will you—"

"Like this," Cade interrupted, then pulled her into his arms. He'd dallied too long with chitchat and preliminaries. Now was the time to make Violet see what she'd been missing. So he did. He lowered his head and took her mouth with his, a prelude to everything that would come next and after. She felt good and warm and eager in his arms, and he felt that he could have kissed her for days and not come up for air. But eventually his lungs protested, so Cade stopped. He gave Violet a loving look, then kissed her once more. "With enough kissing," he explained, "I think your inappropriate dubiousness will go away."

"I'm not so sure," she teased anew. "Perhaps you've lost your touch. Perhaps your kisses have lost their potency."

"Minx." Again he kissed her. And again Cade found *himself* caught up in their coming together. Kissing Violet was like jumping off a cliff…straight into heaven. It was like sunshine and blue skies. It was like needing and *needing*…and getting only a taste of something essential and true. "How do you feel now?"

Appearing dazed, Violet shook her head. "A bit more certain, I guess," she judged with her usual vivacity. "More?"

"More?" She was going to kill him. Any thought Cade might have given to stopping now could not have withstood her provocation. Whether Violet knew it or not, she was giving him exactly what he needed to ignore any lingering doubts of his own. *More, more, more*, she urged him…and Cade wanted to give it.

"Yes, more." She blinked. "Or should I undress first?"

At the thought, dizziness swamped him. The notion of seeing Violet in the altogether, bared and willing and eager, was almost more than Cade could stand. He swallowed. "I'll do that."

"But you're already partly undressed."

"I'll undress *you*." To prove it, Cade toyed with her bodice's topmost button. He contemplated the secrets it hid, and felt himself grow twice as rigid as before. He'd considered what she would look like naked, of course. Any man would have, especially given the time they'd spent together...and the unexpected rapport they'd shared. But to be so close to the reality of that daydream... "Mmm. But first, another kiss."

This time, their mouths met unerringly, in a newly practiced glide that paired heat and slickness and softness in ways Cade had never quite experienced before. With Violet, kissing felt new. *Everything* felt new. New and better than ever.

He raised his head, unable to quit smiling at her. She smiled back at him. Then her mouth made an O. She clapped her hand over her gaping dress bodice, her brows raised. "Oh! You've already started!" A dreamy chuckle. "I didn't even realize it."

"I did." Wolfishly interested in the bare skin he'd revealed at her dress's neckline, Cade traced his finger down the center of her chest. Her cleavage was modest and perfect. With effort, he lifted his gaze to her face. "You're beautiful."

Her expression changed. "I'm not beautiful, Cade. Don't say that. *You*, of all people, know that I'm not—"

"Enough." Sternly, he pressed his fingertip to her lips. It required a serious effort of will not to linger there... not to delight in the luscious softness of her mouth and the sweet bow he found there at her lower lip. But since there were things between them that were more important than simple carnal pleasures… "No more talk like that. I won't have it."

As punishment—and diversion—he deftly slipped a few more buttons free of their confining buttonholes. Her bodice gaped a bit more. The effect was enchanting. Her breasts swelled pertly above her tightly laced corset, ready and waiting and…

"But it's true!" Violet protested. "I'm not even pretty."

"You're *beyond* pretty," Cade said, and in that moment, it became his mission to prove it to her. "You have something no other woman does, Violet. You have yourself, in all your glory, for me to delight in and laugh with and touch this way—"

"Hmmph. No other woman *wants* my so-called 'glory.'"

"Some people are beautiful when you meet them," Cade said, giving her an unyielding look. "Others become beautiful as you get to know them. You," he specified with a lingering touch, "become prettier to me with every minute. You *are* beautiful."

With that, her eyes filled with tears. "Truly?"

"Truly," Cade said, and gave her a kiss to prove it. "I love your freckled face and your wonderful nose. I love your crooked, skeptical smile and your warm, giving hands. I love your body—" He broke off, too distracted to continue speaking as he dared to fill his palms with her breasts, now almost wholly freed from her wide, lace-trimmed bodice. He kissed her instead. "I love everything about you, Violet. And to demonstrate that, I'm going to love every bit of you, starting right now."

Her smile enchanted him. "Even my ankles?"

"Even your ankles," Cade told her, and he knew then that he had won. "So lie back and get ready," he said as he gestured to the waiting bed, "because we've only just begun."

Chapter Eight

With an exuberance born of discovery and curiosity and almost unbearable hopefulness, Violet leaped toward the bed.

She landed amid the tangled covers in a veritable heap of calico skirts and lacy muslin petticoats. Her scandalously unbuttoned bodice allowed her bosom to feel the fresh air; her invigorated skin tingled at her first contact with Cade's fancy hotel room sheets. Her mouth felt swollen and her legs felt weak and everywhere beneath her skirts felt uniquely warm—almost effervescently so—and she wasn't sure how much more of Cade's sweet words she could stand before she simply swooned with joy.

Because Cade Foster loved her. He *loved* her!

He'd just said so, over and over again. *I love everything about you.* And now, just as she had when she'd first heard those words from his lips, Violet felt overcome with gladness.

She'd done the right thing by coming here to be with him. If not for her burst of boldness today, she might never have known that Cade thought she was beautiful. That he thought she was irresistible. That he *loved* her!

"There!" Violet announced. Bravely, she pushed up on her elbows, then regarded Cade from her perch on his bed. Chirpily, she patted the bedclothes beside her. "I'm ready. Now what?"

"Now—" He gave her an adorably devilish eyebrow quirk…one that made her heartbeat race twice as eagerly. "I'll join you."

He did as he'd promised, making the mattress dip beneath his weight. Keeping her in his sights, Cade prowled his way from the edge of the bed to Violet's place in the very center of it.

"You have lovely big muscles," she observed, eyeing the rippled, corded movements of his arms and shoulders and chest as he approached her. Avidly, she let her gaze roam down Cade's chest, following his dark chest hair to his taut belly, then lower to his… Not yet ready, she whipped up her gaze. "I like your muscles. No, I *love* them," Violet said in fond mimicry of him. "I do. Especially when you use them to hold me close."

"That's one of the best uses for them," he agreed.

"I don't suppose it requires much strength to hold cards at a gambling table," she mused aloud, "but still, you're strong."

"And you're talkative." A grin. "But that won't last."

"I can't see why not." Somewhat nervously, Violet watched as Cade stretched out on the bed beside her. "I'm pretty good at keeping a conversation going," she said. "For instance—" She broke off, noticing then that Cade's trousers had gaped a bit near the waistband. His movements made it evident that if he *was* wearing undergarments, they were exceedingly tiny. Which seemed unlikely. Which could mean only that he was naked under there.

Naked. She'd never seen a naked man before. Enthralled by the notion, Violet tried to envision Cade lolling about in the altogether. She only got as far as his hip, which was probably best explained by the fact that she could actually *see* several inches of tawny, fascinating skin just above his trousers. *Hmm.*

Oblivious to her reveries, Cade trailed his fingertips over her arm. His touch incited a riot of goose bumps, but still Violet could not be distracted from her discovery. Naked. *Naked.*

Somewhere beneath his trousers, Cade was naked. Violet had a powerful urge to know what he looked like under there.

"You know, I seem to be at a disadvantage," she ventured in an effort to satisfy her burgeoning inquisitiveness. "Because I am almost completely dressed at the moment, while *you*—" she gestured at his lackadaisically slipped-on trousers "—are…not."

"That's easily fixed." Smiling, Cade kissed her.

She really loved his kisses. Therefore it took a while for her to summon an appropriate response. She had to wait to catch her breath. Then, "You're not going to put on a shirt, are you? You know, to match up with my level of apparel wearing?"

That hadn't been the point of her observation. Besides, she liked that Cade wasn't wearing a shirt. It let her see his brawny chest muscles and his arms and his middle. Every single part of him was different from her. Intriguingly different.

To Violet, Cade looked as though he could shelter and protect her from anything—and would, willingly, if she asked.

A broader smile. "I'm going to undress *you*. Remember?" He eyed her bodice. "It's past time we finished with that."

"Yes," she said brightly. "We should certainly finish!"

His amused look let her know that hers wasn't the response he'd been expecting. But Violet couldn't help that. She was too preoccupied with more vital things—with wondering about the rest of Cade's arresting physique. His shoulders were bunched with muscles. His arms were sinewy with strength. His belly was flat, his hips were slim, his legs were long and undoubtedly flawless.

Even given all that wonderfulness, though, Violet felt *most* intrigued by what lay between all that. Lying next to him this way, together on his bed, she couldn't help wondering…

Was his, well…*manhood* as muscularly proportionate as the rest of him? If so, how would it feel? Precisely?

Breathlessly, Violet regarded him. With an unreadable expression, Cade gazed at her—then at her chest. She remembered feeling his hands on her breasts, just a few minutes ago. Again her nipples budded with eagerness. She forgot to do anything except wish he would touch her there once more, just that way.

Instead, Cade kissed her. *Then* he cupped her breast in his palm, gently gliding his thumb over the pebbled point of her nipple, and Violet couldn't help gasping against his mouth.

"Does that hurt?" Cade murmured, kissing her neck now.

"No." Shocked to feel herself arching against him, Violet nonetheless continued to do it. She had to. "I like it."

He nodded, satisfied. "I told you you would."

"I do!" she confessed in a breathy voice. She flexed her hands against his back, needing to hold on. "I really do!"

"That's good." Sliding lower, Cade nuzzled the curve of her shoulder, then the angle of her collarbone. He nudged aside her dress a bit farther, then kissed the swell of her breast. "Mmm."

Violet couldn't help mimicking him. "Mmm-*hmm!*"

Never had she felt anything more wonderful or more right. With Cade, she *did* feel beautiful. She felt indispensible. She felt as though with him to offer his hand to her, she could fly.

Cade seemed to believe that was true, too. Because for the next several moments, he set about releasing her from everything that held her to her ordinary existence. Moving over her, murmuring sweet words, Cade made sure that Violet felt loved and beloved and needed. He made sure she felt *wanted*...passionately so. And despite the incredible unlikeliness of any of this happening between them, Violet couldn't muster a single protest.

In fact, she couldn't think of anything at all. She couldn't say a word. All she could do was feel: feel Cade's hands slowly stroking her, feel his breath fluttering over her, feel his mouth moving in an increasingly necessary and exciting arc from her breasts to her neck to her mouth and back again.

Caught beneath his incredible attentions, Violet simply gave in. This was real. It was true. It was right. Through half-closed eyes, she watched as Cade loved her…and she knew that she loved him in return, even if she hadn't yet said so.

To celebrate that, even if only to herself, Violet clutched Cade's head and kissed him back. Happily, she surrendered her high-buttoned shoes, her long dark stockings, her dress and her petticoats and even her corset. Or at least she found herself eventually without them—somehow Cade had peeled away all those garments with her scarcely noticing the movements of his clever gambler's fingers. But she gave herself full credit for slipping beneath the bedclothes afterward wearing only her chemise—and for boldly, even cheekily, summoning Cade to join her there.

"Are you sure you're ready?" he asked.

"Would I do *this* if I weren't?" Saucily, she crooked her finger in invitation. "Don't keep me waiting. I need you."

For a fraction of a second, Cade seemed hesitant.

Then, "I need you, too," he said. "*You're* what's left for me after all this is done. I didn't know that until right now."

Violet didn't understand him. But before she could ask what Cade meant, he quashed her ability to ask questions by undoing his trousers and dropping them to the floor. If she'd thought his sporting man's hands were clever before… She'd never imagined they could reveal a sight as fascinating as the one that stood proudly before her at that very moment.

"You *are* commensurately huge!" she blurted, wide-eyed.

This time, Cade was the one who appeared momentarily confused. Also, unabashedly pleased with his endowments. He couldn't have known she'd been wondering if his entire body aligned with his impressive musculature. Yet somehow he seemed to. Otherwise, how else to explain the twinkle in his eyes?

"I'm glad you're pleased," he said as he lifted the rumpled bedclothes to join her atop the sumptuous mattress, "but the proof is in the feeling, not in the seeing."

Still awed, Violet sneaked another glimpse. "I'm enjoying the seeing!" She bit her lip, then lifted her gaze to his magnificent, handsome, beloved face. "But I'm curious about the feeling, too," she confessed. "May I touch you…there?"

Cade closed his eyes. His groan rent the stillness.

"Oh! If that's not done, then I apologize!" Violet said hastily. "It's just that you've done *so* much touching me that I've enjoyed, and I can't imagine why I wouldn't want to do the same for you. Why I wouldn't want to make *you* feel beautiful—"

His gaze met hers. "Then you *do* feel beautiful?"

"I mean *handsome*, of course," she nattered on, "so I…" Struck by Cade's needful expression, Violet paused. "Do you truly not know? *Yes*, I feel beautiful." Warmly, she squeezed his hand. "When I came here today, I wanted the experience of lovemaking. But what you've given me is the experience of being *loved*. It's so much more than I ever could have hoped for."

"I see." His voice sounded husky—whether with unshared emotion or with passion, she couldn't guess. Cade cleared his throat. "But we've barely gotten started," he reminded her.

"I know! Just think how much better it will get!"

His smile dazzled her. "I don't think it can get better than that look of joy on your face right now. But I'll try."

As though proving his intentions, Cade cradled her face in his hands. Tenderly, he kissed her. A bit less tenderly, he slid his tongue against hers in that special way that made Violet's belly turn somersaults and her breath quicken. Grabbing his shoulders with both hands, she returned his kiss as passionately as she could. She *loved* kissing Cade. She loved touching him and looking at him and being next to him. Now all that remained was…

The rest of him. The wholly male, enormously interesting rest of him. Which, at the moment, was hidden by the coverlet.

"So…" Shyly but determinedly, Violet slid her hand down Cade's bare chest. His dark, springy hair tickled her fingers. Already today, she'd dared to touch him quite intimately. She'd even stroked his belly, delighting in the taut feel of his muscles tightening beneath her palm. But none of that contact could compare with what she had in mind now. "May I touch you?"

He knew exactly what she meant. Gazing into her eyes, Cade swallowed hard. He tightened his hand in her hair, then kissed her again. "If you do, I don't know if I can stand it."

"But won't it be nice for you?" Honestly confused, Violet stared at him. Her hand stopped its descent midway to her intended destination. Cade's skin felt *very* warm and a bit more coarsely textured than her own. He looked quite sun-browned, too, in comparison with her, she'd noticed. "Won't you like it?"

"I know I'll love it," Cade said with utter conviction.

"Then what's the matter?" Wriggling with newfound freedom in her nearly sheer chemise, Violet blinked. "Because *I* feel, honestly, as though I can't get enough of your touching. It's as though my skin somehow *needs* to be next to yours. My breasts feel all full and tingly," she elaborated, trying to explain, "and my—" She stopped, at a loss to account for the sensations of heat and pulsing she'd been experiencing elsewhere. She pressed her thighs together, though, and somehow that made Cade understand. "The rest of me seems to need you, too. So why—"

"*Yes*," he breathed. "Do it. *Please*. It can't be any more torturous than hearing you explain why you want to do it."

"Truly? You're sure?"

"Violet…"

"Perhaps you should kiss me first."

Another groan. But Cade complied, exactly as she'd known he would. Because when it came to her, her honor-bound gambler seemed unable to refuse her anything. Even this new intimacy.

Daringly, Violet slipped her hand lower. She encountered Cade's hip, then his thigh, then… *Oh, my*. Silken hardness, a sense of throbbing liveliness and a surprising velvety fullness met her grasp. Thrilled, she stroked the entire length of him. Then, full of exploration and curiosity, she encircled his hot, hard girth in her fingers. Mmm. She quite liked the feel of him.

Cade stiffened. Another moan burst from him. Much too soon, his hand closed on hers, stopping her movements. On the verge of asking him why he'd done that, Violet felt herself being pressed into the mattress. With new urgency, Cade kissed her…and then he just went on kissing her, rolling them both together across the rumpled sheets until she could scarcely reckon out where she stopped and he began. Their limbs tangled; their breath mingled; even their hearts seemed to beat in unison. The only things lacking were fulsome words. But as Cade went on kissing her, as he went on touching her, additional conversation seemed less and less necessary. Everything they needed to share could be conveyed with a look, a moan…another tender touch.

Writhing beneath him now, Violet panted with eagerness. "I *never* imagined lovemaking could be like this!" she blurted. "I feel so…oh, Cade! I feel as though there must be more—"

"There is *definitely* more." Another, deeper kiss.

"And yet I don't know if I can stand it." She wriggled anew, pressing together her thighs to stop the ache that had been bedeviling her for what felt like hours now. Gasping, she delved her fingers in Cade's hair as he kissed her breast. By now, her chemise had been cast aside, yet she didn't feel at all awkward or exposed. All she felt was needful…especially when Cade's tongue slowly swirled over her newly exposed nipple. That only made the ache intensify. "Isn't there something I can do?"

"You've already driven me mad with wanting." Cade grinned, his sapphire-eyed gaze meeting hers with a new, heady sense of closeness. "I can't imagine what else you'd want to do."

"Me neither," Violet confessed, "but there must be something!"

"There is." Soothingly, Cade kissed her. Gently, he pushed back her hair, then gazed longingly into her face. "Enjoy this. That's all you have to do. I'll take care of the rest."

"Oh, but then I won't be doing my share. Surely there's—"

Mmm. The feel of Cade's mouth between her breasts stopped her words. Caught up in that novel sensation, Violet tensed as he kissed her again—this time on her belly. She squealed, unable to hold back another yelp as he slid lower still. His fingertips brushed across the reddish curls at the juncture of her thighs.

"So wet," he murmured. "So sweet. So perfect."

Tossing her head against the pillows, Violet knew she should have thanked him for that—at the very least, because his statement had sounded wholly approving, especially when voiced in that throaty, manful tone of his—but she simply couldn't do so. All she could do was writhe and pant and *yearn.* For what, she didn't know. But Cade seemed to. That's all that mattered.

"Mmm. I love this," he said, but she knew that he meant he loved *her.* At least that's the way it felt to Violet. "I never imagined it could be this way, with you."

Lovingly, he caressed her. "Are you sure you want more? Because if you don't—"

"Yes. Yes!" Violet clenched her fists in the bed linens. Why was he torturing her this way? Already her whole body moved toward him all on its own, her hips thrusting toward his hand, her legs opening wantonly… "Please, Cade—"

"Yes, Violet?"

"I want…" Panting, she tried to conjure up words. "You."

"That's all I needed to know." With a confusing mixture of vulnerability and bravado, Cade looked at her. He stroked her. Helplessly, Violet arched higher. "You feel *so* good," he said.

Good didn't begin to do justice to these sensations. Caught up amid exquisite sensitivity and urgent need, Violet moaned. She simply couldn't help it. Cade's hands felt so skillful. His mouth felt so soft. So good. His mouth felt…as though it was *between her thighs* now. It was! Shocked to feel his lips *there*, of all places, Violet hesitated. Surely this was sinful.

Surely this was…it was… Oh, but it was *bliss*.

These kisses, like Cade's other kisses, were magical. They were gentle and sure and entirely erotic, and as he continued kissing her in places Violet had certainly never expected to be kissed, she discovered very quickly that she needed this new kind of kissing. In fact, if Cade stopped, she would die. That was all there was to it. Eagerly, she raised herself toward him. His tongue swirled and teased in response; his lips pressed and kissed and awakened sensations she'd never even known existed.

By the time he began caressing her with slow, deliberate strokes of his hand, obviously savoring the slick wetness she'd so recently become aware of, Violet knew she could stand no more. Pleading, she cried out to Cade for…something. She didn't know what. But he seemed to. As a new torrent of sensation burst over her, she knew she'd never forget the dexterous, loving, *protective* way Cade held her as the world fell apart…then reassembled itself again. Pulsing, breathless, damp with sweat, Violet looked up. She blinked. Cade smiled.

Then, unbelievably, he said, "There's more."

She exhaled, feeling replete and limp and somehow exhilarated. Her ears were ringing. "I don't believe it."

"I'll show you." Then, sweetly, Cade did. He guided her hand lower, then lower still, all the way to that rigid, heavy part of him. He closed her fingers around him. "Mmm. *Yes*."

Reminded suddenly of everything she still didn't know about, Violet brightened. "*Yes!* I almost forgot about you."

"I'll never forget about you," he vowed. His eyes closed, even as Violet daringly stroked him. "Never, Violet. Never."

"I should hope not!" Feeling bewilderingly energetic now, Violet traced her fingers over him. Delightfully, he leaped in response to her touch. She loved that. So she did it again. "You know," she mused aloud, aiming a speculative gaze beneath the coverlets where all Cade's stimulating nudity lay, "I have all kinds of ideas now that I didn't possess just an hour ago."

"Then you're not regretful? Not bashful or sorry?"

Violet gave a one-shouldered shrug. It was difficult to continue talking while exploring his anatomy this way. "I feel *wonderful*," she told Cade truthfully. "How do you feel?"

He swallowed hard. His eyes opened, then focused on her face. "I feel that if I don't have you soon, I'll die."

Unexpectedly, Violet felt quite protective then herself. Also, her body had begun that curious *throbbing* she'd noticed earlier, all over again. She reckoned Cade could cure that.

"I'm yours," she said simply. "Now and always."

"Ah, Violet." Passionately, Cade kissed her. "I'm yours."

She couldn't help smiling at that—even as Cade chose that moment to pull her into his arms again, effectively ending her explorations of his intriguing manly endowments. An instant later, though, Violet didn't mind as much. Because an instant later, Cade had covered her with kisses, situated himself masterfully atop her and settled himself between her legs.

"Is this the lovemaking part?" Violet asked, suddenly apprehensive. He'd promised it shouldn't hurt much, but—

"With you, *everything* is the lovemaking part." Cade kissed her, even as his body pressed insistently between her thighs. "From the moment I asked you to dance, I was lost. To you."

She smiled. "And I, to you. You're awfully charming."

"And you're chatty." His grin mirrored hers, with a devilish undercurrent of lustiness. With pretend fierceness, he said, "From here on, all I want are moans and squeals and sighs of delight."

"Yes, Mr. Foster," Violet promised. "I'll do my best."

"You don't have to do anything except be you," Cade told her. "That's the part I can't resist—not even now." Seeming newly aware of his own arousal, Cade wriggled teasingly. He kissed her, then gave her a look full of concern and care and passion. "We're about to become one, Violet. Are you ready?"

"For you?" Assuredly, she nodded. "Beyond a doubt."

At her response, Cade closed his eyes. Seeming inexplicably moved by the emotion of the moment, he went entirely still.

Violet thought then that *he* must have felt the same connection between them that she did. As if in proof that he did, Cade truly did make them one: he entered her in one sure stroke. He paused to be sure she was unhurt, then went on.

Having him inside her was…*remarkable.* Feeling filled and fulfilled in a way she never had before, Violet clutched Cade nearer, wide-eyed and astonished and enlightened. *This* was what she'd needed. This and everything that had passed between them until now. This was what she'd been made for…feeling this way.

With soft kisses and tender touches and more and more and *more* skillful thrusting, Cade made love to her in a way that felt unforgettable. His body fit perfectly to hers; his gaze melded seamlessly with hers; and even as he brought them both closer and closer to a new pinnacle of pleasure, Cade never let Violet forget one thing: she was beloved. She was treasured and needed and beautiful to him, and she was *his*. They were united.

"Oh, Violet." With a mighty groan, Cade thrust harder. Beneath them, the mattress dipped and swayed. The bedclothes grew yet more tangled. The coming together of their bodies turned even more frenzied, and still Cade gazed only at her. "Yes," he panted. "*Yes*. You feel *so* good. So right. So...*ah*."

He went still. Then he shouted. With an utter lack of inhibition, Cade lost himself in her body. He moaned anew, wholly lustily. Then, with his hair tousled and his muscles slicked with sweat, he delivered her his most stunning grin yet.

"Does that mean you're pleased?" Violet asked breathlessly.

He laughed. "I'm *beyond* pleased." He cradled her close, hauling her atop his big, sprawled body while they panted for breath. "I'm exhilarated. Buoyant." A hearty swearword. "I've never felt anything like that before." Cade shook his head. He kissed the top of her head, then smoothed her hair. "It must be because of you. You make everything better, Violet. Everything."

Happily, she snuggled against him. "I guess I do!" Wearing a smug—and this time *authentically* sophisticated—smile, Violet stroked her palm over his bare chest. Now she was free to toy with his lovely muscles all she wished. "That's because I love you," she confessed, unable to hold back any longer. Brimful with the knowledge of it, she yearned to fling open the windows and yell it to the world. "I love you, Cade! And now, thanks to everything we've shared, I can tell you so."

Still wearing his bliss-filled, endearingly enamored grin, Cade gazed at her. "Then I'm the luckiest man in the world right now," he said. "I was right about you all along, Violet—you *are* my good-luck charm. And now you're much more besides."

"Much, *much* more," she insisted giddily.

"Yes." Just for an instant, Cade furrowed his brow. Pensively, he gazed at his hotel room's ornate plaster ceiling medallion. He seemed lost in some remembrance—and this time, it appeared *not* to be a happy one. "You are more. Much more." He paused almost ominously. "You're more than I deserve."

"What? Of course I'm not. You're—"

"No one has ever loved me." Cade went on staring at the ceiling, seeing…something she couldn't guess. His bleak-sounding voice scared her. "There's no reason you should be different."

"There's every reason," Violet tried reassuring him. This new melancholic side of Cade confused her. "I love you! I—"

His gaze swerved to meet hers. "Saying it twice as often won't make it doubly true." He grinned. His usual exuberance returned with his smile, bringing with it a full measure of charm. It was as though Cade's brief, brooding descent had never happened. "But making love twice as often *will* make you feel twice as good." He gave her a provocative look. "I'll show you."

"Oh!" Suddenly diverted, Violet smiled, too. She

knew she should address Cade's conviction that he was incapable of being loved. The very notion broke her heart. But just at that moment, Cade was smiling at her and stroking her thighs and gazing at her as though she was the most delectable treat he'd ever encountered, and she simply couldn't muster the mental acuity to cope with his erotic stimulation and his potentially devastating past, all at the same time. She felt too overcome.

"You'll show me, hmm?" Touched and thrilled and aroused, Violet cradled Cade's face. His beard stubble tickled her palm. She couldn't help smiling. "I do hope you're not bluffing."

"With you? Never," Cade swore. "Are you ready?"

His eyes glimmered with mischief, furthering the thought that she'd simply imagined his unhappiness earlier…and making Violet wonder at the abrupt change in him, too.

This Cade—the one who currently charmed her with kisses and scandalous, huskily voiced erotic promises— was familiar to her. *This* Cade looked like a man who'd never entertained a sad thought in his life. He looked like a man who'd always been admired and adored and in complete control of himself and everything around him.

But Violet knew she'd glimpsed something important a moment ago. She'd glimpsed the truth in Cade's face. She meant to explore that truth further. After all, wasn't that what true love meant? Knowing the one you loved and helping him?

But first… "Am I ready for you? Always," she promised.

But she wasn't. Not entirely. Because as Cade surprised her by rolling them both over until *she* straddled him, Violet squealed. Her eyes widened. Her thighs quaked. Even as she splayed her hands atop Cade's massive chest for balance, she realized that she would never be able to predict Cade's next move. *He* was the gambler here, not her. All she could do was hold on and hope for the best. So that's what she did.

"I love you, Cade," Violet whispered as he loved her.

"I love you, too," she would have sworn she heard him say in response. But a heartbeat later, they were both lost to the pleasure they'd found together. Words were beyond them both.

At least they were until later. Then, lolling in a tubful of hot bathwater, laughing as Cade helped her wash up, Violet remembered a few words she'd planned to give Cade herself.

"You really are a good man," she began. "I always knew it."

Cade merely lathered her shoulders, silently and adeptly. His soapy fingers dipped and slid divertingly over her wet skin.

"That's why I'm going to help you," Violet went on. "I'm going to help you live up to the terms of my father's wager."

Cade stopped. His fingers went still. "What wager?"

"His wager with *you*, of course. Since you lost, you'll have to take part in honest labor in exchange for honest wages. Isn't that correct?" Knowing full well that it was, she smiled. "I'm on good terms with everyone in town. I can help you find an apprenticeship as a wheelwright or a cooper or a blacksmith—"

"You said you hadn't spoken with your father this morning."

Cade sounded gobsmacked. She'd thought he might be. That's why Violet hadn't brought up any of these issues until now. They would have interfered with her greater mission: flying with Cade. Experiencing pleasure with Cade. *Loving* him, most of all.

"That's right. But I *did* speak with Papa late last night after he got home from Jack Murphy's saloon." Violet sighed, remembering the rather awkward conversation she'd had with her father in the lantern-lit hours past midnight. "He really can be too overprotective of me at times, I'm afraid. As far as Papa is concerned, no one is ever good enough for me. Not that he's had much opportunity to test that theory over the years, given my dearth of genuine suitors. Most of them," she confessed, "were more interested in my friend Adeline than me."

Slowly, Cade continued soaping her back. "Is that so?"

"It is." Relieved to have this discussion out in the open at last, Violet nodded. "But *you* will be more than good enough for my father. I'm certain of it! In fact, I'm counting on it."

"Counting on it?"

"Yes. So we can be together." Wearing her most joyful smile, Violet tipped up her head. Her new viewing angle brought Cade's hard-edged face into her sight. He appeared thoughtful. "So we can be together, just like this," she clarified, "for as long as we want to be. Isn't that why we're here right now?"

"Right now, yes." Cade continued his sensual soaping. "But I don't plan to stay in Morrow Creek," he reminded her.

Violet found it easy to overlook that detail. Surely Cade would change his mind once he became familiar with his new friends and neighbors. Coyly, she said, "Then I guess we'd better make the most of our time together right now, hadn't we?"

"Minx," Cade said a third time. Then he kissed her and smiled at her, and all was right between them—especially once the soapsuds fight broke out, and a new round of loving began.

Chapter Nine

"I feel certain I'm going to regret this." Full of equal measures disbelief and discomfort, Cade eyed the distant blacksmith's shop. The place hunkered on the outskirts of Morrow Creek, a short walk from the schoolhouse and the town's namesake creek. Even from a quarter mile away, Cade heard the clang of the blacksmith's hammer striking an anvil at regular intervals. The sound came coupled with the persistent smell of smoke. "I once won a racehorse at the faro table. Keeping that beast in horseshoes nearly broke me. I lost it on purpose a week later."

"Well, then. I guess blacksmithing must be lucrative." Striding confidently beside him, Violet looped her arm in his. Her face positively beamed with encouragement. Her voice rang with faith in him. "Besides, you have to start somewhere. You might be excellent at blacksmithing, for all you know!" She gave his arm a heartening squeeze, inadvertently cradling him against her bosom. "You seem to be *very* good at everything else you do."

"Mmm. We're good together, I'd say." Reminded of

the languorous time they'd spent in his bed earlier that morning—and the several mornings before that—Cade quit walking. He couldn't help feeling pleased that he'd impressed Violet. Because of her, he felt hopeful for the first time in years. "At least if the past few days are anything to go by. And I'd say they are."

"They *definitely* are," Violet agreed, holding him close.

"In fact, I think we may have left my hotel a bit hastily this morning," Cade continued, pulling Violet toward a copse of ponderosa pines. He leaned against the nearest tree's thick-barked trunk, then drew Violet closer to join him in that sheltered spot. He twined a bit of her hair in his fingers. Tenderly, he smiled at her. "We should have stayed in bed."

"That would have been nice. And definitely warmer too!"

Agreeing with that in the best way he knew how, Cade kissed her. He still couldn't believe that Violet— gentle, innocent, helpful Violet Benson—had enchanted him so thoroughly. Less than a week ago, she'd appeared at his hotel room door, full of cheeky talk of "reforming" him. She'd gotten under his skin. She'd shown him that love *might* be possible for him, despite the hard lessons of his past. Since then, almost against his will, Cade had begun hoping they could be together—hoping her scheme to help him forge a new, gambling-free life could really succeed.

Not that he felt entirely ready to take up that life straightaway, by beginning the one-day apprenticeship that Violet had arranged for him at Daniel McCabe's smithy shop.

"Maybe we should dally here awhile," Cade suggested instead, lowering his hands to her bosom. He loved touching her there. He loved touching her everywhere. Never had he known a partner more giving or enthusiastic or compassionate. Just being in Violet's presence moved him deeply—so deeply, in fact, that Cade had already blurted out his most shameful secret to her, followed almost instantly by his most strongly felt fear.

No one has ever loved me, he'd confessed to Violet while holding her close. *There's no reason you should be different.*

Yet she *was* different. Cade was powerfully glad of it.

"After all," he went on, forcing himself from that painful memory as ruthlessly as he had on that earlier day, "I haven't yet shown you how stimulating it can be to feel the fresh air on your bare skin—to make love outdoors, where there's no one to hear you cry out in pleasure except the earth and the sky—"

"And that truck farmer working his fields over yonder…"

Cade followed her pointing finger. "Aha." Another kiss. "That only means we'll have to delve deeper into the forest."

She laughed. "You're incorrigible—and apparently immune to the chilly autumn weather, too." She shivered as she glanced up at the cloudy territorial skies overhead. "It's cold outside!"

"I'll keep you warm," Cade promised. He felt full

to overflowing with fondness for her, overcome with a mixture of unaccustomed optimism and all-too-familiar swagger. He'd told Violet he loved her, after all…but he didn't think she'd heard him. That's the only reason he'd risked saying it at all.

Because some things weren't meant to be wagered on—especially not love or the burgeoning promise of it. As much as Cade excelled at gambling, he wasn't reckless. Not usually. Not like this—not the way he was with Violet…with hoping they could have a future together despite the sadness of his past.

But maybe finding Whittier—and the answers he could give—wasn't the only route to the future he needed, Cade had begun to consider lately. Maybe abandoning his search for those answers was.

Not that he was keen to tell Simon Blackhouse as much. He still hadn't informed his benefactor of the wager he'd lost with Reverend Benson—and its subsequent requirement that Cade forgo gambling altogether. With that restriction in place and the faro tournament's qualifying games drawing to a close soon, his chance to find Percy Whittier might be slipping away, Cade knew.

But those were problems for another day—a day when he didn't have an armful of kind, generous woman to love…even if he might have to do so amid the pine trees and nosy warbling birds.

"Be with me," Cade urged Violet, wanting to forget everything except this moment…and this woman. Deftly he worked at her coat buttons, then slipped his hands inside. Blissful warmth, wonderful curves and the promise of Violet's sweet love awaited him there.

He could no more resist those things than he could forget why he'd come to Morrow Creek in the first place.

"You're just trying to delay arriving at the blacksmith's shop," Violet averred, giving him a frisky swat. "Don't worry. You can do this, Cade. If not this, then something else. I have several apprenticeships lined up for you. I'm good at helping people, remember? I won't give up on you, no matter what."

"Maybe you should. You wouldn't be the first."

"There you go, sounding gloomy again." Frowning, she took his hand. She cradled it in hers, gazing intently into his face. "What happened to you, to make you believe such things?"

Yanked unwillingly from the warmth of their togetherness, Cade thought of orphan trains and cold nights and potential foster parents who tightened their lips and shook their heads at the notion of taking in two fast-growing, rascally foundling boys. He and Judah had tried appearing especially angelic once, hoping to lure in a decent caregiver. That had only landed them with a temporary "mother" who thought a swat was as good as a hug and hard factory labor was all that orphaned boys were good for.

Running away had seemed the only reasonable response.

"If I wanted work, would I make my living at cards?" Cade asked, hauling himself back to Violet by dint of sheer will—and doing his best to divert her from her troubling questions. "If I was meant for an ordinary life, would I be a sporting man?"

"*My* life is ordinary." Violet crossed her arms, appearing wounded. "But I have good friends and satisfying work and—"

"And more good deeds to your credit than an angel can claim. I know." With a grin, Cade held up his hands. He knew better than to push her on this. "I already promised you I'd go through with these apprenticeships." Reminded then of another vow he'd made, Cade added, "I also promised you once that I'd make every man in Morrow Creek want you. I'm well on my way to having accomplished that. Getting my hands dirty at a few local businesses will be a good way to test the waters, even if the apprenticeships don't work out. Because if you think I'm going to let just anyone have you without vetting them first—"

"'Have' me?" She snorted. "*That's* not for you to say, Mr. Foster." In a cavalier tone, Violet pressed onward. "What do you think we've been doing together all this time? I've already found the only man I want. While it's true that he can be a stubborn, contrary cuss from time to time, I happen to be—"

"He doesn't sound like much, this man of yours."

"—awfully fond of him." Showing that she meant she was fond of *him*, Violet smiled more broadly. "In any case, I no longer wish to be irresistible to the menfolk in Morrow Creek."

"It would be good for you if you were," Cade protested, warming further to the notion of using his trial employment as a way to fulfill his original promise to Violet. He could scarcely allow her to count on *him* for the future she deserved. She deserved better...much better than him. "Then when I do leave town, you'll have your pick of suitors to—"

"We'll cross that bridge when we come to it," Violet interrupted crisply—almost as though she'd forgotten his vow to her and didn't want to be reminded of it now, despite the bargain they'd made when she'd provisionally agreed to be his good-luck charm…and he'd offered to squire her around town in a sham courtship. "Right now, there are a few things you should know about Daniel McCabe, the blacksmith. He's very happily married to the schoolmarm, Sarah, so don't try to corrupt him as a means of avoiding work at his shop. You know you could do it."

At her dire tone, Cade gave a sober nod. He probably *could* do that, it occurred to him. He possessed both persuasiveness and a knack for forging new friendships. He hadn't thought of that work-avoidance strategy until right now, but if push came to shove and he was stuck in a corner…a bit of harmless, well-meant corruption might do the trick to liven up his workday.

"I would never do that," he pledged, tamping down a smile.

"Don't entice Mr. McCabe's customers into a game of dice to help pass the time, either! That would make them like you, but it would *not* lead to accomplishing a productive day's work."

"Yes, ma'am." Playfully, Cade tipped his hat to her.

"Don't swear. Don't dawdle. Don't forget to be careful around the blacksmithing fire. Whatever else you do, *don't* flirt with the customers, no matter how attractive they are."

"But Violet, farmers wanting their plowshares mended are often *so* appealing." Musingly, Cade tipped his face to the sky. "To say nothing of the lumbermen needing their axes repaired."

"Very funny." Violet's eyes sparkled. "But you told me yesterday when we were having breakfast in bed together after our morning's...*reforming* session—" she broke off, blushing at the undoubtedly racy memory of that clandestine encounter "—that you haven't ever held a traditional job before, so—"

"What I said," Cade protested mildly, "is that it had been a while since I'd had steady employment. I'm not a layabout! I simply happen to be better at collecting foolish men's money than earning a regular working-man's wage. That's all."

"That's enough."

He shrugged. "I can't help it if I have a gift for gambling."

"That's not all you have a gift for." With a devotedly take-charge air, Violet straightened his shirt collar. She patted down his freshly ironed vest, then plucked a bit of errant lint from that selfsame garment. Evidently satisfied, she smiled at him. "Also, *don't* play faro or black-jack at work."

"Right. I'd assumed you'd already covered that with your prohibition on craps. Shall we negotiate roulette next?"

"I just wanted to be certain you understood."

"I would have to be softheaded not to." Cade kissed her. "Has anyone ever told you you have spoilsport tendencies?"

"No." Undaunted, Violet fussed over his hair. She sucked in a fortifying breath. "You'll be brilliant today. So get going!"

"Are you sure you wouldn't rather linger here?" Cade offered her his most winning smile. "Or maybe a little farther along in the forest? I hear the creek is scenic. I could take you there, standing up. Or maybe against a tree." He patted the ponderosa pine behind him, then gave Violet a suggestive look. "You wouldn't even have to remove your skirts. I could just lift them up a bit, slide my hand up your stockings to your garter…"

Hungrily, Cade demonstrated. Beneath Violet's full skirts and layers of petticoats, he encountered warm woolen stockings, snugly fastened garters, delicate drawers…then, rewardingly, warm, soft skin. He stroked her thigh, loving the way she felt.

"All I need is a few inches more, and you'll be mine," he encouraged, feeling aflame at the idea of loving her in such an impulsive, almost illicit fashion. He'd envisioned the notion as a distraction from his impending workday, but now that he'd devised it… "We'd have such fun together, Violet. You know we would. I'd make you tremble and moan—I love it when you do that—and you'd make me forget everything…everything except you."

Urgently, he kissed her. Their mouths met in a bruising pressure, familiar and demanding and passionate. The only thing Cade needed then was a nod, a smile, a breathy *yes*, and he'd be unable to stop himself from making love to Violet right where they stood. He cupped her derriere in both palms and dragged her nearer, grinding himself harder against her, mindless now of the blackbirds and the fallen oak leaves and the steely gray sky.

"Please, Violet," he urged. "Don't say no."

"I won't." She panted, clenching her fists against his shirt. "I can't." She shook her head, even as he kissed her neck, her cheek, her jaw…her mouth. "But I can say… later. *Later*, I promise." With an obvious effort, Violet pulled away from him. Regretfully, she straightened her skirts. Her mouth looked full and luscious, her hair beginning to fall from its twisted knot. Heedless of her own disarray, she smoothed Cade's clothes again. "You're too good a charmer, Cade. You can charm even yourself."

He blinked. That sounded like nonsense to him. "So?"

"So you really need to get to the blacksmith's shop." Violet tucked her fingers in his vest pocket. She withdrew his gold Jürgensen timepiece, then squinted at it. "If you don't go now, you'll be late. I built in some dallying time—"

"You accounted for my wanting to seduce you outdoors?"

"—but that's almost gone now." Smartly, Violet tucked his watch in its place, oblivious to his incredulous look. "You don't want to make a poor impression by being late, do you?"

"At the moment? Truthfully, I don't care."

"You'll care later." She shooed him toward the smithy.

Reluctantly, Cade nodded. He *would* care later. He would care if he had to leave town unexpectedly—in pursuit of Percy Whittier, say, since the man was so cagey and unpredictable—and hadn't had time to find out if there were any bachelor men in Morrow Creek who were good enough for Violet.

For that reason alone, Cade prepared to leave. He might *want* to stay with Violet. He might *hope* they could have a future. But he'd been disappointed too many times to count on that—or to believe that Violet could truly mean what she said when she told him she wanted him, needed him…loved him.

What Cade needed now was a contingency plan. He meant to get one, for Violet's sake. He meant to repay his damn bet to Reverend Benson, too, by proving he *could* perform honest work.

"All right. I'll see you tonight." He kissed Violet again. Their coming together was as tongue-sweet and heady as it always was. "I'll hold you to that promise of yours, too, about our being alone together…*later*. You remember that, don't you?"

"You're dawdling with *me* now," Violet said knowingly. "On purpose." She chuckled. "Did you really think that would work?"

Another shrug—and an answering grin. "It usually does."

"Not with me," Violet alleged with a twinkle in her eyes. Warmly, she hugged him. "I know you far too well to be fooled."

For an instant, Cade feared that she did. Unmoving, he held her. Then he realized…being *known* was nothing to be afraid of. Not unless you were Percy Whittier and deliberately on the run.

Men had been shot, it was rumored, trying to confront Whittier. Men had been knifed and duped and outfoxed. Cade had chased the man at his own peril all these years—but he'd also come closer, he reckoned, than anyone else had to finding him.

Now all he needed was to know if Whittier truly was the man Cade thought he was—and if he was, to get some answers from him.

"It's bad manners to read my mind, Miss Benson," Cade told Violet. "You'll have to quit that pretty soon— or else."

"Or else what?"

"Or else I might find you even more irresistible than I already do. Who knows what wicked ideas you'll spark next?"

She blushed. "Get going, you rascal. I have records to comb through and lists to make. I can't dillydally all day."

She meant for her search for Tobe's mother, Cade knew. *That* was a wild-goose chase he didn't want to involve himself in. On the verge of telling Violet— again—that the boy had been through enough already, he managed to stop himself. "Wish me luck."

"Good luck!" Cheerily, Violet waved him away.

When Cade was partway down the path toward the blacksmith's shop, Violet called out to him again. Inquiringly, he turned.

"Yes?" He nudged his shoulder toward the thickly clustered trees. "Did you change your mind about visiting the forest?"

Violet's expression told him she hadn't. But then she cupped her hands around her mouth and delivered him a statement that was almost as effective as that in brightening his day.

"Did you really mean," she asked, "standing up?"

Helplessly enthralled by her, Cade nodded. He couldn't help picturing the scene, both of them surrendering to a need that was more powerful than common sense *and* a desire to stay out of the chilly autumn weather. He *did* love her. "Indeed I did."

"I thought so. I'm intrigued!" Violet chirped. She gave another jovial wave. "Till later, then. Have a nice day!"

As she turned and headed with her usual vivacity down the path toward the center of town, Cade shook his head. He'd never been more enamored of a woman—or more certain that they probably could not be together for long. Why should Violet love him, the damnably melancholy side of him insisted, when no one else ever had? Why should she stay with him, when everyone else had abandoned him? Clearly there was something wrong with him, Cade knew; something he tried to keep hidden. Inevitably, Violet would discover it—and then she would likely abandon him, too.

Even so, she deserved to be happy. She hadn't asked to be drawn into the complications and secrets that made up Cade's life. If she couldn't love him—not truly—that wasn't her fault.

With those dismal thoughts in mind, Cade strode toward the blacksmith's shop. There was no time to waste. He only had a few days to assess the men of Morrow Creek and set up a backup plan for Violet's future happiness—and it all started with meeting Daniel McCabe and learning to swing a hammer.

Violet was nose deep in a cookery book by the renowned author and home-keeping expert Daisy Walsh, searching for dishes that would be both strengthening and delicious to serve little Tobe, when the boy himself wandered into the kitchen. He wore a knit cap, hand-me-down britches and a shirt liberated from the church's donation box. He carried a stack of schoolbooks bound by a leather strap. He spied her, adjusted that strap so his schoolbooks rode higher on his shoulder, then raised his chin.

That tiny gesture was as close as Tobe ever came to saying good-morning. But Violet was undeterred. "Good morning, Tobe!"

"You don't need to walk me to school today," he announced. Pugnaciously, he frowned at her. "I can get there by myself."

"I know you can. That's what you say every morning."

"I prob'ly don't even need to go to school at all, what with me bein' here in Morrow Creek temp'rarily. I'll be pullin' foot for someplace a little less restrictive pretty soon, I reckon."

Patiently, Violet stood waiting. This happened every day.

"But I can walk there myself," Tobe nattered on, squaring his shoulders as if preparing for a fight. "I ain't a baby."

"No, you're not." Kindly, Violet smiled. "But I aim

to walk you to the schoolhouse all the same. Just like I do every day."

"You're dogged, you know that? Prob'ly on account of your bein' a spinster and all. You ain't got nothin' better to do than pester me." With studied nonchalance, Tobe shrugged. He made a wry face. "But I reckon if I can't stop you doing it..."

"Then you might as well quit trying." With their daily ritual thus complete, Violet hugged him. His copy of *McGuffey's Sixth Eclectic Reader* poked her in the ribs. She didn't mind. It was nice to hug little Tobe—to reassure herself that his scrawny frame *had* filled out while he was in her care and to know that every day he came a mite closer to actually hugging her back.

For now, he stood statuelike in her grasp, stoically submitting to her affection. Tobe had been with her for almost two weeks now. He'd alternated his time among the schoolhouse, the Benson household and—during those occasions when Violet had charitable works to do—the homes of her neighbors. He'd even made a few friends with children his own age—at least he had once he'd come to terms with the necessity of playing jacks or marbles with them instead of poker or vingt-et-un. The boy hadn't asked about Violet's search for his mother, although he knew she'd been diligently combing every possible local record for clues to Mrs. Larkin's arrival in and departure from town.

Violet reasoned that Tobe didn't want to get his hopes up, only to see them cruelly dashed if she failed to locate his mama. In that way, the boy reminded her curiously of Cade. Both males, one younger and one older, seemed to hunger for something more from life...and both seemed to fear that hope was lost to them forever. If she could, Violet meant to help each of them.

Reminded of her imminent daily rendezvous with Cade, Violet released Tobe. She took away his books, then set them on the kitchen worktable. "Go on and eat your breakfast now. I have a few chores to do before we leave for the schoolhouse."

Eagerly, Tobe raced to his place at the table. "Oatmeal!"

"With dried peaches," Violet elaborated, "and cinnamon."

She watched fondly as the boy grabbed a spoon and started in. Tasty vittles reliably brought a smile to Tobe's face, but Violet wasn't sure why that was. Perhaps his mother was an accomplished cook? Or maybe he was simply a pint-size gourmand?

Either way, Tobe seemed thoroughly pleased by his meal. Making a mental note to delve more deeply into Miss Walsh's cookery book for Tobe's sake, Violet offered him some accompaniments. "More sugar?" she asked. "And some milk?"

"Mmm. Yes, please!" the boy enthused. While she sprinkled on maple sugar and poured on milk, Tobe watched her face. "You know, you ain't so bad, Miss Benson. For a preacher's daughter, I mean. For someone who don't like craps playing and ain't fond of saloon girls and skullduggery and everything that's fun."

Violet hid a smile. "What do you know about saloon girls?"

"Plenty!" He spooned up more oats. "I know they like *me*."

"Who wouldn't like you? I certainly wasn't able to help myself. I liked you from the moment I met you."

"Yep." He nodded sagely, chewing with evident enthusiasm. "I reckon that's 'cause I'm a natural-born charmer, like Cade."

"Mr. Foster is probably not someone to be emulated." *But he's wonderful, all the same.* "And I can't help wondering if the 'skullduggery' you just referred to is harmless mischief or something more." She eyed him. "Would you care to enlighten me?"

"Nope. If I tole you, it wouldn't be fun no more." Tobe sent her an exasperated look. "That's why I said you don't like fun. 'Cause you're always tryin' to take it away from me."

"Only in your best interest." Fondly, Violet regarded him. She'd never met a more spirited, bright and resilient child.

Most likely, it occurred to her, Cade had been similar to Tobe in his youth. At least that's the impression she'd gained from their increasingly intimate conversations. She knew Cade had lived in an ordinary home, then an orphanage, then a variety of foster homes. She knew he'd struck out on his own at a young age. She knew he'd done all he could to protect his younger brother, Judah, during those difficult years and afterward.

She only wished she knew how to help Cade now. Because even though they'd spent days together—very *closely* together—Violet still couldn't piece together the scrambled bits of Cade's past. She still couldn't quite understand him. To her, orphanages and foster homes were helpful institutions. They were run by good people. They saved many children who otherwise would have been left on the streets the way Tobe had been. So Violet couldn't figure out why Cade would say the things he did.

No one has ever loved me.

There's no reason you should be different.

Violet wanted to prove to him that she *was* different—that she could restore his faith in himself and other people. Because goodness and kindness and generosity were the norm in the world, not the aberrations Cade seemed to believe they must be. He needed to know that. More than that, he needed to *believe* it.

Violet didn't think Cade had meant to reveal so much of himself to her. But now that he had…it was unthinkable that she would turn away from him. She would sooner sacrifice her own happiness than see Cade disappointed again.

I won't give up on you, she'd told him, *no matter what.*

Maybe you should, he'd replied heartrendingly. *You wouldn't be the first.*

At that moment, Violet had vowed that she wouldn't be included among the people who'd given up on Cade. Whatever it took, she would stick by him. In the meantime…

"Where's your coat?" she asked Tobe, suddenly alerted to the fact that the boy's oversize, much-adored warm overcoat wasn't hanging on its hook where it should have been. "Did you leave it someplace again? It's too cold to walk to school without it. You'll catch your death of cold!"

Tobe quit eating. He gazed downheartedly at his bowl of oats, appearing oddly preoccupied. "My mama used to say that."

Violet went still. "She used to say what?"

"She used to say, 'You'll catch your death of cold!'" His voice was pitched high in mimicry of his mother's. He gave a faint, unsteady smile. "She didn't know it wouldn't be a cold that tore us apart in the end." Tobe's gaze met Violet's. His little brow furrowed. "That's kinda funny, ain't it? All that time spent worryin' about somethin', then…*wham*! I wandered away from that train depot at the wrong time, and that's that."

"Tobe…" Violet hurried closer. "I'll find her. I will."

He looked away, his expression stormy. "For all you know, my mama run off on purpose, the minute I was out of sight that day. For all you know, she was glad to be rid of me."

"That *can't* be true," Violet argued. "It can't."

"My daddy run off like that, too," Tobe informed her bluntly, "when I was just a kid. And what do you s'pose my mama and him had in common? *Me*. That's it." Bleakly, Tobe shifted his gaze back to his bowl of oatmeal. "It was *me* they wanted away from. There's no use saying it wasn't." His lower lip quivered. He swallowed mightily. "But you're awful kind to try an' tell me different. That's what makes you a good person, Miss Benson."

Violet's eyes filled with tears. She simply couldn't prevent them. Her heart felt torn apart at the realization of all that Tobe had been through…was still going through, maybe for a very long while yet. She heaved in a shaky breath.

"Hey." The boy regarded her suspiciously. "Are you cryin'?"

She sniffled. "No. Of course not."

"Because I won't have no truck with cryin'. Not over me."

"I know. You told me that on our first day together," Violet managed to say, "after you had your bath, when you hugged me thank-you and said you were full of joy at being clean again."

Tobe glowered. "You *said* you wouldn't remind me of that!"

"I'm sorry."

"I *like* bein' dirty sometimes! It makes me look fierce. Same way as I *sound* fierce, and not like some smarty-pants city kid, full up on book learnin' and useless good manners."

Well, that philosophy explained a great deal about Tobe's initial appearance. He'd been trying hard to appear—and sound and *seem*—as aggressive and street-wise as possible…probably with the hope of feeling less vulnerable than he was. At that insight, Violet felt a fresh sob well inside her.

"I…I think I might have seen your coat in my father's office at the church," she blurted, searching her pockets for a handkerchief to staunch her tears. "I'll see if I can find it."

"Okay." Tobe nudged her as she passed by him. He held out his hand, offering her a handkerchief. "You lookin' for this?"

"Oh!" Surprised and grateful, Violet nodded. "Thank you."

"It's nothin'." The boy went back to his breakfast, his childish equanimity apparently restored. "Cade told me once that a good man always helps ladies in need." He grinned. "In your case, I reckon a whole lotta bawlin' counts as bein' in need."

His newfound sassiness startled her. Even after all this, Tobe was teasing her? Then Violet realized the truth: just as Cade had done, Tobe had learned to counter misery with charm...to bury despair beneath a grin and a quip.

Her heart ached for them both. She'd been fortunate in all aspects of her life, save the niggling matter of her appearance—which she'd come to terms with anyway. But Tobe and Cade had been stuck beneath an unlucky star for a while now. She'd been blessed with love and support, both before her mother's passing and afterward, when the whole of Morrow Creek had come forward to help Papa raise her. Tobe and Cade had been forsaken.

No wonder they both seemed so hard edged sometimes. It likely took all their strength just to keep moving forward.

Determinedly, Violet cleared her throat. "I'll just collect that runaway overcoat of yours from next door. I'll be back lickety-split."

Her reward was a brief laugh from Tobe. "'Runaway overcoat.' That's a hoot, Miss Benson." He pointed his spoon at her. "If you keep up with them jokes, I reckon there might be hope for you yet."

Chapter Ten

Bustling with resolve and in a hurry to get to Cade for their usual morning rendezvous—after she'd safely seen Tobe to the schoolhouse for his lessons—Violet opened the church doors.

She hastened inside, scarcely pausing to enjoy the calm and orderly atmosphere that greeted her. In the mornings, the church was always empty. The rows of pews stood polished and ready; the stained-glass windows let in just enough autumnal light to give the whole place a cozy and heartening glow.

Inhaling the tart scent of lemony polish, feeling comforted by the memory of the innumerable sermons she'd heard inside these walls, Violet rushed forward. Her woolen coat rustled, releasing the frosty air it had captured outdoors and reminding her that she'd come here to fetch Tobe's overcoat. She had to find it soon or else they would be tardy to the schoolhouse.

She didn't want that. That would mean that Violet might arrive at the Lorndorff Hotel too late to see Cade. Today was his apprenticeship at Owen Cooper's flourishing livery stable, and although taciturn Mr. Cooper had agreed to train Cade readily enough, he didn't seem the sort of man to tolerate tardiness. Violet didn't want to push his good nature too far.

With swiftness utmost in her mind, she scanned the pews. She expected to find Tobe's overcoat in her father's office behind the chancel, but since she was passing this way anyway....

A man knelt in the front pew, his head bowed in prayer.

Startled by the sight of him, Violet changed direction.

Rather than charge down the center passageway as she otherwise would have, she edged toward the outer aisle instead, hoping to avoid disturbing the man. She wished she'd used the exterior door to Papa's office, but now it was too late. Backtracking might prove even more disruptive, she reasoned, than moving stealthily toward the front of the church.

Headed in that direction, Violet glanced again at the praying man. She was passing quite near to him now. She wondered if she should offer to help him or to bring the reverend out to speak with him. Sometimes congregants needed guidance.

Trying to decide, she gave the stranger a more thorough inspection. She didn't recognize him, so he wasn't a regular churchgoer. All the same, there was something familiar about him. Had she seen him at the Territorial Benevolent Association Grand Fair? For some reason, the notion seemed right to her.

As Violet reached the alcove near the office, the stranger stood. He moved slowly, as though burdened, and she couldn't help wondering why he hadn't sought out the minister. Sometimes a bit of counseling eased even the heaviest of burdens. This man, who appeared approximately her father's age, definitely seemed to be carrying more than the usual allotment of troubles.

She paused. "I'm sorry to interrupt, but…can I help you?"

The man's gaze met hers. He looked desolate, almost haunted, and more alone than anyone she'd met. Violet recalled too late—and possibly to her detriment—that some men could not be saved by prayer or helpful intervention. Some men were…lost.

She wished she'd summoned Papa. Or even Sheriff Caffey.

The stranger shook his head, silently refusing her offer of assistance. Respectfully, he held his dark, expensive-looking hat in his hands—hands that appeared, to Violet's eyes, to be unusual in some way. But she couldn't untangle how.

"No, young lady," he said in a low voice, "I don't think you can help me. But if you don't mind, I might stay awhile."

"Please do! I'll try not to disturb you again. It's just that there's usually no one here at this hour. I didn't think—"

He held up his hand. Again, some unusual quality about it nagged at Violet's memory. She still couldn't identify it.

"I'm the one who should apologize to you." He offered a brief, surprisingly chivalrous bow. "I'm sorry I startled you."

Where had she seen him before? Violet wondered afresh. The angle of his shoulders, broad but hunched, seemed strangely familiar to her. So did his striking appearance. The gray in his hair and the lines at his temples only complemented his natural world-weary charm. He wore it like a fine suit of clothes.

Which wasn't to say she felt at ease with him. She did not.

"Have we…met?" Unable to help herself, Violet scrutinized him more closely. "Perhaps at some event in town or at church?"

He shook his head. "It's been a long time since I've been in a place like this." As though dumbfounded to find himself there even then, he gazed in wonder at the pews. "The moment I stepped inside, I half expected the whole caboodle to go up in flames."

Violet gave a discomfited laugh. A sensible woman would have fled right then. After all, the stranger had practically confessed to being a bad man. But it wasn't kind to bolt in midconversation. So Violet settled for doing the next best thing. She offered the man a wave and a conversational dodge.

"All right, then. Well, please stay as long as you need."

"I'm not sure the church will be standing long enough for that. I need a lot of time." The stranger glanced down as though gauging the relative sturdiness of the structure he rested his boots on. "You see, I have a great deal to atone for."

Caught in midretreat, Violet hesitated nonetheless.

The man's regretful tone awakened something empathetic in her.

"The church will hold strong," she said softly. "This is a good place to begin making amends. But eventually your time here will run out." She met his gaze. "After all, no apology is complete unless it's given to the people who've been hurt."

He lowered his head. "And if they refuse to accept it?"

"You can still try to set things right."

The man appeared to consider that. "It's too late for that." He tightened his mouth. "Fifteen years too late."

"It's never too late," Violet disagreed.

"It is if you've done the things I've done."

Again, Violet felt a frisson of unease. Remorse wasn't always enough to keep people from repeating their sins. Was the stranger confessing his wrongdoings to make her understand them—or to warn her away from him? Uncertainly, she took a step back.

"You can't know that unless you try," Violet said. "If you don't try...." She hesitated, trying to decide between telling him the unvarnished truth and mollifying him—which would have been the most sensible option. Sensibly or not, she chose to speak the truth. "Well, unless you try to make amends, all the remorse in the world is nothing more than self-pity in nicer clothes." She gestured toward her father's office. "Shall I fetch the minister for you?"

"I'm not sure. Is he as unforgiving as his daughter is?"

Violet frowned, taken aback by his statement. He

couldn't know she was Reverend Benson's daughter. They hadn't even been introduced. Who *was* he? "The church is all about faith and hope," she told him assuredly. "No one here is unforgiving."

"I beg to differ." The man lifted his gaze from his hat. "*You're* mighty unforgiving, Miss Minister's Daughter. No wonder I've stayed away from 'right-minded' folks all these years."

She couldn't resist asking the obvious question. "What makes you think I'm the minister's daughter?"

"It's not tricky to figure out." He aimed his chin at her. "You walk like you own this place. You dress like a nun. And you talk like a damnable do-gooder." He shuddered. "I hate most do-gooders. No offense to present company intended, of course."

"Of course." Violet bristled. "How could I take offense when you've tried so hard not to give it?"

At that, the man guffawed. His laughter transformed him, turning him from a downtrodden charmer to an irredeemable rogue.

"You're feisty. I like you, Miss Minister's Daughter. I can see why—" Shaking his head, the stranger broke off. Wearing a regretful expression, he clapped his black hat over his heart, then gazed directly at her. "It's only too bad I embarked on this cockeyed salvation mission on my way out of town. Otherwise, we might have gotten to know one another better."

"We might have," Violet agreed, halfway to being charmed in spite of herself. "You don't have to leave Morrow Creek if you don't want to, you know," she added in an impulsive rush. "Your destiny is in no one's hands but your own, Mr.…?"

"Oh, no. There'll be none of that now," he warned, tsk-tsking with a sparkle in his vibrant blue eyes. "I've gone to great pains to keep my name my own business. I won't surrender it to a chatty, gutsy girl with more courage than compassion."

"I'm plenty compassionate!"

"All the same, I'm afraid I'm leaving." With smooth and nimble fingers, the stranger tugged on his hat. He gave another brief bow. "Thank you kindly for the advice."

"You're welcome. Will you be taking any of it?"

"Probably not." Seeming oddly cheered, he shrugged. "But it's been nice saying something besides 'ante up' or 'how much for a night?' for a change. So thank you for that, as well."

Violet considered his first remark, overlooking his obvious allusion to arranging a liaison with a prostitute. She'd lived in the West her whole life. She didn't find soiled doves or their customers particularly shocking. "You're a sporting man, then?" she asked with interest. "Are you in town for the private faro tournament? I know someone who's in the final rounds."

The man's eyes gleamed with wariness. He didn't deny her guesses, though, and Violet was about to ply him with more questions—such as an inquiry about whether he knew Cade, since she was powerfully curious about Cade's life outside their time together—but at the moment she began to, her father bustled in.

"Oh, you're here, Violet! That's good. I was about

to run to the house with Tobe's overcoat—" he lifted the boy's favorite gargantuan garment in demonstration "—when I heard your voice out here and realized you must have come to collect it yourself."

Reverend Benson stopped in midstride, his face alight with genial inquisitiveness. Doubtless he'd glimpsed the stranger in their midst. Knowing that her father could likely extract the man's name where she had failed to, Violet turned to make a helpful introduction. But she was too late. The man was gone.

Even as she looked, the church door swung shut behind him.

"Not a very friendly fellow," her father observed. "But an early riser and a wearer of very spruce suits! Who was he?"

"I don't know." Violet glanced to both sides, unable to believe the man had simply ducked out—entirely unobserved—when her father had arrived. "He seemed in need of guidance, though."

"I trust you did your best to provide some?"

"I did." She hesitated. "Did he look familiar to you?"

Her father squinted in thought. He shook his head. "No."

"He did to me. There was something about him...."

Still trying to reason out what it was, Violet considered the few things she'd learned during their conversation. The stranger was a gambler, a rogue, an admitted sinner...and he possessed smooth palms and uncallused fingers—fingers uniquely suited for reading altered playing cards, detecting loaded dice and excelling at games of chance.

Just like Cade.

What's more, the stranger had been pointedly secretive about his name, his past *and* his business in Morrow Creek.

Again…just like Cade.

All at once, several pieces of the puzzle fell into place. Starting with something Cade had once told her about Percy Whittier, the man he'd been searching for at the tables…

I want answers from him, that's all, Cade had said on the day he'd asked her to be his lucky charm. *I want to know why he ran out on his family back East. They loved him and needed him.*

Shocked, Violet stared at the church door. Could it be…?

"I think I might know who that was!" Determinedly, Violet snatched Tobe's overcoat from her father. Then she hugged him goodbye. "I'll see you tonight, Papa! Right now I have to hurry Tobe to school. I have a new project to see to!"

"Don't you always?" Ever resigned and proud, her father smiled at her. "This time, make it a less dangerous one than trying to reform that gambler, Cade Foster, won't you? When you took up with him, I endured no end of sleepless nights."

Guiltily, Violet shifted. "You worry too much."

"I worry exactly the correct amount," her father disagreed sternly. "You're my only daughter. Before your dear mother passed on, she made me promise I would look after you, and that's all I'm doing."

"I know." Affectionately, Violet hugged him again.

"But Mama would not have wanted you to tire yourself out with the effort. I worry about you, too, sometimes. After all, I should already be married by now. I should be taking care of *you*—"

"Pshaw," her father disagreed. "I won't hear of it."

"—in your dotage," she went on with a teasing grin, "not remaining an old maid living dependently in your household forever. I'm a drain on your strength and your income." Suddenly distraught at the notion, Violet frowned. "I'm sorry, Papa! I never quite thought of it that way before, but it's true. If I never marry, you'll be worried about me forever and ever."

"There now. Don't concern yourself over things that won't ever happen." With a reassuring sound, her father enfolded her in his strong embrace. "You'll get married someday. Just as soon as you find a man who's worthy of you. It won't be easy—"

"Nonsense. There are a multitude of men in Morrow Creek."

"Exactly so. But not one of them has proven himself."

"Not many of them have tried," Violet reminded him, filled with fondness for her overprotective father. "But even if a million men courted me, I doubt you'd approve of a single one."

"Well, he'd have to be mighty special. That's true." With a twinkle in his eye—and a mysterious smile on his lips—her father nodded. "But I could be moved to approve of the *right* man. The man who could make you as happy as you deserve to be."

Violet wished he meant Cade. *He* made her happy. But Papa didn't know that. Reminded of her multiple secret meetings with her honor-bound gambler, she felt swamped with guilt.

She ought to confess everything to her father, Violet knew. It wasn't right keeping such a secret from him. But if she could truly help Cade meet the terms of his wager with her father, then maybe that would help soften the news of her deception. If she could truly help Cade, she would have done a good, charitable deed. How in the orld could Papa disagree with that?

Meaningfully, her father cleared his throat. "Didn't you say you had to rush off to Tobe's school?"

"Oh! Yes!" Newly reminded of all she meant to do, Violet hastily clutched the boy's overcoat. "Bye, Papa! I love you!"

"I love you, too," he said. "Far more than you know."

But the last of his words came indistinctly…almost too softly for Violet to hear clearly as she raced down the aisle and hurried away, intent on telling Cade what she'd learned.

The most surprising thing about doing an honest day's labor, Cade discovered midway through his apprenticeship at Owen Cooper's livery stable, was that he liked it.

He liked using his mind in new ways. He liked using his muscles. He liked lifting and straining, putting in an effort and earning results that were less transient—and harder to lose—than poker chips or gold nuggets. He liked knowing that the results of his labor meant something to people. Most of all, he liked seeing the look of pride on Violet's face when she met him at the end of the day and listened to him talk about his work.

What was even more amazing to Cade was that *he* was proud of himself, too. By now he'd probably done enough labor to repay his lost wager to Reverend Benson—and then some. But somehow Cade had passed the point of working merely to repay his debt to Violet's father and protect his honest name. Now he was working to catch a glimpse of the life he'd thought he'd never have…and maybe to grab ahold of it, too.

Because these days, with Violet, that charmed life felt almost at the tips of Cade's fingertips…his newly callused, almost-worthless-for-cardsharping, workingman's fingertips.

Ruefully, Cade staked his pitchfork in a nearby pile of hay. Alone in one of the unoccupied stalls at Cooper's stable, he lifted his hands. His palms were roughened with those aforementioned calluses; his fingers ached with the aftereffects of the varied and unfamiliar work he'd done. Muscles in his arms and shoulders twanged with every exertion, letting Cade know that honest labor required more effort than gambling ever had.

Of course, lately he'd done more than his usual share of exerting himself in other more enjoyable ways, too. Recalling all the times he'd spent with Violet in his bed, Cade felt a smile sneak across his face. Feeling gratified, he leaned on his pitchfork's handle and recollected some more.

Violet kissing him. Violet loving him. Violet promising him that no matter what, they'd be together.

Cade prayed she was right. Since his apprenticeships

had gone so well, he'd even begun planning for a future where she *was* right and they *could* be together. He'd begun daydreaming, for the first time since he was a boy, about happier days.

It could work, Cade thought with renewed hopefulness. He could speak to Owen Cooper or Daniel McCabe or the lumber mill owner, Marcus Copeland, or any of the other tradesmen who'd taken a chance on him, and convince them to hire him full time. He could work hard, save his money and eventually build a home for him and Violet. He could abandon his search for Percy Whittier—because it had never brought him anything but misery, after all—and just get on with living his life. He could do it.

It would be a gamble. It would take a long time to set up a sufficient nest egg. It would be a while before he made himself worthy of asking for Violet's hand in marriage. He wouldn't be able to rely on his "sinful" gambling skills, either—not given the reverend's stated opposition to such gambits. But Cade was a patient man. He could hold out, no matter how long it took.

The only question was…could Violet do the same?

Could she wait for him to start their future together? Or would some other man—newly aware of her and beguiled by her, thanks to Cade's initial pursuit of Violet at the charity ball—chase Violet and win her for himself? After all, the local men had a head start on honest living—one that Cade couldn't hope to match. Violet insisted she didn't want anyone else. But if she were faced with a choice between marrying a good man who was ready for her today and Cade—who might not be ready to reputably make her his until years from now—who would she choose?

Alarmed by the query, Cade frowned. He hoped Violet would choose him. On the strength of her faith in him, he could do all of it. He could become a new man with a new life. All he'd need was a straight talk with Blackhouse first, a conversation to free himself of their arrangement, and he'd be ready to begin.

"Well, now. Isn't this a sight?" Wearing an amused look, Simon Blackhouse strode confidently into the livery stable. He glanced around, seemed to assess the unlikelihood of there being a roulette wheel stashed among the draft horses and mules, then stopped at the door to Cade's stall. "I heard it was true, but I didn't believe it—Cade Foster, pitching hay when he could be pitching woo to any number of nubile young ladies in town."

Cade frowned at him. "You're unsurprisingly single-minded, Blackhouse. Everything on earth doesn't revolve around women."

"Not once you've already settled on one of them, I guess." Blackhouse gave the stable another speculative look. He wrinkled his nose with distaste—undoubtedly at the place's earthy aroma—then shook his head. "That's so…limiting of you, Cade. It's too bad *your* chosen ladylove wants you to do things like *this*."

Meaningfully, his benefactor frowned at the stable and its dirty environs. He came no nearer, almost as though he worried that Cade's newfound willingness to perform hard labor might be contagious. After all, Blackhouse wouldn't want to risk his reputation as a renowned bachelor and ne'er-do-well by engaging in productive employment. His expression said as much.

"*I* want to do this." Deciding he'd lollygagged long enough, Cade forked up more hay. With a mighty effort, he lobbed it into the waiting hayloft. "This or something else like it."

Blackhouse boggled at him. "You can't be serious."

"I'm as serious as I've ever been about anything."

"Oh. I see. I thought you were working some game or other. That *is* serious." Blackhouse seemed distressed. "Damn."

"I'm afraid you'll have to find someone else to go carousing with," Cade told him, cutting straight to the point. The truth was long overdue. "I'm thinking of staying here."

"In the stable? But it stinks!" Blackhouse aimed an agitated glance at his boots. He stepped back, his frown deepening impressively. "I don't know if you've noticed, but there's manure on the floor. *Manure.*" He shuddered. "There's a reason I hire people to take care of these things for me."

"I'm thinking of staying in Morrow Creek, I mean," Cade elaborated with a grin. "Settling down here for good."

"Aha. I see." Blackhouse frowned. Musingly, he fiddled with his waistcoat. "Adams will have to burn this damn suit, I guess, now that it's been contaminated with the stench of labor."

"*That* is the stench of manure. You're understandably confused, having not encountered either of those things up close before."

As in old times, they shared a grin. Their partnership may have been rocky on occasion, but it had been fun more often than not. In many ways, Cade and Blackhouse were kindred spirits.

At least they were…until Blackhouse sobered.

"I'm afraid I can't have you quit on me, Cade. You promised you'd find Whittier for me. You haven't done that yet."

Cade offered a good-natured shrug. "I won't be the first to fail," he pointed out. "There's that Pinkerton man who quit on you after he got knifed in a fight with Whittier—"

"Damn coward," Blackhouse muttered. "He had a derringer!"

"—and that U.S. Marshal you were paying to monitor the official reports of arrests. He collected your bonus money—"

"When all he'd seen was a drunk, deadbeat miner who resembled Whittier," Blackhouse complained, "*if* you were drunk too, and squinted just right." He heaved a sigh. "That's why I partnered with *you*, Cade. That's why I risked sponsoring *your* search. Because you were motivated by more than just money."

"I still am." Stopping work again, Cade leaned on his pitchfork. In the stalls nearby, horses shifted and blew. One whinnied, probably calling out to the freer beasts trotting by on the bustling street beyond Cooper's stable. "Truth be told, I'd still like those answers I've been after," he admitted. "But maybe finding Whittier isn't in the cards for me."

At the livery stable's wide, double-door opening,

Cade suddenly spied Violet. Just then, all she was doing was chatting with Owen Cooper, grinning and gesticulating with typical warmheartedness, but all the same, Cade's heart leaped in response.

They hadn't been together that morning. Cade wished they had been. Although he knew Violet must have had a good reason for skipping their usual meeting, he'd missed her. Now, merely at the sight of her, everything inside him felt gladdened.

"Maybe I'm meant for something else—for some*one* else," Cade said. With his mind made up, he faced his benefactor. "I have a future now, Blackhouse—one that can't include gallivanting all over multiple states and territories tracking a man who doesn't want to be found. Whittier dodged me. It's done. *I'm* done."

Now Blackhouse appeared even more distressed than he had upon noticing the dirty, hay-strewn stable floor. He put his hand to his brow. He paced from side to side. He wheeled around to confront Cade again. "You can't quit on me. You can't!"

Surprised by his vehemence, Cade frowned, too. "Why not?" He gave his benefactor a measured look, trying to decipher him. "What's your interest in Whittier anyway? You never told me."

"You never asked."

Cade grinned. "If I remember correctly, that was a condition of our arrangement. We agreed not to ask questions."

"Not even of one another," Blackhouse specified. "That was our stated policy, and it's worked out very well until now." Convivially, he spread his arms, plainly hoping to cajole Cade into resuming his search—or at least dropping his questions about his unknown motivations. "Why spoil a good thing?"

Cade looked at Violet. "Because things have changed."

"Oh, really? They have? I—" Blackhouse broke off. Astutely, he followed Cade's glance to the livery stable's doors…and the one-of-a-kind woman silhouetted in that gap. "I see."

"I still want to know why you're after Whittier," Cade pushed. "It's important." It *was* important—partly because he'd never seen Blackhouse this upset before. His reaction could not be due solely to Cade's quitting his search. "Maybe if you'd told me your own reasons for finding Whittier, it would have helped my search."

"'Would have'? Are you saying you won't continue your search if I don't tell you my interest in finding Whittier?" Blackhouse wanted to know. "Is that your price?"

Cade remained silent. There wasn't much more to say.

Obviously unaccustomed to accepting defeat, Blackhouse offered him a stiff smile. "Fine. I'll tell you." With reluctance—and no small measure of gravitas—he announced, "The reason is… Well, it's a matter of honor. My *honor* is at stake."

He delivered that certain bluff in as straight-faced a fashion as Cade had ever experienced. In spite of everything, Cade was impressed. He'd have sworn Blackhouse believed his own lie. But then all the best liars did. Just like all the best gamblers bought into their own bluffs. They had to, to win.

All the same…Blackhouse thought he possessed *honor*? Truly?

Still boggling at that remarkable idea, Cade guffawed.

His benefactor did not so much as crack a smile.

"You're serious," Cade observed with amazement. He examined Blackhouse through new eyes. "You actually believe that finding Whittier will preserve your *honor* somehow."

Blackhouse was silent. With a tight expression, he swiped his hand over the stable wall. He frowned with distaste.

"I'll make you a wager," he offered in an obvious bid to regain control. "If you find Whittier, I'll tell you why my honor is at stake. I'll tell you everything you want to know."

Cade shook his head. "You're overestimating my curiosity about your past."

"Am I?" Blackhouse simply gazed at him. "Am I also overestimating your inability to resist a juicy wager?"

Hell. Blackhouse had him there. Cade had always had a hard time turning down a bet. He'd proven that much already by wagering with Reverend Benson. But still Cade refused to commit.

"I already know who Whittier is to *you*," Blackhouse pushed, undoubtedly sensing he'd struck a nerve. "If you want to know who Whittier is to me, then find him." Blackhouse paused. "I'll pay you triple the amount we agreed upon. For a man in your position, that much money could set you up quite nicely."

With a significant glance toward the livery stable entryway where Violet and Owen Cooper were still conversing, Blackhouse nodded. It wasn't difficult to guess his meaning. He would give Cade everything he needed to begin a new life in Morrow Creek—*if* in return Cade gave him the means to restore his alleged honor.

"You'll need a stake," Blackhouse pressed. "I can give it."

"I'm not gambling. I haven't been for days. So I don't need a stake of any kind. Not anymore. Not from you." Stubbornly, Cade eyed him. "Besides, some things aren't wagering material."

"Some things," Blackhouse agreed. "But not many, in my experience." He held out an engraved card. "Bring this with you to my private train car tonight. I'm having a party to celebrate the first night of the tournament. I want you to come."

Cade gripped his pitchfork. "I already have plans."

"I'm sure you do." Blackhouse offered a wide smile. He tucked his invitation card into Cade's vest pocket anyway, then gave it a pat to secure it. He delivered him a breezy wave. He turned, seeming for all the world to be completely carefree. "Think about my offer. Give me your answer tonight. And bring your paramour with you, why don't you. I'd love to meet her."

"She won't want to meet you."

"Are you sure about that? She looks friendly." Blackhouse winked at a surprised-looking Violet. Flirtatiously, he tipped his hat to her. She blushed. "Maybe I'll invite her myself."

Cade tightened his grasp on his pitchfork, unhappy with the idea of allowing Blackhouse unfettered access to Violet. There were things Blackhouse knew about him that Violet should not.

Grudgingly, Cade nodded. "We'll be there."

"Aha. Good!" His benefactor smiled more broadly. "I thought you might find a bit of leeway in your busy schedule. You'll be glad you did, I promise." Blackhouse offered another, almost mocking tip of his hat to Cade. "It can't be all manure shoveling and horse wrangling and shoe dirtying all the time, now, can it? That's no kind of life for a man like you. Besides, if all goes well, I may have a surprise for you."

With that cryptic statement, Blackhouse walked off toward a patiently waiting Adams, who stood outside the livery stable with a cigar box, an umbrella and a bulging satchel. Blackhouse passed Owen Cooper and Violet, gave Cade's beloved a second audacious tip of his hat, then hied off to prepare for his soirée.

Chapter Eleven

Feeling flustered and eager, Violet hastened from the livery stable doorway to the empty stall where she'd spied Cade.

"Whew!" Energetically, she fanned her face. "I thought I'd never get here to you! First I had to thank Mr. Cooper for providing you with this apprenticeship, of course. Then I had to inquire about his usual helper, Gus, and find out how he's doing. Then I wanted to talk about Mr. Cooper's daughter, Élodie, who goes to school with Tobe." After pausing for a gulp of air, Violet rushed on. "She's the sweetest little girl—she lost her mother when she was just a baby, poor thing, but everyone in town is helping Mr. Cooper raise her. At least as much as they can, of course." Confidingly, Violet leaned nearer to a bemused-looking Cade. "Confidentially speaking, Mr. Cooper can be a bit of a lone wolf, I'm afraid. He's a hard man to help—a bit like *another* rough-and-tumble Western man I know."

"Hmm," Cade rumbled. "I can't imagine who that would be."

"Oh, me neither!" Violet fibbed with joyful exuberance. She loved teasing Cade. She'd *so* missed seeing him this morning. She'd been too late after all, between fetching Tobe's coat, meeting the mysterious stranger at the church and speaking with her father, to arrive at the Lorndorff Hotel in time. "All the same, though, I do appreciate Mr. Cooper's apprenticeship. It looks as though you're doing wonderfully over here!"

Aiming an admiring glance at Cade's physique, Violet nodded. She'd appreciated the way he looked in his fancy gambler's duds, of course—any woman would have—but she thought he looked mighty fine in his workingman's clothes, too. With his shirtsleeves rolled up, she could glimpse several tantalizing inches of muscular, sun-browned arms. With his shirt partly unbuttoned, she could savor the sight of his tawny throat and intriguing chest hair. With his vest loose, she could see the braces that held up his trousers...and remember herself slipping off those selfsame braces to brazenly help *remove* his trousers. She'd taught herself that particular maneuver just yesterday.

With hardly any provocation at all, Violet sighed dreamily. She sent her gaze roaming over Cade's personhood all over again.

"I won't be able to think about working at all," Cade told her roughly, "if you keep on looking at me that way."

Another sigh. Daringly, Violet sneaked her fingertip beneath his rightmost brace, testing its strength. If she tugged a bit, it would fall. With another skillful flick of her finger, so would his left brace. After that, with

just the merest nudge, so would his trousers. Hmm...
"I can't help it."

"You seemed to be able to help it a few minutes ago.
Then, you only had eyes for Simon Blackhouse." Cade
offered the name as though it were arsenic. "The world's
most famous layabout."

Violet blinked. "Blackhouse? You were talking with
Blackhouse just now?" She'd wondered about that.
"Your mentor?"

"My sometime *benefactor*," Cade clarified, his jaw
tight. "And yes—he's the one you were flirting with a
while ago."

"Flirting?" Filled with disbelief, Violet hooted with
laughter. "I wasn't flirting! I wouldn't begin to know how.
You know me—I've been a veritable dormouse all these
years."

Grumbling, Cade said, "You blushed at him."

"Blushed *at* him?" Growing more amused now, Violet
gave his arm a good-natured poke. "Exactly how does
one blush 'at' someone? Especially me? I don't possess a
single feminine wile that I know of." When Cade didn't
relent, she sighed. "Honestly, Cade, if I didn't know better, I'd think you were jealous."

With a powerful, obstinate gesture, Cade crossed
his arms. He gazed into the middle distance toward a
passing wagon, silently refusing to say more. His profile faced her, all hard and determined...and grouchy.
Very, very grouchy.

Realizing the truth at last, Violet boggled.

"You *are* jealous!" she crowed.

"You needn't sound so all-fired happy about it."

"Happy? I'm *thrilled*!" Violet admitted unabashedly. "No one has ever been jealous of my affections, Cade. Not ever."

"They should have been. This town is full of fools."

"You're sweet to say so." She beamed at him. She couldn't help it. *How* could he possibly be so smitten with her? She'd done nothing at all to deserve him. "I remember when your Mr. Blackhouse tipped his hat at me, of course. It did excite me a little. But only because I'm not used to the attention. Frankly speaking, he *is* quite a handsome man, of course, so anyone—"

"Handsome?" This time it was Cade's turn to boggle. "You think he's handsome?" He released an annoyed gust of air, then turned his attention with new zeal toward the street. "I guess some people might think so. If they like the slick type."

His gruffness was beyond endearing. He *did* care. What's more, he was obviously unused to caring as much as he did.

"I especially fancy Mr. Blackhouse's lovely hair," Violet teased further. "It's so very blond, with all those gorgeous waves in it." Unable to resist joshing Cade, she gave a teensy squeal, then clapped her hands together in apparent exaltation. "It makes him look like a sun-kissed angel! Don't you think so?"

Cade snorted. He shook his own dark, tousled hair, undoubtedly without realizing he did so. "The only thing *less* angelic than Simon Blackhouse is old Beelzebub himself. Don't be fooled by his stupid hair," he warned ominously, "or his pretty face or his impeccable manners or his crates full of money—"

"Is this meant to put me off him?" Violet interrupted pertly. "Because you're making him sound like quite a catch."

"—or his private luxury train car," Cade went on relentlessly, "or his valet or his damnable mysterious past—"

"Ooh, how intriguing!" Violet gushed, clasping her hands girlishly. "A mystery man! With his own valet, to boot!"

"—or his constant offers of reckless wagers—"

"Oh! That reminds me!" Violet butted in, forgetting to josh Cade for the moment. "I met someone today, and I think—"

I think he might be the man you've been searching for all this time.

"—because Simon Blackhouse is a damn blackguard, through and through," Cade growled in a plainly possessive and resolute tone before Violet could tell him her news, "no matter how harmless he might seem. He's no good for a woman like you."

With her jaw fully dropped now, Violet stared at him.

"He's not nearly *good enough* for a woman like you," Cade continued relentlessly, "and if you can't see that, well…"

"Well?" Breathlessly, Violet waited. "Well, what?"

"Well…" Exasperatedly, Cade cradled her cheek in his hand. He drank in the sight of her. He drew in a deep breath. He shook his head. Despairingly, he said, "Words aren't enough."

"Enough for what?" All of a sudden she was scarcely keeping up with him, Violet realized. Jealousy, it seemed, was a powerfully confusing emotion for all parties concerned. "What are you trying to tell me? What am I supposed to see? Are you—"

Before Violet could finish asking questions, Cade's mouth was on hers. In the earthy stillness of the livery stable, he kissed her…so expertly, in fact, that Violet forgot all about the dimness and hay and soberly painted wooden stalls. All she could think about were Cade's lips, soft and insistent on hers, and Cade's mouth, warm and wet and delectable against hers, and Cade's hands, steady and arousing against her neck and jaw, and even as she tried to formulate her last, almost-forgotten query—just to assure herself that she could— all Violet could do was grab ahold of Cade's vest and just hang on. There was something about the way Cade kissed her, with slow, lazy strokes and tiny rousing bites and gentle, soothing glides of his lower lip, that made her entire mind simply shut down to all other sensation.

"You're supposed to see that *I'm* all you need," Cade announced when he was through kissing her. "You're supposed to remember that, now and always, whether I have the words to say so or not." His gaze remained rapt on her face, his vivid blue eyes dark with passion. "But if you need another demonstration just to set that lesson for certain—"

"I do!" Violet avowed, feeling all aflame. With her last dredges of wit, she added, "You'd better hurry up, too, before I run after Mr. Blackhouse and launch myself a comparison scheme."

Growling against her hair, Cade gave her neck a tender nip. The combination of his rumbling voice and naughty mouth made shivers race down her spine. Blindly clutching his shoulders, Violet gasped. They were still in the stable, she remembered belatedly, in public, where anyone could see them. This was risky. It was foolhardy. It was—she realized as Cade framed her face in his hands and brought his mouth to hers again—utterly and completely necessary. She'd stop breathing without this.

"*Ahem*," came a voice from nearby.

Unwilling to acknowledge that intrusion, Violet squeezed her eyes shut a little bit tighter. She went on kissing Cade, telling herself that the sound she'd heard had most assuredly been a snuffling horse or a kicking mule or a distant bit of thunder...never mind that autumn storms were rare in Morrow Creek, and she'd yet to meet the beast of burden who could sound like—

"*Ahem*." That intrusion came again, more loudly this time.

Oh, no. Possibly it was Owen Cooper. She would ruin Cade's apprenticeship! Urgently, Violet pulled away. Through her dazed vision, she glimpsed Cade's face, impassioned and wonderful.

He wore the same expression he always did when he kissed her, which was besotted and determined and arresting in equal measure, and before Violet knew precisely what she was doing, she'd put both palms to the beard-stubbled sides of his jaw and was kissing him again, crowding herself closer and closer...

"You're going to have to let the man do his work sometime," someone said from nearby. Very loudly.

"Otherwise he won't be able to repay his gambling debts—especially his debt to *me*."

With effort, Cade wrested himself from Violet's embrace. In obvious shock, he stared. "Reverend Benson!"

"Papa!" Violet gaped, too. For indeed it *was* her father who'd been futilely trying to get her attention for the past few minutes. He stood beside a curt-looking Owen Cooper, both men impatiently waiting for her and Cade to quit spooning in the stable like addle-headed lovebirds.

Too late, Violet recalled that the livery stableman had famously shunned all things frivolous and sinful, from gambling to drinking to carousing with women. Although he was still young and vibrant, widowed Owen Cooper had become the most straitlaced man in Morrow Creek…all for the sake of his little daughter, Élodie. He would not approve of Cade and Violet's behavior.

Of course, neither would her poor beleaguered father.

Chin held high, Cade stepped up. "This was not Violet's fault, Reverend Benson." He put out his palms in an appeal to be heard. "I encouraged her to see me. I took advantage of her naïveté. I know it was wrong, and I'm sorry. But I care about—"

"No! It was me! All me." Violet crowded aside Cade in her haste to take the blame. Earnestly, she faced her father. "I knew you didn't want me to see Cade, Papa, but I did it anyway. I did it because he needs me! Because I care about—"

"It was me, sir," Cade insisted, head bowed. "All me."

"I won't have it!" Determinedly, Violet shook her head. "I knew you made that wager with Cade to make him quit seeing me. But I also knew I could help him repay his debt to you, so I set out to help him, and everything just ballooned from there—"

"Only because I allowed it to," Cade contended with new and convincing forcefulness. "I should have known better, but—"

As he continued, Reverend Benson and Owen Cooper exchanged an inscrutable look. Then Mr. Cooper piped up. "Isn't anyone going to apologize to *me*? It's *my* stable you're besmirching."

Was that a glimmer of amusement behind his equable facade? Violet wondered. No, it couldn't be. Not with Owen Cooper.

Instantly, Cade did as the stableman wished. "I'm sorry, Cooper," he said in a contrite and resolute tone. He frowned. "I never meant for this to happen, especially here. If you want me to leave, I understand. I'll collect my things and—"

"Of course he won't want you to leave!" Instantly loyal, Violet shook her head. "You've been doing a good job here. Anyone can see that. Mr. Cooper is an understanding man. He—"

At that, Cooper put up his hand, signaling her to stop. Then he *did* grin. He *was* amused! "Enough. I have customers to see to and work to do." He tipped his hat to the reverend. "I trust you can manage this all on your own, Reverend?"

Gravely, Violet's father surveyed her and Cade. He gave a solemn nod. "With some prayer and divine guidance…yes, I can."

Even as she watched Owen Cooper amble away,

Violet swallowed hard. Whenever her father decided he needed the help of the Almighty to deal with her, it was not a positive sign.

Seeking assurance—or maybe trying to give away a smidgeon of it—she shuffled closer to Cade. Behind her skirts, she took his hand. She squeezed it. Cade squeezed back, delivering her a world of comfort in that single familiar gesture.

After her father bade goodbye to Mr. Cooper, he turned again to Violet and Cade. His spine was stiff, his face filled with censure, and at the sight of his obvious disappointment, it was all Violet could do not to crumple in dismay herself.

"I never meant to let you down, Papa," she said.

"I know that, Violet." Contemplatively, her father examined her and Cade. He took in their close-together posture, their tightly clasped hands…even their heads, automatically tilted to faintly and supportively touch. "I also know that you're capable of ignoring my wishes if that's what's needed to follow your heart. Otherwise, you never would have taken to delivering meals to the prisoners at Sheriff Caffey's jail, for instance, entirely against my better judgment and my explicitly stated wishes."

Violet squirmed, remembering that incident from last year. Papa had thought she wouldn't be safe at the jailhouse. She'd insisted on doing her charitable work there anyway, arguing that no one needed aid more than those people who'd been forsaken and separated from the people who knew them and cared for them.

She guessed she still maintained that philosophy—

after a fashion—with Tobe and Cade. Her feelings for them had grown far beyond the compassion she'd felt toward the inmates, though.

"It wasn't that I wanted to defy you," Violet said in her own defense. "I had to do what I thought was right."

"I understand that," her father told her. "I realized then that that's the sort of person you are—the sort of person you've always been. You're helpful and kind and determined, and I rightly cherish those qualities in you. I'm proud of you."

For a moment, confusingly, all her father did was smile at her. Violet began to nurture a burgeoning hope that her father would neither disown her nor begin praying for her redemption—nor decide to march her and Cade down the aisle by force. Not that that last consequence would have been entirely unwelcome....

Unfortunately, her father dashed her newfound optimism by frowning at her in a troubling fashion. He inhaled deeply.

"But that incident taught me one important fact—you *do* have a contrary streak, my dear. That streak, coupled with the fact that you're about as wily and cynical as a newborn puppy—"

"Papa!" Violet exclaimed, thoroughly taken aback.

"—meant I could hardly ignore what was going on when you became enamored of a hard-bitten, hard-drinking, dangerous-looking professional gambler who was willing to slip me an 'improving card'...and was able to discern that I would use it." Somewhat sheepishly, her father glanced at Cade. "But I could hardly just rush ahead willy-nilly, either," he told Violet. "Approving your friendship would have sent the wrong message. Yet if I forbade you outright from seeing Mr. Foster, you might have rebelled and begun a relationship purely *because* I'd prohibited it. I'm sure you appreciate the fix I was in."

Violet did not. She felt much too baffled for that.

"I didn't want to increase Mr. Foster's rascally allure by putting him off-limits—" astonishingly, here her father *winked* at Cade "—but I felt duty-bound to step in and protect you if I could. Because the truth is, Violet, you've given too many foolish men far too many opportunities to hurt your feelings—and all because you insist on seeing the best in people."

He meant the times, Violet knew, when she'd given someone a chance to become close to her, only to learn that he was solely interested in her as Adeline Wilson's best friend—as someone who could offer an introduction to the most beautiful woman in town.

"Seeing the best in people is what you taught me to do," she said in her own defense. "It's the Christian thing to do."

"It is," her father agreed. "But it can be dangerous, too. Seeing good where there's also plenty of bad can be misleading. People are a fickle mix of both." He slanted a perceptive glance at Cade. "So when you told me about your Mr. Foster and I saw that telltale sparkle in your eyes, I knew I had to…intervene."

"You mean you had to separate us," Cade guessed in a knowing tone, "before we became too involved in one another."

Astonishingly, her father nodded. "Yes. As a result

of my wager with you, Foster, I reasoned that either you would realize my gullible daughter was *not* easy pickings for a scoundrel—"

Violet frowned, unhappy to hear herself and Cade described that way. "I'm not gullible, Papa! And Cade is no scoundrel."

"—or you would rise to the occasion and prove yourself. Either way, I reckoned things would work out in the end—*without* my inciting Violet's more defiant instincts. Judging by the way you two have been mooning over one another since I've been here, I'm guessing everything is coming along just fine."

"I wish you'd trusted me, Papa," Violet protested. "I wish you'd let me make my own decisions about this."

"But I did!" Her father blinked. "You didn't have to know what I'd done to acquit yourself splendidly—from arranging these apprenticeships for Mr. Foster to helping him quit gambling and drinking. You did all that on your own." At Violet's look of bewilderment, her father explained, "The desk clerk at the Lorndorff told me you'd been visiting Mr. Foster to help reform him of his debauched habits. That's admirable work, my dear."

Violet and Cade exchanged a guarded glance. Violet bit the inside of her cheek, suppressing an urge to confess everything. Too late, she recalled that her father knew just as many—if not many *more*—residents of Morrow Creek as she did. It made sense that he would learn of her comings and goings without much effort. How could she have been so blind? So blithe? So foolish?

At least her father apparently thought that *all* she'd done was legitimately reform Cade by helping him quit drinking and gambling and carousing, though. There was a blessing in that.

"But all that generous charitable work would mean nothing," her father continued in a more fired-up tone, warming to his usual oratory vigor now, "if your Mr. Foster hadn't done his share. I put as many obstacles in your path as I could, sir, but you hurdled them all." Briskly, he saluted Cade. "Well done. I approve of you, *and* I approve of your courting my daughter. The two of you officially have my blessing and my well wishes."

Violet felt delighted. Cade appeared gobsmacked.

"You were *testing* me?" he asked, skipping over her father's hard-earned approbation for the moment. "You weren't trying to get rid of me? You were testing me?"

"I had to." Reverend Benson's tone sounded matter-of-fact. "I had to know if you truly cared for Violet or if you were simply using her for your own nefarious and immoral purposes."

Cade scowled. "I would never abuse Violet that way."

"Well." Her father chuckled. "Of course, I know that *now*. But I also had to know if you were worthy of my daughter, too."

I could be moved to approve of the right man, Violet recalled her father saying earlier. *The man who could make you as happy as you deserve to be.*

Cade *had* been that man, just as she'd hoped.

"You *liked* Cade," Violet accused her father. "You liked him!" She shook her head in astonishment. "Why didn't you just tell me so? We could have avoided all this subterfuge."

Her father gave her an unreadable—but quite possibly playful—look. "Where would have been the fun in that?"

"Fun? Papa!" Exasperated, Violet waved her arms. "What is *fun* about sneaking around, meeting in smithies and stables—"

"You *will* have to quit smooching in public," her father cautioned her. "I can't condone that. I'm old-fashioned that way."

"—and not knowing if your love is doomed?" Growing suddenly overwhelmed, Violet inhaled. Beside her, Cade squeezed her hand. "Don't you know? I worried every day that I would have to choose between you and Cade, Papa. That I would want to be with him and you would say no. That a decision would be forced on me that I was in no way prepared to make. It was crushing me!"

Her father sobered. "I finally guessed as much." He touched her shoulder, then gazed into her eyes, his full white whiskers and earnest expression ever comforting. "I had a feeling there was something you weren't telling me. Just this morning, when we were talking about that stranger in church, I knew it. I knew you were keeping something from me. I knew it was bothering you to do so. That's why I followed you here, so we could talk about it. You, my girl, are not someone who keeps secrets easily."

"That's for certain!" Violet laughed, even as grateful tears sprang to her eyes. She felt *so* relieved to finally have things out in the open. "I can't tell you how many times I wanted to tell you about something wonderful Cade had done—"

At her side, Cade grew suddenly alert. She hoped he didn't think she wanted to confide anything *intimate*. Silly man. She might be a freethinking woman, but she wasn't entirely daffy.

"—and had to rein in my thoughts for fear you wouldn't approve. I meant to tell you everything, Papa," Violet assured him, "once Cade had finished his apprenticeships. I thought I could present the whole thing as another of my charitable accomplishments!" Giddy with relief, she waved her arms and enthused, "You know, just another lonesome soul, brought from darkness into light, saved from demon drink and the perils of gambling…" She paused, grinning. "Something like that."

On the heels of her own dramatic oratorical triumph, Violet became aware that Cade had grown quite still beside her. He'd turned verifiably wary when she'd begun discussing his overall wonderfulness and her wish to describe that wonderfulness to her father. But that previous guardedness was nothing compared with the way Cade seemed now. His face looked stony, his eyes impassive, his muscles rigid with what appeared to be…anger?

"I'm not anyone's charity case." With his jaw tight, Cade clenched his fists. "Especially not yours, Miss Benson."

His gaze swerved to Violet's. In his eyes, she glimpsed deep hurt, abundant confusion…and no small measure of defiance.

"I don't need some self-proclaimed do-gooder looking out for me. I had all the 'charity' I'll ever need when I was just a boy." Cade swept Violet and her father with a damning look. "As a grown man, I sure as hell don't need the blessing of a tippling, wagering, deceitful 'man of God' like yourself, *Reverend*. I can get along just fine without either of you."

Motionless with shock, Violet stared at Cade. Didn't he know she'd only been chattering on, only half thinking? She hadn't meant to conjure up painful memories of foundling homes and abandonment. But that seemed to be exactly what she'd done.

"Cade, no!" Violet cried. "I didn't mean that. I don't think of you as a charity case. I don't! I couldn't—"

Determinedly not listening, utterly closed off to her, Cade grabbed his pitchfork. He stabbed it into a nearby pile of hay, his face as emotionless and fearsome as she'd ever seen it.

From nowhere, Violet recalled Tobe's childish assertion.

I like bein' dirty sometimes. It makes me look fierce!

But likening Cade to Tobe made no sense. Not in this context. Cade was no child. And he legitimately *was* fierce, now more than ever. He was streetwise and aggressive, too. If the hay he was pitchforking didn't burst into flames beneath his gaze, Violet thought in a dither, it would be a miracle.

Which only served to remind her, in a scrambled and nonsensical fashion, of the stranger in church today. In a flash, his words came rushing back to her. *The moment I stepped inside, I half expected the whole caboodle to go up in flames.*

If that man really was Whittier…

"I think you both should leave," Cade said roughly.

"But I was only joking!" Violet grabbed Cade's arm.

He shook off her grasp, then went on working. "Cade, you must know I don't think of you that way—as one of my charity projects. I—"

Love you, she wanted to say. But his condemning expression and frighteningly lethal gaze left the words stuck in her throat.

Indomitably, Violet tried again. "I was only relieved! I was happy to have our courtship out in the open, that's all. I spoke out of turn, without thinking clearly. I'm so sorry."

"I don't want your apologies."

"But I *am* sorry! Please listen to me."

Cade refused. Obdurately, he shook his head. Again, Violet was reminded of the stranger in church—of his grim expression, his tellingly dexterous hands, his unshakable belief that it was too late for him to apologize for the bad things he'd done.

It's too late for that. Fifteen years too late.

All at once, Violet had an inkling of what the stranger had meant—and she didn't like it. If this misunderstanding hardened between her and Cade, she didn't know how she would cope.

"This is silly," she insisted. "You can't really believe—"

"Just go." Cade turned his back to her. He forked up more hay, then tossed it into the nearest stall. "Leave. Now."

"I won't leave!" Violet planted her feet. "I said I won't give up on you, Cade, and I won't. Not now and not ever."

Cade gave her a bleak look. "Spoken like a true do-gooder. Don't you see? I'm a lost cause—a hopeless case. Just get out."

No one has ever loved me, she recalled him saying. *There's no reason you should be different.*

Well, she *was* different. Determinedly, Violet rallied.

If she couldn't reach Cade with caring or mulishness, then perhaps she could influence him with the pull of something she knew he wanted. "I saw Percy Whittier today. I met him. I talked to him."

Cade gripped his pitchfork. Although his back was turned to her, she thought she glimpsed new tension in his shoulders. Before she could be sure, though, her father touched her elbow.

"Come along, Violet. What's done is done. You can't mend a sock that's still coming unraveled, no matter how fast you darn it."

Totally confounded, Violet shot her father a confused look. Her father knew nothing about mending. What was he saying?

"The reverend's right," Cade said roughly. "You don't want to be here when I come undone." He stabbed his pitchfork again. "A soft, sweet, *kind* person like you could get hurt."

Violet couldn't miss his embittered tone. Cade didn't think she was kind. Not now. Not at all. Maybe not ever. Because just then, everything they'd ever shared felt as insubstantial and unreal as this conversation did.

"It's too late," she said. "I already am hurt."

Then Violet picked up her skirts, nodded to her father and hurried away from the stable just as quickly as she could.

Chapter Twelve

For a man with his own personal valet, Simon Black-house required far too long to answer his own front door—or at least what passed for a front door: his train car's rear hatch.

Unhappy with that fact, Cade frowned at the gaily painted hatch. He lifted the bottle of mescal he'd brought, waved it in the air, then bellowed, "Blackhouse! Open the damn door!"

Sounds of a hurried conversation drifted toward him from inside the train car. Thumping footfalls could be heard.

The door's twin locks were disengaged. The door opened.

To Cade's surprise, Blackhouse himself—he of the angelic blond curls and hellaciously cocksure de-meanor—stood there in the entryway. His gaze lit on Cade's liquor bottle.

"Foster! You're early. The party's not for hours yet. But you brought libations, so all is forgiven." With out-right merriment, Blackhouse reached for the mescal. "Thank you."

Cade held it out of reach. He took a deliberate swig.

"Courtesy demands that you surrender whatever gifts you bring." Blackhouse appeared puzzled. "That's what's done."

"What do you know about 'what's done'? You can't even manage your own valet." Tipsily, Cade scowled. "I expected Adams to open the door, not you."

"Adams is busy preparing for the party later," Blackhouse told him. "I'm perfectly capable of opening a door by myself."

"Hmm. And here I thought I'd witnessed a miracle." With sham concern, Cade peered at him. "Opening a door by yourself is almost akin to work, Blackhouse. Does your hand hurt?"

"My hand is fine." Blackhouse stifled a swearword. He narrowed his eyes. "Which is more than I can say for you, by the way. What happened? You look as though you picked a fight with your conscience—" here, Blackhouse gave a typically devilish grin "—and then crushed that bothersome nag to smithereens."

"Very astute of you." Feeling himself waver slightly, Cade pointed his mescal bottle at his friend. Confidingly, he said, "I'm undoing all the reforming Miss Benson has accomplished on me. So far, I've cleaned house in faro, drank a third of this bottle of firewater, flirted with four saloon girls *and* delivered a mighty sockdolager to a mouthy saloon patron who was rude to one of those fine dancing ladies." Upon remembering that last occurrence, Cade flexed his fingers. He winced. "*My* hand *does* hurt. It's been a while since I've been brawling."

"I see." Blackhouse gazed at him with uncharacter-istic—and in all likelihood, imaginary—sympathy. His erstwhile benefactor stepped aside. "Well, come inside, then. You won't find any brawls in here, but in a few hours you *will* find all manner of other distractions. We'll have drinks and hors d'oeuvres…"

As Blackhouse nattered on describing the evening's upcoming festivities, Cade listened with half an ear. Clutching his mescal bottle, he entered the train car. It smelled of exotic fragrances, owing to Blackhouse's en-thusiasm for Eastern-influenced objects and incenses. It looked posh, thanks to Blackhouse's affinity for luxuri-ous fabrics, rare polished woods and expensive metals. It felt safe inside, Cade thought in a nonsensical and prob-ably drunken fashion, as a result of Blackhouse's insis-tence on sturdy locks and close-at-hand weaponry. He'd hung multiple knives, one wicked rifle and two—no, *three*—pistols on the train car walls like fine artwork.

Frowning, Cade considered all the firepower on display. Why did Blackhouse—ostensibly a carefree pleasure-seeker with no ties to anyone—need to have a veritable arsenal at the ready?

"…will have music, too, of course," Blackhouse was saying as he ushered Cade into the train car's parlor area, "at least whatever this innocuous mountain town can provide for us…"

Cade swallowed more mescal. The liquor seared a path to his gut, joining with the bitterness there to make an unholy brew. After Violet and Reverend Benson had left the stable, Cade had toiled awhile in blind confusion, abrading his hands with fresh calluses and trying to work off the memory of Violet's words.

I thought I could present the whole thing as another of my charitable accomplishments! Cade recollected unwillingly. *Just another lonesome soul, brought from darkness into light, saved from demon drink and the perils of gambling...*

Violet hadn't seemed to realize what was wrong with that boastful statement. But Cade had, and he'd worked tirelessly to forget it soon after. His efforts had been stymied by a surprisingly compassionate-seeming Owen Cooper, though, who'd wrestled the pitchfork from Cade's hands and made him leave.

Cooper couldn't possibly have understood the demons driving Cade. Yet he'd done everything but shove Cade forcibly out the stable doors. For that intervention, Cade had decided—eventually—to be grateful. At least he had once he'd found himself standing outside Jack Murphy's saloon...and realized he could rid himself of unwanted "salvation" once and for all.

Hell. He should have known he was nothing more than an altruistic exercise for Violet, Cade told himself now as he followed Blackhouse farther into the train car's well-appointed depths. No woman as pure as Violet Benson could have loved a man like him—a man full of flaws. What had he been thinking?

He was lucky he'd escaped before he'd fallen even harder.

"...and a high-stakes game, just to whet their appetites," Blackhouse rambled on. Cade hadn't heard more than one-tenth of what his friend had been saying, but that didn't seem to matter to Blackhouse. Even now, he turned with an excited flourish.

"But all those things pale, I'd say, compared with what's up next." Confidently, Blackhouse gestured to the settee. "I'd planned this to be a surprise for later. Remember? I mentioned it to you at that dingy stable?" He grimaced. "But now that you're here, Foster, and in such a sorry state at that…"

Blearily, Cade tried to concentrate. "You can be damnably long-winded, Blackhouse. Come to the point, why don't you?"

"Fine. But first I'd better take this from you." With gentle insistence, his friend prized the bottle of mescal from Cade's grasp. "I wouldn't want you to drop it in surprise."

"Surprise?" Vehemently, Cade swore. He wanted his alcohol back. He wanted this charade of pleasantries done. He wanted…

Damnation. He wanted Violet. He wanted her to think of him as a man, not a down-on-his-luck recipient of her benevolent good deeds…not a lonesome drifter needing her angelic embrace.

Angelic. Blast. She and Blackhouse had that much in common. They'd both become idealized versions of the people they'd started out to be. They'd both lifted themselves. Cade had sunk. For a while, he'd thought Violet was lifting him, too, but now…

"Nothing surprises me," Cade grumbled. "Not anymore."

Blackhouse disagreed. "Are you sure about that?"

Cade fired off another expletive. He shouldn't have

come here. Except something Violet had said—something about seeing Whittier today—had pushed him inevitably toward Blackhouse.

Most likely, some pathetic but still-hopeful part of him wanted to take Blackhouse's triple-the-money offer, Cade knew. Some part of him insisted on hoping that he could still find Whittier in Morrow Creek, get the money he needed to start a new life, impress Violet, make her his...

His pesky, newly awakened optimism had more kick than he'd reckoned on. Annoyed by that, Cade frowned. "Give me my mescal."

"I'll give you something even better!" With a flourish born of innate confidence and inborn good manners, Blackhouse waved his arm. His grin widened like a child's on Christmas morning. "Behold! Your surprise!"

Wearily, Cade glanced in the direction he indicated. A young man sat patiently on the settee, all angular arms and long legs and broad shoulders, wearing a grin that looked several degrees more uncertain than Blackhouse's. His hair was dark, his eyes blue, and in their depths, Cade glimpsed a million close-held memories—memories that stretched from boyhood till now.

"Hellfire, but you've developed a thirst for mescal," the young man said in a husky, emotion-choked tone. He rose, his gaze fixed firmly on Cade's face. "I haven't tried any of that Mexican liquor myself, but I guess I'm going to have to sample some now. If my brother says it's drinkable—" he stretched out his arms for an embrace "—then I reckon there'll be no arguing."

He stood there a moment, leaning markedly on one

leg. He kept his arms outstretched, his attitude full of buoyant hope and unabashed optimism—full, in fact, of the selfsame optimism that Cade was currently at war with. This could only be one man.

Cade blinked, still disbelieving. "*Judah?*"

Hunched on her bed, wrapped in a quilt that her mother had stitched long ago, Violet lugged another leather-bound ledger onto her lap. On the bureau beside her bed, her oil lamp cast a golden glow over the pages. Next to it sat an untouched cup of tea—brought a while ago by her father—and beside it, a jumble of jacks belonging to Tobe. They'd played a few games earlier, but Violet had been unable to keep her mind on the diversion.

All she could think about was Cade—and the way she'd hurt him. It had been an accident, of course, but did that really matter? In the end, he was as wounded as if she'd kicked him on purpose. She might as well have screamed that she didn't want him—that, just like those foster families who'd passed over Cade and his brother, Judah, she'd found him lacking and unlovable.

I had all the "charity" I'll ever need when I was just a boy. Of course Cade thought that. He might have experienced poorly given charity, but he'd never encountered real love.

It was Violet's mistake that he'd somehow confused the two. She'd offered love. He'd experienced charity. Violet had no idea, especially now that they'd parted, how to bridge that gap.

Feeling more distraught than ever, she wrenched open the train-station ledger that Joseph Abernathy had given her. Rows of penciled-in names and dates met her gaze, adrift in a sea of swirling cursive letters and numbers. The task before her suddenly seemed nigh impossible. It would have even if she hadn't been despairing and upset just then. Who was she to think she could find Tobe's mother, where others had failed?

Except there had been no others, Violet reminded herself staunchly, forcing herself to rally as she always did, especially when someone needed her. Tobe had not gone to the authorities, she remembered. He'd feared Sheriff Caffey would toss him in his jailhouse or send him to do forced work. He'd worried a "reformer" like Violet would march him onto an orphan train or enlist him in church service. So rather than look to responsible adults for help, Tobe had fended for himself. He'd banded together with vagabond youngsters in similar circumstances, and he'd made himself seem as akin to them as possible, and he'd gotten by somehow.

But that wasn't good enough anymore. Determined to help him, Violet rubbed her eyes. She refocused on the ledger. If she concentrated hard enough, she would think about finding Tobe's mother, Mrs. Larkin, and not about Cade. She would grant herself some reprieve from worrying about Cade and maybe do some good in the process. That's what she always did, wasn't it?

Sometime later, a knock at her door dragged her away from her records. Drained and gritty-eyed, Violet glanced up. "Yes?"

Her bedroom door creaked open. Adeline Wilson, her very best friend, stuck her head around the door frame. She smiled. "It's about time you heard me. I've been knocking for ages!"

"You have?" Violet blinked. "I didn't hear a thing."

"I thought as much. Let me guess—you were engrossed in one of your helpful projects, weren't you?" With a familiarity born of longtime friendship, Adeline bustled in. Her pretty face was full of empathy as she sat at the edge of the bed; her hands were clutched in worry. "How are you doing? Are you all right?"

"I suppose I will be." Violet's tentative smile, already shaky at best, didn't improve under the pressure of Adeline's sympathetic expression. "I tried to find Cade to apologize," she said, having already confided everything to her friend during an earlier talk, "but he wasn't in his room at the Lorndorff."

Wide-eyed, Adeline regarded her. "You went to his hotel?"

Violet nodded. "And to the places he's apprenticed, and even to the saloon. Mrs. Murphy had to escort me, though. My arrival at that last one wasn't too popular, let me tell you."

"I'll bet! Those men can be bullish when they're drinking."

"The only place left to try is his friend's private train car." Violet explained about Simon Blackhouse, his mysterious existence and his relationship to Cade's search for Whittier. "Mr. Blackhouse is hosting a party tonight. He's invited me."

"I heard about that shindig!" Eagerly, Adeline grabbed her arm. "You should go! You can have fun, forget about Cade—"

"I don't want to forget about Cade."

"—and enjoy some of that long-ignored popularity

that Mr. Foster's interest bestowed on you." Knowingly, Adeline nodded. "That's what I'd do. Why not? You knew this day was coming, after all. You must have considered what you'd do after—"

"After what?" Violet felt her gaze sharpen. Her heart pounded. "How was I supposed to know this day was coming?"

"Well…" Adeline appeared uncomfortable. "I only meant this isn't the first time you've been disappointed, Violet," she said gently. "You must have known this fling with the gambler couldn't possibly last…and planned what you'd do accordingly."

Now it was Violet's turn to feel uncomfortable. She made a face, unhappy to realize that even Adeline, her very closest friend, hadn't believed she and Cade could make a lasting match.

Had *she* believed it herself? Violet wondered suddenly. Or had she blurted out that thoughtless statement about reforming Cade with her charity work as a means of protecting herself?

After all, Violet mused, if the whole world thought she was simply *helping* Cade—not falling vulnerably in love with him—then she wouldn't be pitied if he didn't return her feelings.

The notion wasn't unthinkable—it was only disillusioning. She'd thought she was stronger than that. She'd thought that, with Cade's help and encouragement, she'd gotten *much* stronger.

Evidently, she'd only gotten strong enough to hurt him.

"Come now! Don't look so sad!" Adeline broke into

her downhearted thoughts with a cheerful poke. "You still have a lot to look forward to. It's not every day that an heir to a world-renowned industrial fortune invites you to his soirée."

"Heir?" Baffled, Violet wrinkled her nose. "Who's an heir?"

"Mr. Blackhouse, silly!" Adeline tilted her head. "You honestly don't know? You've never heard of him? He's notorious."

At her friend's tone of scandalized delight, Violet perked up. "Well, Cade *did* mention that his friend was an infamous layabout," she considered. "But that's as far as it went."

"Typical male." Adeline tsk-tsked. "He left out all the most pertinent details. Everyone knows about Simon Blackhouse—he's been in all the newspapers back in the States. He's the black sheep of the Blackhouses. They're famously estranged."

Violet frowned. "He sounds like a bad influence on Cade."

At that, Adeline laughed. "I can't believe you're still worried about your gambler's well-being! You really are too kind, Violet." She smiled fondly at her. "Anyhow, I reckon Mr. Blackhouse is a bad influence on everyone. Men like that usually are. Not that *I* care, now that I have my beloved Clayton by my side." She flashed her new engagement ring in genuine elation, having gotten very practiced at that showy gesture lately. "But when it comes to you—well, you're long overdue for a proper dose of adoration and flirtation! You deserve it."

Her friend's loyalty was touching. Her concern was

sweet. And Adeline *did* have a point about Violet being overdue for her turn as the belle of the ball. Over the past weeks, she'd received invitations of carriage rides and picnic lunches and sightseeing excursions to Morrow Creek in the company of local gentlemen. She'd turned down all those offers in the interest of spending time with Cade. But if *he* thought of her only as a starchy, prudish Goody Two-shoes—if he didn't love her, to boot, then why *shouldn't* she enjoy herself at a party for once?

Belatedly, Violet recalled Cade's insistence that Simon Blackhouse had been flirting with her. Well, maybe he had been!

Tentatively, Violet glanced at the nearby rocking chair where she usually stowed her knitting. Today, in place of balls of yarn with knitting needles stuck through sat a gorgeous spray of apple blossoms, wrapped with greenery and organza ribbon, all done up in a festive bow. Beside it perched an engraved card.

"Well…Mr. Blackhouse *did* deliver all those lovely things with his invitation," Violet divulged, nodding toward them. "He genuinely does seem to want me to attend his fancy party."

Adeline looked too. Her mouth formed an O. She rushed to the chair, then returned a heartbeat later cradling everything.

"A corsage? Ribbons?" A gasp. "An *engraved* card?" Holding it clasped to her bosom, Adeline let everything else fall. "Oh, Violet. You simply *must* attend this party. Do it for all of us."

"But what will I wear? What will I do? What will I

talk about?" Clutching her most recently examined ledger to her upraised knees, Violet frowned at her threadbare, well-loved quilt—and the very ordinary calico dress she had on beneath it. "Who am I to go to a party like Simon Blackhouse's party?"

"You are Violet Benson, a *wonderful* person," Adeline said. She took away the ledger, then seized the quilt to wrest it away as well. It billowed across the mattress. "You will wear your best dress—the one that brings out the stunning red in your hair. You will have a nice time. And you will talk about—"

Here, her friend hesitated. Violet feared she'd run out of steam. Heaven knew, *she* was stumped on this issue.

But then Adeline came through, just as she always did.

"You will talk about your search for Mrs. Larkin," her friend suggested brightly, "and maybe even enlist Mr. Blackhouse's help in your quest. How about that?"

"Well…I can scarcely resist an opportunity like that, now, can I?" Violet asked, feeling cautiously cheered. "It would be churlish of me to pass up any chance, however remote, to help Tobe find his mother," she told Adeline. "Besides, Cade did tell me that Mr. Blackhouse has buckets of money. Maybe he *can* help!"

"That's right. It's decided, then." Looking pleased, Adeline shooed Violet to the wardrobe to select her gown. "You'll be doing a good deed, as usual, *and* I'll bet you manage to do a little dancing, too. So let's get going!"

"*Judah?*" Cade repeated. "You're really here?"

His brother laughed. "You'd better believe it."

Their host, Blackhouse, laughed, too. "You didn't see that one coming, did you, Foster?" Jovially, he returned Cade's mescal. "Have your bottle. No, wait! I can do that one better." Blackhouse hastened to the sideboard, then rattled around inside it. "We'll have a toast to celebrate. Just as soon as I find—"

"Don't strain yourself with looking." Cade shifted his gaze briefly to Blackhouse before feeling his attention drawn inexorably back to his younger brother. He stared in wonder. "You've already wearied yourself with opening the door, Simon," Cade said abstractedly. "You'd better call Adams. Quick."

At that, Blackhouse grumbled. But he didn't mention Cade's lapse—he'd uncharacteristically called Blackhouse by his first name—and for that, Cade was grateful. He was also damn humbled.

How had Blackhouse known that seeing Judah was exactly what he needed? Not as a push to find Whittier, not as a threat of having his search usurped by his younger brother, but simply as a means of remembering… everything that meant anything to him.

He wished then, foolishly, that Violet was there, too.

In the sudden silence that fell next, Judah shook his head. He hauled Cade close for a hug—a hug that felt far too brief.

His brother felt thinner, taller… Hell. He had to be imagining those changes in him, Cade decided roughly, just the same way he was imagining the dark circles beneath Judah's eyes.

With a final hearty clap on the back, they ended their embrace. Judah gazed at Cade, doubtless in the same dumbfounded fashion that Cade himself gawked just then—as though he couldn't believe they were standing face-to-face again after so much time apart. Unwilling to let go completely, Cade put both hands on his brother's shoulders. He shook his head in wonderment.

"It's in here somewhere!" Blackhouse said jollily. "Hang on another minute, and we'll have a proper reunion toast."

Cade quirked his mouth. "I think I hear Adams laughing in the next train car. You'll never find anything by yourself."

"Aw, ease up, Cade." Judah grinned. "Simon was kind enough to bring me here, after all. I arrived on the train just today."

"But you're not well enough to travel," Cade protested instantly. Protectively, he looked downward. "Your leg is—"

"Almost healed," Judah insisted, "which is more than I can say for my pride. *That's* pretty well trampled, thanks to that rampaging stallion." He shook his head, undoubtedly remembering the horse that had gotten spooked, thrown him, then accidentally stomped his leg to pieces. "So…where's that drink, Simon?"

Judah pulled away abruptly, ending Cade's contact. He maneuvered, only a little awkwardly, to the sideboard just as Blackhouse emerged triumphantly with a whiskey bottle. Cade stood alone, wondering how it had come to pass that Judah was here at last. He hadn't known how much he'd needed him till now.

From nowhere, it occurred to Cade to wonder: Did Tobe have a brother? Or a sister? He couldn't remember if he'd ever asked the boy those questions. Although they'd spent a bit of time together, Cade had always kept himself at arm's length. He'd been afraid to hurt the little sharper by getting too close…then leaving him behind one day.

Maybe, Cade thought for the first time while watching Judah and Blackhouse salute each other with their whiskeys, he'd been wrong about Tobe. Maybe Violet had been right. Maybe the boy *did* need hope. Even if that damnable emotion had kicked Cade in the teeth a time or two, it might be different for a child.

Especially for a child whom Violet was intent on helping.

Decisively, Cade cleared his throat. "Simon—"

Again, his lapse in calling Blackhouse by his Christian name went unremarked upon. It was almost as though Blackhouse had expected Cade to soften eventually, all along.

"If you were going to find a missing woman," Cade pushed on, ignoring his own newfound pliancy, "where would you begin?"

Blackhouse blinked, whiskey in hand. "Have you mislaid one?"

"Not again!" Judah clucked in disapproval. "How many times have I told you? If you're going to juggle women, you have to have a system for keeping them straight in your mind."

Cade leveled his brother an inquiring look. "Oh, really?"

"Yes." Judah drained his whiskey, then held out his glass for more. He watched with relish as Blackhouse poured a refill. "You have to assign them code names or numbers, something like that. Otherwise you'll be—" Catching sight of Cade's frown and Blackhouse's inquisitive expression, his brother regrouped. He cleared his throat. "A missing woman, you said? Who is missing?"

For a moment, silence descended. Blackhouse caught Cade's eye. "It seems your brother isn't the innocent you described."

Cade couldn't believe it. But that was a problem for another day. "The missing woman is Mrs. Larkin," Cade said. "She's the mother of a friend of mine." Briefly, he described Tobe's predicament and his mother's disappearance. "If you were to track her, with all your resources, how would you begin?"

Blackhouse arched his brows, still nursing his first whiskey. "What makes you think I'd succeed? After all, I've been on the hunt for Whittier for years now with little success."

At his mention of that name, Judah went still. He shot Cade an anxious look. "You're not still looking for him, are you? Simon told me you'd quit. He told me you'd fallen for a titian-haired saint and were out of the manhunt business for good."

Titian-haired saint. That was one way to describe Violet.

Wielder of cruel kindnesses was another, more accurate way.

Cade wished he'd never swept her into that first dance they'd shared. Maybe then he wouldn't have learned to love her at all. Maybe then he wouldn't have learned to hope for more.

"I'm not still looking." Cade delivered that assurance brusquely. He'd always told himself he was on the hunt for Whittier because Judah wanted it—because Judah needed it. But the truth was…Cade had wanted and needed it enough for the two of them combined. There had been times Judah had tried to make him quit. Cade had refused to take them seriously.

"Good." Judah nodded. "That search was killing you."

Shocked by that, Cade stared at his brother. Belatedly, he remembered that this wasn't the first time Judah had said something like that. But it *was* the first time Cade listened.

In that spirit, Cade aimed a supplemental frown at Blackhouse. "That means I won't be taking you up on your latest offer, Simon. I've given up on Whittier." *And, by extension, on Violet, too.* Without Blackhouse's money, Cade would not be able to support her the way she deserved, anyway. "And I think you can find Mrs. Larkin," he added, returning to the matter at hand with a determined edge to his voice, "because unlike Percy Whittier, *she* is not trying deliberately *not* to be found."

Seeming content with that, Blackhouse nodded. "All right, then." He set aside his whiskey, then began pacing. He wheeled about to confront them both. "If I were searching for a runaway mother, I would begin by wiring the police, the hospitals and the mental institutions. I would hire a detective. I would—"

"I doubt she ran away, turned loony or got herself stuck in the clink," Judah grumbled. He poured himself more whiskey, evidently growing tired of waiting for Simon to offer another glass. "That's putting a grim spin on the situation, wouldn't you say? Maybe she's just been…misplaced, as Cade suggested."

Helpless not to remember their own mother's untimely passing, Cade frowned. "Mrs. Larkin might have gotten robbed or attacked. Even now she could be trying to get back to Tobe."

"'Robbed or attacked'?" Blackhouse repeated with a frown. "Nice. And you two think *I'm* the grim one?" He shook his head, then delivered Cade a more serious look. "If you're asking me to look into this, I will. All I need are the details."

"For that, I'd have to ask Violet. She knows all the facts about Mrs. Larkin." No one remarked on the fact that Cade had accidentally quit calling his lost love "Miss Benson." "Or I'd have to speak with Tobe. But he's staying with the Bensons right now, so that would mean confronting the reverend. Or Violet."

Caught, Cade hesitated. He never should have embroiled himself in that little sharper's troubles. From the moment he'd agreed to a game of craps, purposely lost his warm overcoat…

"Your lady friend is a *reverend's daughter*?" Judah boggled. "Damnation, Cade. That ought to be as easy as pie! You just pull out the charm and take whatever information you need from her."

Blackhouse saw the situation differently. "Miss Benson isn't your typical reverend's daughter. And if Foster's pie-eyed appearance—and the mescal he's murdered—are any indication, he's had a falling-out with her anyway. We need another course."

"No, we don't." Suddenly resolute, Cade straightened.

As a boy, he'd wished someone had stepped in to help him. He'd wished he hadn't had to shoulder the burdens and concerns of raising himself and Judah all alone. If he'd had a lost parent out there somewhere, if they could have been reunited….

Hell. He'd have wanted that more than anything. He still wanted the family he'd never had. How could he stand in the way of seeing Tobe brought together with his long-lost mama now?

He couldn't. Not if all he had to do was set aside his own heartache for a night and ask Violet for some information.

"If I get all the details about Mrs. Larkin," Cade asked Blackhouse, "will you do what you can to find her?"

Equably, his friend raised his whiskey. "I promise I will. If your faith in me and my money is justified, I might even succeed."

Blackhouse's lopsided grin gave Cade hope—one more morsel of that precious stuff than he'd entered the train car with. As a gambler, Cade knew that meant his odds were improving. From here, no self-respecting sporting man would have failed to push the limits. Not while there was still a chance of winning.

"Fine." Cade nodded. "Then I'm off to get more details."

"Wait." Blackhouse raised his hand, a frown marring his privileged, irksomely perfect face. "Am I dreaming?

Or are you actually planning on engaging in an act of selfless generosity?"

Judah shuddered. "That sounds suspiciously like charity work. I hate charity work—and charity workers, too." He made a face, undoubtedly prompted by bad memories. "Bunch of damn good-for-nothing nuisances. They should mind their own business."

"That's what I used to think," Cade told his brother. "Until I met one who wanted to be with me more than she wanted to change me." *It was true,* he realized as he said it. Violet had never honestly tried to reform him. She'd never pitied him, even after he'd shared so much with her. In fact, with her zest for sinful romps in his bed, Violet had mostly engaged in the opposite of reformation and pity. She'd *adored* him. Openly.

In return, Cade had made her leave him after the first mistake she'd made. His own hoary doubts—his fears that he could neither love nor be loved—had forced him to do so.

Those fears had been too strong to resist. After all, Cade realized, he'd spent years polishing them up. He'd worried over them like crooked dice in his pocket, turning them over until their sides were worn smooth and familiar. Then he'd rolled his fixed dice and spoiled his chances in the worst imaginable way.

It was almost as though it had been fated to happen. Cade hadn't even granted Violet the same easy tolerance that a dissolute bachelor and a travel-weary youth had managed to grant *him* tonight, when his need for friendship had overcome his need to be hardened and remote. When he'd needed them, Simon and Judah had been there for him. If he was lucky, Violet might be there for him again, too.

If not for his sake, then at least for Tobe's.

"Have fun at the party. I may be gone awhile." Cade hesitated, then gave Judah another heartfelt hug. "I'll make this up to you later, I promise. In the meantime, don't get too pie-eyed yourself." He nodded at his brother's third—fourth?—dose of whiskey. "If I can convince Violet to forgive me—" which at that moment he realized he'd have to do to enlist her help "—I'll want you sober enough to meet her—and remember it later."

Accepting his brother's careless nod, Cade left behind his mescal bottle, left the train car and left his damnable doubts in the dust. In their stead, he set out to face the only woman who'd ever made him want to become a better man—and to try to convince her that he was well on his way to doing so now.

Paradoxically, Violet had changed him by *not* trying to change him, Cade realized as he reached the road beyond Blackhouse's parked train car. Violet's openhanded acceptance, all on its own, had been enough to free him—to make him want to do more with his life. But now none of that mattered. All that mattered to Cade, as he loped off into the cold autumn night, was that he found Violet, begged her forgiveness and asked for the answers he needed: new answers, to new questions.

He had to do this. For his own sake. For Violet's sake.

Most of all…for Tobe's sake. Because if Cade could save that dirty-faced, fast-talking, craps-playing, itinerant shyster of a boy from a life spent wondering about his own ability to love and be loved…well, that's what he damn well planned to do. And no one had better try to stop him.

Chapter Thirteen

Cade's newfound courage lasted *almost* all the way to the Bensons' snug, cozy home on the other side of Morrow Creek. It lasted him past the train depot and the saloon, past the stable, past the Lorndorff Hotel and the jailhouse and the telegraph station and the homespun idyll of the central town square. It lasted as he strode through drifts of dried fallen scrub-oak leaves. It lasted as he clenched his hands at his sides to warm them—he really had to replace the overcoat he'd lost to Tobe—and it lasted as he pushed past gossiping townspeople with their friendly faces and even friendlier greetings. It lasted…

Hell. It lasted until the moment when the Bensons' modest house came into view down the street, with its lace-curtained windows aglow with lamplight and its chimney puffing wood smoke. Then his damnably fickle courage fled like the fair-weather friend it really was. When the chips were down, Cade's bravado deserted him in two seconds flat. Frankly, he resented that.

Grumbling a swearword, Cade quit walking. His

boots thumped on the hard-packed dirt street for a final time. There, shielded by darkness, he squinted at the Benson household and tried to imagine what it would feel like to be welcomed inside it.

His mind turned blank. Hellfire. Panicked and impatient, he tried again. Again he could not conceive of being forgiven.

It's too late, Violet had said. *I already am hurt.*

Feeling regretful and beleaguered, Cade frowned anew. What he needed was an approach, a maneuver, a fail-safe plan of the variety he'd managed to spin for half his lifetime now. But faced with a real problem—with a real need—Cade felt stymied.

Maybe he was no good at selflessness. Maybe among all his other faults, self-interest was seated as king of them all.

Or maybe he simply needed a new dose of courage. With his mescal forsaken, he'd have to look elsewhere. Casting about for a solution, Cade glanced to the church. That would have to do.

Gussied up, polished up and not entirely comfortable with either process, Violet stepped into her family's front parlor. The skirts of her second-best gown rustled softly. The gems in her borrowed earrings and necklace sparkled. The hammering of her heart was most assuredly, she thought, audible to everyone.

Her father sat reading in his armchair. Tobe squatted on the rug, frowning in concentration as he assembled a painted jigsaw puzzle that the McCabe family had given him. Between them, Papa and Tobe were the very picture of warm conviviality.

Loath to disturb them, Violet turned—and almost ran smack into poor Adeline, who'd been following close behind her. Her best friend, undoubtedly sensing what Violet had been thinking, firmly took Violet's shoulders and spun her to face her family once more. It wasn't for nothing that they'd been chums since girlhood. Adeline Wilson knew exactly what she needed.

"Look, everyone! Doesn't Violet look beautiful?"

Reverend Benson glanced up. He smiled. "Very lovely!"

Behind his assurance lay several unasked questions. Violet could glimpse them in his drawn-together brows and pensive look. But she was grateful, just then, that Papa didn't push her.

"Tobe?" Adeline prompted. "Did you see Violet?"

The boy nodded. He inserted another puzzle piece.

"Doesn't she look nice? She's going to a party tonight."

A shrug. "Git goin', already. I ain't gonna applaud you for leavin', if that's what you're waitin' for. So just go on. Git."

"Tobe." Feeling an enormous tug of affection for him, Violet plunked down on the rug. Heedless of the need to protect her fancy dress, she crawled close to him. "I'm coming back, you know. If that's what you're worried about, you don't have to."

"I ain't worried." His little face screwed up tight. "I done survived bein' deserted once already. I can do it again." Tobe refused to look at her. But he *did* drag something forward from around his neck—something grimy, hung on a tied length of twine. "See? I got me the trophy to prove it an' everythin'."

Violet squinted. "The 'trophy'? What's that?"

Confused, she caught hold of it. It appeared to be a rectangular scrap of paper, printed with dates and destinations, punched with a hole for the twine to fit through. It was almost too discolored to make out its original function. Almost.

"Where did you get this? I've never seen it before."

"Sure you have." Tobe tucked it beneath his shirt again. "It's on me every single day." He shook his head as though she was being silly. Peevishly, he went back to his puzzle. "I don't never take it off. Well, 'cept for sometimes, for them baths you make me have, even though I don't want no part of *them*—"

"Tobe, that's a train ticket," Violet said.

"So?" His one raised eyebrow formed a perfect pint-size imitation of Cade's oft-cynical demeanor. "You want one? Git it yourself, why don't you? Maybe after your blasted party."

Aware of her father's and Adeline's gazes fixed on her, Violet inhaled. Sometimes she had to fight to remember that, despite having survived partly on his own, Tobe was only a little boy. He was neither mature nor capable of true cynicism.

What he was, she remembered, was vulnerable and alone.

"Can I please see that ticket again?" Violet asked.

Tobe raised his skinny shoulders in a shrug. "I reckon."

With his permission, Violet shakily brought her fingers to the loop of twine around his neck. Carefully, she pulled the train ticket forward. She read the issuing date. The price paid. The departure and destination stations. This could only be...

"I don't know why you're so int'rested," Tobe complained. "That ticket didn't help me none, not when I was in the clutch. Not like it was s'pposed to. Not like my mama promised."

"Your *mother* gave this to you?"

Tobe nodded. "In case I got lost or missed the train."

Violet gawked. "But you *did* miss the train!"

"No, I didn't," Tobe insisted with the inimitable indignation of a misunderstood child. "My *mama* did. Not me. I was right there, at the train, and she wasn't. I looked."

Openmouthed, Violet gawked at him. Tobe must have gotten confused about which train to board, she realized. On a crowded platform during a hasty stop, it was easy to get separated and confused. Especially for a woman and her son traveling alone.

"Did you ask the stationmaster to help you?"

Another boyish shrug. "He tole me the train I needed was gone already. He tole me he'd have to call the sheriff about it." Tobe frowned. "I didn't want him to turn me in to some mean ole' lawman. I'd heard some older boys on the train talkin' about what *that* meant. That meant I wouldn't never see my mama again, if the law got me and sent me away someplace. So I skedaddled away when nobody was lookin'."

In dawning enlightenment, Violet stared down at her

hands. She held the key to locating Mrs. Larkin. It had been so close, all this time. All she'd needed were the right questions to ask.

"Why didn't you ever show this to me before, Tobe?"

The boy gave her an impatient look. "Can I do my puzzle?"

"In a minute. Please, Tobe. Why didn't you show me this?"

Now he only seemed perplexed. "T'weren't no big secret or nothin'," Tobe said blithely. "I figured you'd rifled through my stuff when I was havin' that very first bath on chicken-dinner night. That's what people do, you know, if you don't keep watch over your kit—they pilfer things. When you didn't pinch that ole' trophy of mine, I reckoned it didn't mean nothin' to nobody."

Violet could scarcely believe it. "*This,*" she said, "is everything we need to reunite you with your mother, Tobe."

He scoffed. "No, it ain't. You're pullin' my leg." He set another puzzle piece in place. "My mama was wrong 'bout what that dumb ole' train ticket could do for us. I know that."

There in the parlor, Violet held her breath. Beside her, Adeline stood stock-still, doubtless sensing the drama of the moment. Her father clutched his copy of the *Pioneer Press* newspaper, gazing from Tobe to Violet with evident solemnity.

"Tobe," the reverend said, "that ticket can take you home."

In the flickering lantern light, the boy glanced up.

His gaze swerved to Violet's face, obviously seeking confirmation.

She gave a brief nod. Tobe swallowed hard. His chin wobbled. Wearing an impatient frown, he grimaced peculiarly.

He was trying not to cry, Violet realized. *He was trying to remain strong—to remain fierce, just as he'd done for so long.*

"You ain't fibbin'?" Tobe asked in a choked voice.

Silently, Violet shook her head. So did her father.

"I can really go home?" Tobe asked. "To my mama?"

"Yes," Violet said. "Just as fast as we can get you there."

Suspiciously, Tobe examined her face. He frowned once more.

"I'd like that," he said simply, then he began to sob.

Soon the whole room was ablubber with tears. Violet bawled with happiness and relief, Adeline cried with sentimentality and sympathy, and Reverend Benson... well, he was the worst of all.

"I don't know what I was thinking, reading that awful heartrending story just now," her father complained as he dabbed at his red-rimmed, tear-filled eyes. "It's plainly affected me."

"Papa, that was just the boring newspaper," Violet said.

"Tsk-tsk, daughter. You go on to your party now. I'm going to help Tobe with this puzzle, then look up train schedules."

Still concerned, Violet glanced at the boy. She'd been hugging him close until quite recently, but Tobe had finally wiggled successfully from her grasp and gone back—contentedly—to his waiting puzzle. He truly was an irrepressible, rascally boy.

"Will you be all right if I go, Tobe?" she asked.

"*Pshaw.* Go on. I'll be right as rain now!" he said in an immodest tone. "Nothin' could get me down now that I done solved the mystery of how to git myself back home to my mama again."

"*You* solved—" On the verge of correcting him, Violet stopped. Instead, she smiled. "Is that what you'll tell your mother? That you solved the problem all by yourself?"

Tobe gave her a mischievous grin. "Nah. My mama ain't half so credulous as you, Miss Benson. She won't never believe me. I'll tell her the truth—that a kindly spinster helped me out."

Flabbergasted, Violet stared at him. Then she laughed.

She would have expected no less from such a unique boy.

"All right, Tobe." After giving him another hug and a quick tousle to his hair, Violet stood. "I guess I'm off, then!"

Stepping into the humble clapboard church that stood closely adjacent to the Benson household, Cade held his breath.

He didn't make a practice of seeking divine guidance. Undoubtedly, a repeat sinner like him would have been denied it. And although he'd come here not long ago to donate his gambling winnings to the church collection plate as a means of seeing Violet again, Cade did not feel comfortable inside the church.

Ostensibly, it was peaceful. Even he could appreciate that. From the bracketed wall sconces, lamplight filtered over the pews. On the air, the aromas of old hymnals and lemony furniture polish lingered faintly. Underfoot, the floorboards creaked as Cade stepped forward. Belatedly, he snatched off his hat. Holding it in hand, he made his way to the rearmost pew. A short prayer couldn't possibly hurt. If the Almighty took pity on him…

Well, if the Lord took pity on him, Cade would be equipped to help Tobe *and* himself—and maybe Violet, too, by dint of loving her. He would have to try very hard to make things up to her.

Guardedly, Cade stepped into the row of pews. He held his hat over his heart. He bowed his head, preparing to begin.

Tarnation. He didn't remember how to pray.

Surely he'd done this as a boy. Urgently, he tried again.

"Well, if this don't beat all," a man said from nearby.

Cade recognized that voice—that laconic drawl and that elusive tone. Instantly alert, Cade wheeled around.

A tall, well-dressed, partly gray-haired man stood inside the church's entryway, studying him with what appeared to be cynical detachment. It shone from his eyes like the glimmer of fool's gold, obscuring his true emotions in a fashion that Cade recognized well. He'd used that tactic himself a time or two. Like that worthless rock's shine, the man's expression was meant to mislead. Doubtless it usually succeeded—especially when aimed at the gullible. But Cade didn't count himself among them.

"Whittier."

A nod. "That's what they call me."

Muddled by the man's appearance in church, Cade stared. He lifted his weapon a mite higher, realizing just then that he'd automatically drawn it. His hat, which he'd been holding, now lay sideways, abandoned on the pew where he'd dropped it.

"I should have known you'd sneak up on a man," Cade said.

"That's rich, coming from the boy who's been tracking me all this time. I can barely turn around without seeing your face." Whittier strode farther inside. His boot heels clunked against the pristine floorboards. "You sneaked in here just like I did the first time," he observed with a sidelong glance, "as if you expected the whole place to go up in flames."

"With you in it? I still do." To Cade, it felt as though Whittier's presence sullied the church. A man like him didn't belong there. Not after everything he'd done. Not when he was probably packing firepower—never mind the pistol that Cade had drawn. He'd never killed anyone with it. "Show me your hands."

A head shake. "That's not necessary. I'm not armed."

Cade aimed his chin at Whittier's hip. "I can see your gun belt from here." He felt curiously disappointed as he added, "Your bluffs aren't what they used to be, old man."

A frown. "I mean I would never draw on you."

Well, there was that. *Why* hadn't Whittier drawn on

him? Cade wondered suddenly. By all accounts, he was a dangerous, amoral professional gambler—one who backed down from no one.

Certainly he didn't voluntarily get himself cornered. Yet there he was, in the church, making his presence known to Cade. Whittier could just as easily have ambushed Cade where he stood.

Befuddled, Cade kept his pistol aimed at his target.

Evidently unconcerned to find himself at gunpoint, Whittier raised his palms. Amiably, he nodded at Cade's elaborate watch chain. "Still carrying the Jürgensen, I see."

Tensely, Cade nodded. He'd be damned if Whittier didn't seem oddly pleased to glimpse his former timepiece. "If I recall correctly, you didn't seem motivated to keep from losing it."

An easy shrug. "I wanted you to have it."

"You've got things backward," Cade told him. "I took it."

Even as he said it, though, Blackhouse's onetime musings returned to him. *Do you think Whittier lost on purpose? Maybe he wanted you to have that Jürgensen. Just because you didn't know who he was doesn't mean he didn't know who you were even then.*

"You've changed since then." Whittier gave Cade a measured look. He seemed peculiarly...nostalgic? "You look...meaner."

Cade didn't want to discuss his own progression from a green youth to a hardened man. If he was right, Percy Whittier was partly responsible for those changes in him.

Trying to cut to the heart of the matter, Cade squinted

at Whittier. It felt impossible to match the man before him with the man in his recollections…or with the man in the faded tintype he always carried. It had been years since he'd seen Whittier this close.

It had been many more years since he'd seen.…

Cade gestured with his pistol. "Come closer."

Obligingly, Whittier did. Cade still wasn't satisfied.

"Where did you get that Jürgensen?" he asked.

He wished he'd asked that question years ago, when he'd first won it. But it hadn't been until later that Cade had spied the message engraved on the back of the time-piece—the message that had made him connect Percy Whittier with…everything.

Whittier lowered his arms. "It was a gift from my wife."

"The truth." Cade cocked his pistol. "Please."

That courteous touch was Violet's influence, Cade reckoned. He couldn't help feeling a little bit proud of himself for that.

As if sensing her angelic inspiration even now, Whittier glanced around. "Have you seen a little redheaded gal around here anyplace? She and I had a talk the other day. She told me—"

He had to mean Violet. "Answer the question."

Tight-lipped, Whittier glanced to the door. Then he relented. "My wife, May, gave me that watch on our wedding day."

Cade's hand wavered. "My mother's name was May."

It was her name that had been engraved on that watch, along with his father's name and the year of their marriage. For that reason alone, Cade had considered himself lucky to have come across it, even by capricious gambling—even by winning it from a man whom he hadn't recognized when sitting down with him. At that point in his life, Cade had only been trying to find his way in his new world of cardsharps and roulette-wheel spinners.

Then, he hadn't been as good—or as lucky—as he was now.

Then, he hadn't deserved to win that watch. But he still had. Those paradoxical facts had niggled at Cade for years.

Whittier gazed at him, not speaking. But Cade could still hear his last words reverberating in his head, all the same.

My wife, May, gave me that watch on our wedding day.

At the recollection, Cade felt dizzy. His heart hammered. He willed it to slow down, but it didn't work. He wondered…

No. He'd come here looking for courage, not a damn miracle.

"That little redhead." Whittier rambled on. "She seemed to think it was never too late to say you were sorry. I reckon—"

"But my mother, May *Foster*, never married Percy Whittier." Regaining his nerve, Cade clenched his pistol more tightly. His shoulders felt as hard as granite. His feet felt rooted to the floor. "So here's what I think. I think you met my father, and you stole that watch from him, and then when I won it from you—"

"Cade—"

"Don't call me that." His father would have called him that. This could not be his father. Not after all this time. Not like this. The only thing that had gotten Cade through the past years was believing his father was dead—believing he'd left his family not by choice, but by a cruel quirk of fate. Knowing this could not be happening, not like this, Cade closed his eyes.

Unfortunately, that paltry act was not enough to shut out Whittier. He just kept on talking, talking as if he'd kept the words bottled up for years and couldn't hold them in now.

"You know Whittier isn't my real name," he said in an uneasy, falsely jocular tone. "You've known that all along. *You* of all people—you weren't fooled by my name or my running away—"

At that, Cade snapped open his eyes. "You're wrong about that. Your running was too real to ignore. For all of us."

Whittier swallowed. His gaze looked imploring. "Is Judah—"

"Stop." *This couldn't be happening.* Cade strode sideways. His grasp on his pistol slackened. He glanced at it with sudden dismay, then rammed it into its holster. "You're dead." He shot an angry glance at Whittier. "I mean you're not him. *He's* dead."

"If you mean Ben Foster…then I guess you're right."

At the sound of his father's name, Cade quit moving.

"Ben Foster might as well be dead," Whittier went on, "for all the good he did for his family. His wife. His two boys—"

"You're lying," Cade insisted. He mustered up a

mighty scowl, a fearsome expression designed to show the world that *he* should be feared. He balled his fists, refusing to look squarely at Whittier. "You're standing in church and you're lying to an armed man. You really are crazy."

"You put away your weapon," Whittier pointed out. "And this little church happens to be the only reason I didn't skedaddle already, like I usually do—or at least that redheaded girl I met in here is. She talked to me, and she made me see some things, and she convinced me to stay in town awhile."

Violet. Again. At the irony of that, Cade shook his head. He didn't want to believe it had been Violet, not him, who'd stumbled upon Whittier. Violet who'd talked to him. Violet who'd persuaded him to stay in Morrow Creek. But she'd told him so herself. *I saw Percy Whittier today. I met him. I talked to him.*

"If not for her," Whittier went on, "I'd have pulled foot for the next town already. I'd have kept right on running, just like I have been. But I wouldn't have found any peace in it."

"You don't deserve any peace."

"That may be true." Whittier gave him a level look. "But you do. Judah does. Once I realized that, I couldn't leave."

Hell. Whittier talked like his father would have. He looked a little like his father would have—at least like Ben Foster would have looked, years later. But after all this time, Cade couldn't risk believing this *was* his father. Feeling newly shaky, he searched the ceiling, looking for courage. For so long, he'd wanted answers. But now that they were imminent...

Cade wasn't sure about any of them. This wasn't the conversation he'd imagined. This wasn't the man he'd imagined. This wasn't the reunion he'd longed for, alone in the unfamiliar households where he and Judah had been fostered, put to work, ignored in their idle time, then made to leave when the harvesting season was through or the factory work was done.

"There's nothing you can say," Cade told Whittier in a harsh tone, "that will explain away everything that's happened. Maybe, when I was still a boy, if my father had come back then—"

"I couldn't come back. I left for *you!* I left to protect you and Judah and your mother—" Whittier broke off, his careworn face full of regret. "I didn't hear she'd taken ill until it was too late. By then, you and your brother were gone, on your own."

"I don't believe you." Mulishly, Cade shook his head. His feelings veered, wildly, from belief to fear to skepticism. "Maybe, before you stole that watch from my father, you heard him talk about us. Maybe *he* missed us." That had always been Cade's secret hope. "Maybe *he* wanted to come back and couldn't."

Whittier only gazed at him. "You were stubborn like this as a little boy, too. You didn't believe the fire was hot till you touched it. It didn't matter how often we warned you away—"

Cade wished someone had warned him away from *this.* "Stop."

"I can't. Not now." Whittier shook his head. "That's

what that little church gal told me, and I believe her."
Raggedly, he inhaled. Loudly, he blurted, "I'm sorry,
Cade. I'm so sorry for everything I put you through! I
didn't mean for any of it to happen. I made a wager and
I lost—I lost so much more than I knew I would. If you
knew the kind of people I was indebted to—"

"*I know them.*" Seemingly from nowhere, Simon
Blackhouse appeared. Wearing a troubled, deeply determined look, he strode nearer. He glanced at a dumbfounded Cade. "Hell, I'm *related* to them, and I wish I
wasn't. He's right, Cade—they're bad people."

"*Simon?*" He had to be imagining things, Cade realized.

Simon Blackhouse—the Simon Blackhouse he knew—
was neither this serious nor this stealthy. The Simon
Blackhouse that Cade knew was an irresponsible layabout with nothing on his mind beyond the next willing
woman or the next pleasurable game.

But *this* Simon Blackhouse…this Simon Blackhouse
proved his transformation by continuing in stark, plain-
speaking terms.

"If you hadn't gone on the run, you would have been
killed," Blackhouse told Whittier. "They meant their
threats."

Thoroughly confounded, Cade stared. Again, "Simon?"

"*My uncle* meant those threats," Blackhouse continued relentlessly. "He meant to have you—and probably
your family—killed if you didn't repay that rigged wager
of his. For years, that's what my family has specialized
in—extortion, cheating, legalized stealing…all in the
name of business or 'pleasure' or whatever caught their

fancy. I'm the first to break the mold," he said, "and believe me, the Blackhouses don't like it much."

So *that* was why Simon was estranged from his family, Cade realized. The situation was much more dire than he'd thought—much more dire than the idle society gossip had implied.

"But me, being me... Well, frankly, I don't care what they think about what I do." Here, Blackhouse offered a vivid grin. "I forgive your debt, Mr. Foster—" upon saying that name, he aimed a decidedly confirming glance at Cade "—which is something I have all rights to do. My uncle's death passed his authority to me. What's more, I have the money you lost in that rigged wager to repay you with, with interest, at my private train car. If you'd like to come with me, I'll give it to you."

Now Whittier *and* Cade both gawked in astonishment.

"I can't trust you!" Whittier said. "This must be a trick."

"You can trust him," Cade said, astonished to hear himself admit it aloud. "*I* trust him. It's not a trick. It's...incredible, but it's not a trick. I'd stake my whole bankroll on it."

"Thank you, friend." Gratefully, Blackhouse inclined his head toward Cade. "That, all on its own, makes sponsoring your search worthwhile." He turned to Whittier. "It *isn't* a trick," he emphasized, "but I knew you might think so if you heard I was looking for you with the stated purpose of giving you money."

Whittier gave a cynical snort. "Sounds like a trap

to me. I haven't survived all these years by keeping up with long odds."

"All I want in return," Blackhouse said, "is for you to accept the money, the settled wager and my humble apologies. No one will bother you again. You won't have to run anymore."

"I see." Still seeming rather dazed, Whittier gave him a chary look. "If I do all that... What do you get out of it?"

Cade knew the answer to that one. "He gets back his honor. Or at least a little piece of it." Still stunned, Cade shook his head at his friend. "Because it really *was* a matter of honor to you, wasn't it? Why didn't you tell me, you bastard?"

Blackhouse shrugged. "I thought your reason for conducting your search was more compelling than mine. Finding your father—"

"He's *not* my father," Cade interrupted willfully. "He—"

"—was more important than correcting another heinous familial wrongdoing, even if I *have* been traveling the country doing exactly that for years now. I have a long way to go, too. Your father's was one of the simplest cases to resolve."

"He's *not* my father!" Cade insisted. "He can't be."

Simon gave him a sorrowful look. Behind them, the church's door slammed shut. Steady, measured footsteps could be heard.

"Are you sure about that, Cade?" Judah asked. Painstakingly, he made his way to their position, his gaze fixed on Whittier all the while. "Are you sure he's not?

Haven't you seen what he's been doing with that match safe in his hand?"

Taken aback, Cade looked. Whittier froze in place, his attention fixed, too, on the silver match holder in his hand.

It rested now, its glimmer temporarily dimmed, between his agile fingers. But until seconds ago, Cade realized with a perception he'd lacked until just that moment, Whittier had been tumbling that match safe between his fingers like a magician with a conjuring trick, juggling it with scarcely any effort at all.

"That's what Papa used to do whenever he was worried," Judah said. "Don't you remember, Cade? He taught us how to do that trick, too. You were especially good at it, I recall."

Mutely, Cade shook his head. He was afraid to believe…

Whittier tossed him the match safe. Without thinking, Cade caught it. He juggled it as he did so—in the same showy way—to prevent it from falling to the floorboards.

"Well done," Blackhouse observed. "Like father, like son."

Like father, like son. Dumbstruck, Cade stared at Whittier.

But Judah only smiled. "I *knew* we'd find you!" His injured leg scarcely slowed him as he went to Whittier with a smile on his face. Gruffly, he embraced him. "Simon said he'd almost tracked you down. I wanted to be here when he did."

Near them, Blackhouse nodded. He glanced at Cade.

"How much more proof do you need?" he asked. "Just look at your hands."

Cade did. He was, he saw instantly, still nervously juggling that match safe—exactly the same way his father had just done.

A huge wellspring of emotion surged inside him. Buffeted by it, Cade watched silently as Judah and Whittier—*Foster*—parted.

They both looked at Cade. He cleared his throat. "Papa?"

The smile on his father's face erased all doubt. "I'm sorry, Cade. It wasn't right, what I did. I need you to know—"

For once, Cade didn't need answers. "It's *really* you?"

His father nodded—or at least Cade thought he nodded. It was hard to tell, because his vision went blurry, his eyes stung…and he could as soon have flown as he could have spoken past the lump of emotion stuck in his throat. He tried to move—

But his father moved faster. With urgent strides, he crossed the short distance separating them. He gazed at Cade, who was trying desperately not to bawl, then hugged him.

He felt different from the man Cade remembered. He felt leaner and tougher and older, but he still felt…right.

A heartbeat later they separated, curtly and awkwardly. There were more apologies, more promises—and more vexing, perceptive grins from the likes of Blackhouse and Judah.

Feeling overcome, Cade scowled at them. He swiped

at his eyes, then demanded, "What are you two doing here anyway?"

Blackhouse shrugged. "You didn't think we'd let you go on this adventure all alone, did you?" he queried with his usual jauntiness. "We followed you from the train car, of course."

"That's right," Judah agreed with a nod. For the first time, Cade noticed he was tottering—probably on account of the whiskey he'd drunk. "I've just found you again. I wasn't going to let you sneak away so soon after our reunion. I'm a little slow these days, on account of my leg—" he gave that appendage an impressive frown "—but I'm pretty hard to stop, all the same."

"We thought we'd be witnessing your groveling to Miss Benson," Blackhouse admitted, "but as a secondary feature—"

"This is mighty fine, too," Judah alleged. He slung his arm around Whittier's shoulders with genial—and possibly drunken—aplomb. "Although I *was* keen to meet the minister's daughter."

Blackhouse clucked with dismay. "Yes, that's too bad."

Violet. Suddenly reminded of her, Cade went still.

Nothing had gone the way he'd planned this night. But everything had turned out providentially, all the same. Could it be, he wondered, that his good luck was back for good?

He would have been a poor gambler not to think so.

Filled with new resolve, Cade raised his hand. He turned to Whittier—to, remarkably, his *father.* "I have more questions for you. There are so many things I want to know. But first—"

"First he has to settle accounts with a girl," Blackhouse said, a knowing grin on his puckish face. "With a special girl."

"With a damn go-gooder of a reverend's daughter," Judah specified, plainly having learned a few more pertinent details from Simon—and then having editorialized them further, "with lovely red hair, an excess of kindness and—near as I can tell—woefully poor eyesight, if she's smitten with my big lummox of a brother."

Cade let that insult slide. He felt too relieved just then—too amazed and grateful and hopeful—to quarrel with Judah.

"A redhead?" Whittier raised a brow. "Is she skinny? Fearless? Fond of calico and cockeyed pep talks?"

The trio of Cade, Blackhouse and Judah nodded.

"I think I know her," Whittier mused. A nod. "Nice girl."

Cade only shook his head. "I let her get away from me once. I couldn't forgive myself if I didn't try to get her back."

With that, his friend, his brother and his long-lost father all agreed to return to Blackhouse's train car. "After all," Simon eagerly pointed out, "I'm having a party tonight!"

Watching them make plans, Cade knew it would take a while to resolve everything. It wouldn't be easy to come to terms with the Fosters' long separation and decide where to go from there.

For the first time, though, Cade felt the stirrings of belief that they could do it. For now, that was enough.

Determinedly, Cade tossed back his father's silver match safe, then straightened his shoulders. "I'll be next door," he announced with twice the bravado he felt, "winning back Violet, finding the means to locating Tobe's mother, dazzling Reverend Benson with my wholesome good intentions and—now that I won't be carousing through town—possibly saving the whole of Morrow Creek from descending into debauchery."

Blackhouse raised his eyebrows. "That's a mighty tall order you've set for yourself."

"I know," Cade replied with a grin. "But I feel up to it."

At least he *did* feel up to it—until he arrived at the Benson household and learned, too late, that Violet had left for the rest of her life as the belle of the ball…without him.

Chapter Fourteen

It was an altogether different experience, Violet realized as she wandered through the crowded, elaborately decorated rooms of Mr. Blackhouse's luxurious private train car, listening to the music provided by a small group of musicians and carrying a fluted glass filled with an assuredly alcoholic beverage, to attend a party as a woman of interest, rather than a person who hung decorations and cheered up all the wallflowers.

Where once she'd spent her energies volunteering, fetching refreshments for elderly friends or chatting with other plain girls on the fringes of events, now Violet found herself smack in the middle of things. Handsome men flirted outrageously with her. Popular ladies pursued her with invitations to their own upcoming soirées. Even the waiters—and the kindly gentleman valet, Adams, who'd admitted her to the private gala—seemed to treat Violet with a mixture of burgeoning respect and interest.

Feeling overwhelmed by the newness of it all, Violet maneuvered to the train car's window. Through it, she saw that the town she knew and loved—and had been born in—might as well have vanished for good. From her vantage point, only the barest hints of Morrow Creek's existence remained. Some lantern light could be seen, faintly, coming from establishments like the Lorndorff Hotel and Jack Murphy's saloon—and the nearby train depot, of course. Otherwise, all the houses looked dark. From inside the warm, festive, brightly lit train car, the entire town could have disappeared with a snap of her fingers.

If it had, Violet never would have known it—and just at that moment, she realized, she'd already lost enough. Her first real love. Her pure-hearted motivation for doing good works. A part of her innocence. She didn't want to lose Morrow Creek, too.

Why had she come here, anyway? She no longer needed Mr. Blackhouse—or his fortune—to help her track down Tobe's mother. She no longer needed the validation of other men's interest to make her feel beautiful. All she needed, truly, was Cade. And he was as lost to her, just then, as the lights of her friends' and neighbors' houses were. They stood nearby, it was true; but it felt in the evening darkness as though they were gone forever.

Then Violet remembered something—something Cade had once said to her: *the real tragedy in life isn't failing to believe that hope exists, Violet. It's convincing yourself that you don't want any hope, even when it's right in front of you.*

Was hope right in front of her? What if Cade was here—what if her second chance was *here*—and she was overlooking it?

She was no gambler, Violet assured herself. But maybe it was time she took one more chance with her life. After all, it was possible that Cade *was* at his benefactor's party. With a little looking—and a little luck—maybe she could find him.

Determinedly, Violet gulped down her drink. She set down her glass. She straightened her shoulders, then faced the animated crowd of partygoers again. They were a mix of visiting strangers, professional gamblers and their associates, and townspeople who either knew Simon Blackhouse or wanted to.

None of those smiling men was Cade.

But if he was here, Violet knew she could find him.

She began in the parlor car, weaving through laughing women and groups of cigar-smoking men. No Cade. She progressed to the library car, where a variety of games of chance were taking place. Cade was not among the sporting men there, either. She sneaked into the rearmost quarters, where the staff was bustling with gala preparations. Cade was not there, unsurprisingly, but the valet, Adams, was. He rebuffed her with cordial firmness.

"I'm sorry, Miss Benson, but you shouldn't be back here."

"I know, Adams. But I'm searching for someone."

"Mr. Foster, perhaps?" His respectful face betrayed no sign of where he'd gained the knowledge that Violet knew Cade. "Have you tried the central car, miss? That's where the musicians are. It's the liveliest by far. If Mr. Foster has returned—"

"He was here and now he's *gone*? Where did he go?"

"—that's undoubtedly where he'll be." A bow. "Good luck."

"But where did he go?" Violet persisted. "I must know."

"I'm afraid I'm not at liberty to disclose that." Adams offered a regretful expression. "I'm terribly sorry."

Frustrated, Violet considered pressing him for more. At the same moment, Adams crossed his arms. He offered a slight frown. He was, it occurred to her, quite formidable when he had to be. Why on earth did Mr. Blackhouse need such an intimidating valet?

"Thank you, Mr. Adams," she said. "I'll try elsewhere."

Feeling increasingly dismayed, Violet hurried back to the central train car. Strains of rollicking music reached her, carried on the same currents of air that held the fragrances of ladies' perfumes, exotic incenses and cigar smoke. The party had grown even more crowded during her short absence. Now she could scarcely see past all the packed-together men and women.

Where in the world was Cade? Had he left town altogether?

Just as she conceived that awful notion, someone touched her shoulder. "There you are!" a man said from behind her, in a firm, self-assured voice. "You're missing our dance!"

She'd heard those words before, from Cade. But he couldn't be here. She'd have seen him. This was an unkind joke. It was…

It was…*wonderful*, Violet realized as she turned. It was wonderful because Cade stood there, close enough to touch, looking handsome and manly and exactly as dapper as he had on the night they'd met—the first time she'd heard those words.

He also appeared, she noticed with a second distressed glance, a little beleaguered…and a little apprehensive. Did he truly believe that she might refuse his invitation to dance?

There you are! You're missing our dance!

Well, if he did believe that, Violet had the perfect solution to offer. Stepping into his outstretched arms, she gave him her sauciest smile. "Oh no I'm not!" she said, just as she had on the very same night. "I'd never miss a dance!"

Like magic, Cade whirled her into the dance. Never mind that the train car was jam-packed with revelers. Never mind that they risked stomped-on toes and jostled shoulders. With the same command that he'd displayed on that oft-remembered night, Cade drew Violet into the crush of the celebration…and then made her feel that they were alone in the midst of all the frivolity.

"I was afraid," Cade said, "that you'd say no."

"To you?" She could scarcely believe he was here. "Never."

"You appeared engrossed in something. I saw you rushing from car to car, but I couldn't catch up. If not for Adams—"

"Adams?" Maybe that rascally valet *did* know much more than he let on.

"—slowing you down and then sending you back here, we might not have crossed paths all night." Cade twirled her. His hand felt warm against hers; his hold on her waist felt perfect. "Do you need help finding something? You seemed to be searching—"

"I *was* searching. I was searching for you."

He didn't seem to know what she meant. "I was trying to find *you*," Violet said. Smiling with relief and hopefulness, she explained, "You've been searching, yourself, for so long now. I thought it was about time that someone came looking for *you*."

At that, Cade appeared humbled. "I won't be searching anymore. Tonight I found what I was looking for." He gave her a tender smile. "It turns out it was right here, all along."

"You found Whittier?" Excitedly, she grabbed his arm. "See? He *was* in Morrow Creek! I knew it. I told you I'd seen him."

"Yes. I did find Whittier," Cade confirmed. "I found even more than that, too. I found my father, and my brother—"

"You *have* been busy! No wonder Mr. Adams couldn't explain."

"—and I found some of the answers I needed. But that's not what I meant. What I meant…" Here, Cade pulled Violet to the side. Away from the frolicking dancers, he brought his hand to her face. He gazed at her, exactly as though she were precious. "What I meant was that I was looking for *you*. I needed *you*, all along. But because I was foolish and cruel and too blind to see the truth—"

"No!" Violet hurried to stop him. "It wasn't you. It was me. I was so unkind, Cade. When I suggested that I was helping you as one of my charity projects… I never meant that! I was only afraid. I was afraid to love you—afraid to believe that you could love me! Because who am I? Only plain Violet Benson—"

Just as she'd hoped, Cade kissed her. Hard and fast.

"Plain Violet Benson," she tried again, breathlessly.

Another kiss. This time, Cade hauled her against him, too. He'd told her so many times not to refer to herself that way.

With her heart hammering, Violet managed to stammer, "P-plain Violet Benson, who's never known a courtship that lasted and who's never—" She broke off, casting Cade a mischievous glance. "What's wrong? Aren't you going to kiss me this time?"

Cade's answering smile beguiled her. "Vixen. You were hoodwinking me all along. I'm fairly certain that *I*, as the professional sporting man here, should be taking that role."

"Oh, I like the role you're playing just fine." Feeling happy and effervescent, Violet grinned. She *knew* she'd manage to take advantage of Cade's unusual method of "chastising" her with kisses eventually. "Whereas when it comes to *me*, plain Violet Benson—" She stopped. Suggestively, she arched her brows.

"When it comes to you," Cade growled obligingly, *not* kissing her yet, "I can't get enough. Before I met you, I was lost. After I met you, I thought all I wanted was a dose of good luck—a bit of good fortune to see me through my lonesome days and the games of chance that filled them. But now—" Seeming downright overcome, Cade broke off. He kissed her again. "Now I know that what you gave me, Violet, was more than good luck. What you gave me was love. Like a fool, I almost threw it away—"

"Not while I'm here to have a say in it!"

"—but I came to my senses just in time. Or at least I hope it was just in time." With a concerned glance at the revelers surrounding them, Cade frowned. "I know you could have your pick of men here. I know that I'm not nearly good enough. I have a long way to go before I settle down, quit wagering and stop feeling a need to indecently ravish you any chance I get—"

"And the trouble with ravishment is…what exactly?"

"I know you deserve an upright husband," Cade said, "a *good* man to call your own, a protector and a conqueror and a hero—"

"Oh, Cade." Violet sighed. Adoringly, she stroked his jaw. "Don't you know? You already *are* all those things to me."

"But I love you, Violet," he forged on, sounding raspy and determined and fierce. "I think I've loved you from the start, from the moment when I pulled you into that dance. You looked at me with that impish grin of yours, and you took my hand as if we were meant to be one, and you trotted onto the dance floor with me without the least hesitation. I was so grateful for that. I was so grateful for *you*. I couldn't take my eyes off you."

Violet knew she must be blushing. Raptly, she gazed into her beloved gambler's face. While looking at him, it was easy to ignore all the hullabaloo and revelry going on around them.

"That's because I must have loved *you* from the start," she insisted. "You spun me into that dance and straight into another way of being. Without you, I would have contented myself with giving and volunteering and working. Without you, I would have had friends, and my family, and maybe even a husband someday." Here, Violet clutched his hand, needing him to know everything. "But I wouldn't have known how it felt to be carried away—to be made to feel special and lovely and beautiful—"

"You *are* beautiful," Cade swore. "You've never been anything less to me. All I had to do was open my eyes."

"—and I wouldn't have known how it felt to love someone with all my heart and soul. Because that's the way I love you, Cade. If I could give you contentedness, I would. If I could give you surety, I would. But all I can give you is *me*. I hope it will be enough. If only you would consider staying here, in Morrow Creek, I know that eventually things will work out."

"They already are working out," Cade told her. "Even with your father. I saw him when I came for you—when I went to your house this evening, after leaving Judah and Blackhouse and my father. That's who Whittier was, you know, all this time."

Violet boggled. "I *knew* it! I almost guessed as much when I saw him at the church." The truth of it all was remarkable. "You actually left your long-lost *father* to come find me at home?"

Cade nodded. Assuredly, they would need to have a long catching-up conversation when all this was through.

"He's with Judah. For now. We'll talk again later," Cade continued, surprising her anew with the news of his brother's arrival in town. "Your father told me that you found Tobe's hidden train ticket. I knew you'd persist until you found the lead you needed." Proudly, Cade smiled at her.

Violet nodded. "Now all we have to do is take Tobe to see his mother. If our guesses are right, she's just a skip away."

"Hmm. I think I know someone who'd be willing to undertake that mission." Cade cast a slanting glance at Mr. Blackhouse, who'd arrived at the train car sometime during their reunion. His former benefactor gave a somber nod. Cade regrouped. "But the whole point is," he said, "that I spoke with your father tonight—"

"Well, of course you did. You just said so."

"—and I made my case as best as I could, without resorting to flattery or beguilement or outright professional charm—"

"Well, now. For you, that sounds impossible!"

"—and eventually I made Reverend Benson see the truth."

"Oh." Perplexed, Violet inhaled. "Which was?"

"That he's going to have to come to terms with having a reformed, scoundrelly sporting man in his daughter's life," Cade said. "Because I can't live without you, Violet. I tried, and I can't. Without you, there's no substance to life. There's no laughter. There's no joy—" Cade stopped, quite obviously searching for more. "There's not even any fun to be had with drink or dice or dancehall girls!"

Feeling vexed, Violet arched her brows. "Oh, really?"

"What I mean is…" Soberly, Cade held her hand in both of his. He lifted his gaze to join with hers. "I want you to be mine. Please. I love you, Violet. Having you as my good-luck charm is not enough. It never was." Watching her closely, Cade drew in a fortifying breath. "I want you as something more."

For a single, heart-stopping moment, Violet thought he was asking her to be his mistress. After all, these were sophisticated people in very sophisticated surroundings. And she was *almost* prepared to accept.

But then, astonishingly, Cade dropped to one knee, right there in front of Mr. Blackhouse and everyone who stood nearby and the dauntingly intimidating but well-mannered valet, Adams, and all the most daring gamblers in the whole territory, and then Cade—her very own honor-bound gambler and the man who'd unrepentantly stolen her heart—took on the very biggest risk of them all.

"Please, Violet. Will you marry me?" he asked. "I know I'm not what you probably hoped for, but I love you. And if you give me half a chance, I swear I'll make you happy. I know I can."

"Yes." Filled to overflowing with love for him, Violet dropped to the floor, too. Her skirts fanned out in a majesty of color. They should have been trodden upon, but partygoers miraculously made way for them. Her knees wobbled. They should have buckled, but Violet amazingly managed to remain steady. Her voice broke as she repeated her answer. Somehow, again, she managed to say, "Yes! Of course I'll marry you."

Smiling almost too broadly to pucker, Violet leaned forward and kissed Cade anyway. At her instigation, he pulled her into his arms, lowered his head, then made her his more thoroughly than he had all night—and through it all, all Violet could do was rejoice. She'd reunited with Cade. She'd made him hers and rightly become his. Now all that remained was one final detail.

"I will be *delighted* to marry you," Violet said when at last they parted amid the cheers of the crowd. Blushing for certain now, she added, "I have just one tiny stipulation."

Cade appeared concerned. "Stipulation?"

"Yes."

In his face, caution warred with an evident determination to fulfill whatever demand she made. "What stipulation?"

"Earlier tonight," Violet told him, "you said that you weren't a good enough man—that I probably hoped for more."

Cade nodded. "I'm *not* a good enough man for you. I—"

Determinedly, Violet kissed him. Hard and fast.

He appeared perplexed. "I'm not good. I gamble. I drink—"

Again she kissed him. This time, Violet wrapped her arms around his neck and devoted her entire being to the task. But when she'd finished—when she next peeked expectantly at him—Cade merely drew a breath and forged onward. "I'm *not* good enough—"

Wholeheartedly, Violet kissed him once more. Then she reared back to give him a serious look. "You *are* good enough," she insisted vigorously, "for me and anyone else. But you're mighty slow to recognize when someone's giving you a dose of your own medicine."

Coquettishly, she smiled. "Shall I demonstrate again, or are you catching on to this game at last?"

Then—only then—Cade seemed to understand her meaning.

With a knowing gleam in his eyes, he adopted a very pensive demeanor. Elaborately, he furrowed his brow. "I'm not—"

Her punishing kiss almost bowled him over. Laughing, Cade caught her in his arms and then raised them both. He'd never looked happier—or more handsome—than he did in that moment.

"I have a feeling," he said as he cradled her close before rejoining the party, "that you're going to keep me on my toes."

"With me," Violet promised, "life will *never* be dull."

With that much settled for certain, they turned delightedly to face their friends and neighbors. As one, the people of Morrow Creek cheered. The shadier visitors to town offered gamblers' odds on the probable wedding date they would set. In the center of the melee, a satisfied-looking Mr. Blackhouse encouraged everyone to raise their glasses in a toast.

"Three cheers for lasting love!" he roared. "However improbable, however difficult, however unlikely it is to occur for *some* of us—" Here, Blackhouse stopped for a properly dramatic pause. He glanced at an older man and a younger, dark-haired man standing nearby. "—we can see tonight that sometimes Lady Luck delivers more than a bounteous payout. Sometimes she delivers us a second chance at living our lives. And for that—"

"He always was a bit of a show-off," Cade grumbled

privately in Violet's ear. "We'll be here for days before he's done."

"For that," Blackhouse finished, "we salute her. To Lady Luck! To Miss Benson! To Mr. Foster!" With a triumphant flourish, he raised his glass. "And most of all, to love!"

Together, the women nearby swooned. The men downed their whiskeys. And Violet tugged Cade's arm. Smiling, she whispered, "Let's dance before Mr. Blackhouse starts in again."

"Ah. A woman after my own heart," Cade pronounced.

Then, with an even broader smile, he danced them both into the party, long into the night, and all the way to tomorrow…with all the wonderful tomorrows that lay beyond it still to come for them both to share.

Chapter Fifteen

There was nothing like a wedding to bring out the good spirits of everyone involved, Violet thought. Women commended the bride and told her how lovely she looked. Men congratulated the groom and joked about the coming wedding night's ribaldry. Even children, who were rightly oblivious to most adult goings-on, seemed to sense the crackle of celebration in the air. They participated by whooping, hollering and teasing each other mercilessly. Now, eyeing those selfsame boisterous youngsters as they raced down the aisle of her father's church, Violet sighed.

Upon hearing that telltale sigh, her longtime friend, Adeline Davis, stopped on her way out of the church. Together in their best dresses, she and Violet watched through the open church entryway as the ring bearer and his cousins chased two of the tiny, squealing flower girls down the steps outside.

Beyond the children, autumn-leafed trees embellished the townscape of Morrow Creek. Above those trees, clear territorial skies stretched forever, promising that the mild weather they'd enjoyed would last. In the distance, a train whistle called.

Upon hearing that sound, Violet started. She sighed again.

Adeline gave an empathetic smile. "Still missing Tobe?"

Swallowing hard, Violet nodded. "I know he's been happily reunited with his mother in California, thanks to Mr. Blackhouse's generosity—" the enigmatic magnate had employed his private train car to see to that mission personally, surprising everyone except Violet "—but I still miss the little scamp." Violet smiled at the memory of him. "I'm not at all certain Tobe will write me as often as he promised he would." She hoped he would. "I'm afraid I grew awfully attached to that boy."

"I did, too," Adeline admitted. "He was very sweet."

With a commiserating nod, Cade stepped up. Sentimentally, he added to their reminiscences. "That little sharper," he said fondly of Tobe. "He took my best warm overcoat with him."

"That was *your* overcoat all along? I never knew that!"

At that, Cade smiled. If his attention had been on the many townspeople exiting the church around them, it wasn't now. Now his attention was all for Violet. Dotingly, he took her hand.

"With Tobe, I lost a bet on purpose," Cade said. "With you, I won a lifetime of riches by accident. I'll take those odds."

With a chuckle, Clayton Davis approached. As befit his wedding day, he was decked out in his finest suit. He stopped beside Adeline, his blushing bride, then hugged her tightly.

"I still say I got luckiest of all, Foster," he said. "But if you take away anything from your attendance at our wedding…"

Clayton paused, even as Adeline cast him a curious look.

"…it's that you ought to elope when it's your turn." With a beleaguered grin, Clayton shook his head. "The planning, the decorating, the meeting up with all the distant relatives—I swear, we should have just run away to Avalanche to exchange vows. We could have skipped to the 'married' part straightaway."

"However it happened, I'm glad it's done." After a loving smooch, Adeline caressed his cheek. "When it comes to matters of the heart, you know I can be a mite…*impatient* myself."

Clearly that was a private joke between them, because Adeline gave her groom a teasing, enigmatic wink. Clayton winked, too, then grinned right back at her.

The two of them were so full of love and admiration and wonderment that Violet would have found herself hopelessly consumed with envy…had she not had a partner by her side who'd brought her every bit as much happiness. So rather than feel covetous, Violet only smiled. She was glad that Adeline had finally wed her long-beloved Clayton, glad that Tobe was finally with his mother and glad—*so* glad—to have Cade by her side, now and forever.

As though illustrating his willingness to stand by her, help her and love her, Cade extended his arm in a decidedly romantic and chivalrous fashion. "Shall we head to the party?"

"Oh yes, *please*!" Violet said.

As a group, she and Cade and Adeline and Clayton tromped down the church steps, heading for the back room of Jack Murphy's saloon where the wedding reception was to take place.

Spying her father on his way from the other direction with some congregants, Violet waved and blew him a kiss. He'd been wonderful since her engagement. He'd even gone so far as to invite Cade to live with them—in the room Tobe had vacated—while he and Violet made their own wedding plans and got settled in.

"If we get to the reception early," Violet enthused as they walked onward, "there will still be plenty of cake!"

"Spoken like a woman who knows her mind." With a grin, Judah joined them, not seeming to notice when they all slowed their pace to accommodate his injured leg. "I approve, Cade."

"You approved of Violet from the moment you met her at Simon's party and she allowed you to beat her at billiards," Cade said. "You would approve of anyone who did that."

"There's more to it than that!" Judah insisted earnestly. To Violet, he tossed a flattering smile. It looked *almost* as charming as Cade's smiles did…only a shade darker and more evocative of sin. "I approve of Violet because I approve of your new life, Cade," Judah said as he moved with a determined effort to keep up. "It's been good for you, settling down."

Cade tilted his head as if considering his new position as a purchasing agent—an unusually persuasive and hard-driving one, at that—at Marcus Copeland's lumber mill. He smiled.

"You ought to consider doing the same," he suggested to Judah. "Settling down, I mean—now that you're here in Morrow Creek and intend to stay."

But his brother merely laughed. "If only I could find the angel who'd have me!" he pronounced with an almost Blackhouseworthy sense of drama. Hand over his heart, he surveyed Violet and Cade, then Adeline and Clayton, each in turn. "I'm afraid you four have laid claim to all the available love and locked it away. Poor romantic fools like myself have no recourse at all."

This time, everyone *else* guffawed. "The last thing *you've* faced is a shortage of romantically minded company," Violet pointed out as they arrived on the main street. They all took to the raised boardwalk to traverse farther. "The women in Morrow Creek are all aflutter over you, Judah, and you know it!"

"Hmm. Maybe so." Enigmatically, he sighed. "But all the spooning in the world doesn't add up to love, Miss Benson."

"If anyone's made a thorough study of that supposition," Cade said as they arrived at the saloon, "it's my brother."

Wearing good-natured smiles, they all trooped inside. In the newly decorated saloon, Grace Murphy welcomed them. So did all the gamblers, drinkers, partygoers… and one very special faro dealer. Wearing a handsome suit and tie, he came forward.

Violet hugged him. "How is your work progressing,

Mr. Foster? Is Mr. Murphy treating you fairly? Are the gamblers all tipping you generously? Are the dance-hall girls all flirting with you between sets, the way I told you they would?"

"Very well. Yes. Yes. And not nearly enough, but I think I'll remedy that soon." Cade's father gave her a boyish grin. It was easy to see where the Foster boys had gotten their devilish ways. "Some of the sporting men in town are a little confused about my new—*old*— name." Since Simon Blackhouse had freed him from his unfair debt, Cade's father had reclaimed *Ben Foster* as his name instead of Percy Whittier. "But here in the territory, things have a way of sorting themselves out. I'm just happy to have my name and my rightful reputation back." He widened his grin to include his two sons. "I'm happy to have *all* of it back. If not for you, Miss Benson—and that cagey Simon Blackhouse, too—things might have progressed very differently."

"Well, I *do* have a powerful knack for helping people," Violet admitted with a dose of pride. She hugged him again. "If you find a break in the wagering, please come join the party."

"Yes, please do!" Adeline and Clayton agreed. Even as they spoke, strains of fiddle music came from the saloon's back room, luring them toward the nuptial festivities. "We'd love to have you there. The more the merrier!"

Seeming grateful to be included, Cade's father nodded. He turned to Cade and Judah. They recognized their cue to nod as well, letting him know they wanted him to be at the party, too.

The Foster men hadn't yet resolved all their concerns. They had many years of separation and misunderstandings to make up for. But between themselves, with Reverend Benson's wise help and Violet's ongoing support, the three were well on their way to forging a new kind of family. Violet could not have been more pleased about that…especially for Cade's sake.

There could be no denying that her now-retired gambler had thrived since he'd decided to make Morrow Creek his home. As though that little town of theirs possessed some sort of magical good luck that even Cade hadn't counted on, it had carried him and Violet forward from their first dance to their latest…from their first meeting to their own upcoming wedding. And despite Clayton's advice that they should simply elope and have done with it, Violet had some very specific notions about that event.

Because of that, as everyone headed into the next room for the party, Violet hung back. To her surprise, Cade did, too.

She raised her brows. "Is everything all right?"

"With you? It couldn't be better." He smiled, then held out his arm to escort her. "I was only thinking about *our* wedding."

Violet laughed. "That's serendipitous. I was, too!"

"And I think," Cade went on, "that we should—"

"Have it sooner," they said in unison.

"Tomorrow?" Violet proposed.

"The next day," Cade amended. "I'd like to give Marcus Copeland at least that much notice. I wouldn't want

to leave him in the lurch at the lumber mill. After that…
I'm all yours."

"And I am yours." Violet couldn't help smiling with
new anticipation. "If ever I'd wondered whether a
charming, wagering, altogether disreputable rascal of
a gambler could settle down and become a good husband," she mused aloud, "I don't anymore. You're perfect for me, Cade."

"And you, for me. Why else would I bother giving
up all the glories of my previous life of pleasure and
debauchery?"

With an undoubted twinkle in her eyes, Violet
thought about that. "I'd wager there will still be *some*
pleasure and shared debauchery in our lives from now
on. Wouldn't you?"

"Absolutely." Cade caught on to her naughty teasing
right away. With a roguish grin, he leaned forward to
kiss her. Then he kissed her again, even more linger-
ingly. "That's one bet I'd be happy to break my with-
drawal from gambling to make."

"Good. It's settled, then." Taking his proffered arm
at last, Violet headed into the wedding reception.

For today, she was not the belle of the ball. Adeline
was, and rightly so. But as Violet glanced at Cade and
saw him standing proudly beside her while they greeted
several of their friends and neighbors, she knew one
amazing fact for certain.

When it came to Cade, she *was* the belle of the ball.
Now and forever.

With him in her heart, she could not have asked for
more—not even if it made her beautiful in the eyes of

everyone in town. Because for the first time in all her life, Violet realized then, she *felt* truly beautiful, both inside and out…and it was loving someone that had made her feel that way.

Love was the magic in Morrow Creek, she understood in that moment. And with the good people of the town to keep that love flowing, there really was no end to the magic that might occur…for every single one of them.

* * * * *

REQUEST YOUR FREE BOOKS!

HARLEQUIN® HISTORICAL:
Where love is timeless

2 FREE NOVELS PLUS 2 **FREE GIFTS!**

YES! Please send me 2 FREE Harlequin® Historical novels and my 2 FREE gifts (gifts are worth about $10). After receiving them, if I don't wish to receive any more books, I can return the shipping statement marked "cancel." If I don't cancel, I will receive 6 brand-new novels every month and be billed just $5.44 per book in the U.S. or $5.74 per book in Canada. That's a savings of at least 16% off the cover price! It's quite a bargain! Shipping and handling is just 50¢ per book in the U.S. and 75¢ per book in Canada.* I understand that accepting the 2 free books and gifts places me under no obligation to buy anything. I can always return a shipment and cancel at any time. Even if I never buy another book, the two free books and gifts are mine to keep forever.

246/349 HDN F4ZY

Name	(PLEASE PRINT)

Address		Apt. #

City	State/Prov.	Zip/Postal Code

Signature (if under 18, a parent or guardian must sign)

Mail to the **Harlequin**® Reader Service:
IN U.S.A.: P.O. Box 1867, Buffalo, NY 14240-1867
IN CANADA: P.O. Box 609, Fort Erie, Ontario L2A 5X3

Want to try two free books from another line?
Call 1-800-873-8635 or visit www.ReaderService.com.

* Terms and prices subject to change without notice. Prices do not include applicable taxes. Sales tax applicable in N.Y. Canadian residents will be charged applicable taxes. Offer not valid in Quebec. This offer is limited to one order per household. Not valid for current subscribers to Harlequin Historical books. All orders subject to credit approval. Credit or debit balances in a customer's account(s) may be offset by any other outstanding balance owed by or to the customer. Please allow 4 to 6 weeks for delivery. Offer available while quantities last.

Your Privacy—The Harlequin® Reader Service is committed to protecting your privacy. Our Privacy Policy is available online at www.ReaderService.com or upon request from the Harlequin Reader Service.

We make a portion of our mailing list available to reputable third parties that offer products we believe may interest you. If you prefer that we not exchange your name with third parties, or if you wish to clarify or modify your communication preferences, please visit us at www.ReaderService.com/consumerchoice or write to us at Harlequin Reader Service Preference Service, P.O. Box 9062, Buffalo, NY 14269. Include your complete name and address.

HHI3R

*Lauri Robinson's THE COWBOY WHO CAUGHT HER EYE
will make you fall in love with the Wild West and its cowboy
heroes all over again!*

"What's your dream, Molly?"

Having been stuck in the past for so long, she struggled to offer the truth. "I've so many regrets, wishing I could change things… I can't say I have a dream."

He ran a single finger down the side of her face. "That's not right, Molly. A person needs to have dreams."

Her insides atremble, she had to close her eyes for a moment. "Have you always had them?"

"Yes. I'd have never gotten here without dreaming of how better things could be."

Molly didn't want to be this hopeless, but the truth was very little could compare to what was in her future. "What if they can't?" she asked.

"Everything can always get better, Molly."

She knew the opposite. And she didn't need to drag him down with her. Dredging up what she hoped resembled a smile, she said, "I better get back to the store."

Carter frowned and his features turned hard. His hand slid from the side of her face to grasp her chin firmly. "I won't let anyone hurt you, Molly."

She did know that, but she couldn't ask him to stay, to right her wrongs, to give up his dreams. The things that made him who he was. A truly remarkable man. "Thank you, Carter. For all you have done. It's made a world of difference." She broke from his hold then, started walking away.

"I'll take you to Montana," he said from behind her. "You and Ivy and Karleen, if that's what you want."

The struggle within her was fierce. Half an hour ago that had been exactly what she'd wanted him to say. She even contemplated it for a moment as she stood, staring toward the big house with its storefront and the outbuildings surrounding it. But she had more than many people had, and she wouldn't give it up, wouldn't make her sisters give it up. "Thank you, but no. That's your dream, Carter, and I don't expect you to share it with me."

It's Carter Buchanan's job to know about secrets and Molly has something to hide. But she touches a place he thought long ago dead, and those eyes have got this cowboy considering exchanging his pistol for a band of gold.

Look for Lauri Robinson's
THE COWBOY WHO CAUGHT HER EYE,
coming July 2013 from Harlequin® Historical.

SADDLE UP AND READ 'EM!

This summer, get your fix of Western reads and pick up a cowboy from some of your favorite authors!

In July, look for:

ZANE by Brenda Jackson
The Westmorelands
Harlequin Desire

THE HEART WON'T LIE by Vicki Lewis Thompson
Sons of Chance
Harlequin Blaze

OUTLAW LAWMAN by Delores Fossen
The Marshals of Maverick County
Harlequin Intrigue

BRANDED BY A CALLAHAN by Tina Leonard
Callahan Cowboys
Harlequin American Romance

Look for these great Western reads and more, available wherever books are sold or visit
www.Harlequin.com/Westerns